ACCLAIM FOR THE TRIPLE THREAT SERIES

"Only a brilliant lawyer, prosecutor, and journalist like Lis Wiehl could put together a mystery this thrilling! The incredible characters and nonstop twists will leave you mesmerized. Open [*Face of Betrayal*] and find a comfortable seat because you won't want to put it down!"

—E. D. HILL, FOX NEWS ANCHOR

"Who killed loudmouth radio guy Jim Fate? The game is afoot! *Hand of Fate* is a fun thriller, taking you inside the media world and the justice system—scary places to be!"

—BILL O'REILLY, FOX
TV AND RADIO ANCHOR

"Beautiful, successful and charismatic on the outside but underneath a twisted killer. She's brilliant and crazy and comes racing at the reader with knives and a smile. The most chilling villain you'll meet . . . because she could live next door to you."

—DR. DALE ARCHER, CLINICAL
PSYCHIATRIST, REGARDING *HEART OF ICE*

ACCLAIM FOR *SNAPSHOT*

"...the writing is strong and the plot is engaging, driven by the desires (both good and evil) of the characters and the reader's desire to know who killed a man decades before, how it was covered up, and whether an innocent man has been charged and imprisoned. The book offers a 'snapshot' of the civil rights movement and turbulent times."

—*PUBLISHERS WEEKLY*

"A pitch-perfect plot that tackles some tough issues with a lot of heart. *Snapshot* brings our world into pristine focus. It's fast-paced, edgy, and loaded with plenty of menace. Lis Wiehl knows what readers crave and she delivers it. Make room on your bookshelves for this one—it's a keeper."

—STEVE BERRY, *NEW YORK TIMES* BESTSELLING AUTHOR

"*Snapshot* is fiction. But it takes us along the twisted path of race in America in a way that is closer to the human experience than most history books."

—JUAN WILLIAMS, BESTSELLING AUTHOR OF *EYES ON THE
PRIZE: AMERICA'S CIVIL RIGHTS YEARS*

"Inspired by actual historical events and informed by Lis Wiehl's formidable personal and professional background, *Snapshot* captivates and enthralls."

—JEANINE PIRRO, BESTSELLING AUTHOR OF *SLY FOX*

"Riveting from the first page . . ."

—PAM VEASEY, SCREENWRITER AND EXECUTIVE PRODUCER

ACCLAIM FOR *A DEADLY BUSINESS*

"The second Mia Quinn mystery is action-packed from the first page. Layers of lies and deception make for a twisting, turning story that will keep mystery lovers entranced. This is a thrill ride until the very end, so hang on tight and enjoy the trip!"

—*PUBLISHERS WEEKLY* REVIEW, 4 STARS

"Wiehl's experience as a former federal prosecutor gives the narrative an authenticity in its depiction of the criminal justice system. Henry's expertise in writing mysteries and thrillers has placed her on the short-list for the Agatha, Anthony, and Oregon Book awards. The coauthors' . . . fast-paced detective series will keep legal thriller readers and John Grisham fans totally engrossed."

—*LIBRARY JOURNAL* REVIEW

"Wiehl has woven a wonderfully multi-layered story that will have readers on the edge of their seats . . . *A Deadly Business* delivers everything we love in a massively good mystery."

—CBA RETAILERS & RESOURCES REVIEW

ACCLAIM FOR *A MATTER OF TRUST*

"This suspenseful first in a new series from Wiehl and Henry opens with bang."

—*PUBLISHERS W*

"Wiehl begins an exciting new series with prosecutor Mia at the center side storyline about bullying is timely and will hit close to home for m

—*RT BOOK REVIEWS,*

"Dramatic, moving, intense. *A Matter of Trust* gives us an amazing ins the life of a prosecutor—and mom. Mia Quinn reminds me of Lis."

—MAXINE PAETRO, *NEW YORK TIMES* BESTSELLING

"*A Matter of Trust* is a stunning crime series debut from one of m authors, Lis Wiehl. Smart, suspenseful, and full of twists that only like Wiehl could pull off. I want prosecutor Mia Quinn in my co murder's on the docket—she's a compelling new character and I lo to seeing her again soon."

—LINDA FAIRSTEIN, *NEW YORK TIMES* BESTSEL

LETHAL BEAUTY

LETHAL BEAUTY

A MIA QUINN MYSTERY

LIS WIEHL

WITH APRIL HENRY

Thomas Nelson
Since 1798

NASHVILLE   MEXICO CITY   RIO DE JANEIRO

Published in Nashville, Tennessee, by Thomas Nelson. Thomas Nelson is a registered trademark of HarperCollins Christian Publishing, Inc.

Thomas Nelson titles may be purchased in bulk for educational, business, fund- raising, or sales promotional use. For information, please e-mail SpecialMarkets@ThomasNelson.com.

Library of Congress Cataloging-in-Publication Data

Wiehl, Lis W.
  Lethal Beauty : a Mia Quinn mystery Lis Wiehl with April Henry.
     pages ; cm. -- (A Mia Quinn mystery ; 3)
  ISBN 978-1-59554-905-1 (hardcover)
1. Women lawyers--Fiction. 2. Murder--Investigation--Fiction. I. Henry, April. II. Title.
 PS3623.I382L48 2015
 813'.6--dc23   2014036424

Printed in the United States of America

15 16 17 18 19 RRD 5 4 3 2 1

For Dani and Jacob. You are my inspiration.

Love always, Mom

CHAPTER 1

A faint scream drifted up from the basement. Lihong shifted from foot to foot on the peeling linoleum, waiting in line to use the tiny bathroom. The girl named Chun bit her lip and avoided his eyes. A muscle flickered in Feng's jaw.

Was it a shriek of pain or fear? Or simply a continuing protest? Ying was probably okay, Lihong told himself. She was just getting acclimated. Life in America was not what she had expected. Ying must still be thinking that if she made enough of a fuss, things would change. That she would get what she had dreamed of, the American life where she would drive a Mercedes and live in a big house and wear expensive clothes.

What she had gotten instead was the expectation that she would work nearly one hundred hours a week at a restaurant that served "Chinese" food that tasted nothing like what they ate at home and live crammed in a small house with eighteen other people.

Ying had been handcuffed in the basement for refusing to work. It had been explained to her over and over. Both with words and with blows. She owed a debt to the snakeheads for smuggling her over here, and her life would not be her own until she paid them back.

They all owed so much. Every day simply pushed them deeper into debt. It wasn't cheap, their owner explained, to put them up in this house, drive them to work and back each day, provide them with food. So he would have to charge them for all these things. Lihong had tried to work out the total on scraps of paper, but he had learned only a little math in his few years in school. Whatever the answer was, it was a lot. It would take years to earn it back.

And to make sure they all kept up their end of the bargain, they were warned that their families would be killed if they did not. None of them had known each other back home, and some of them spoke dialects that were hard for the others to follow. There was no loyalty among them, not when whispering a secret to the owner might earn favor.

Lihong never left the house by himself. Even if he went to the store, it was as part of a big group, while one of the minders watched them and translated as needed. Of course, it didn't take much watching. Not when everyone was so afraid.

Hu slipped out of the bathroom, her dark head tilted down so that her hair fell over her eyes. The bathroom didn't have a door, just an orange window curtain tacked onto the frame to give the illusion of privacy. It was the only curtain in the house. The other windows were either bare or covered with yellowed Chinese newspapers. Chun slipped into the bathroom and they all shuffled forward. Ping took her place in line behind Lihong. There were only two bathrooms, and to get to them you had to wend your way through bunk beds filling every space.

When he first came to America, Lihong had agreed to the terms, made his mark on the paperwork, and handed over his identification. So had everyone else in this house. They all worked at the restaurant, taking orders, busing tables, refilling pots of hot tea, or standing for hours over flaming woks. Lihong washed dishes and sometimes cooked if they were shorthanded. He was clumsy, though, and often burned himself.

Lihong had worked with Ying on her first—and so far, last—day. She had been filling one of the metal tea carafes with nearly boiling water when Lihong dropped a plate that exploded into shards. She jerked at the sudden clatter. The hot water burned her forearm, immediately forming a red fluid-filled blister. Ying had started weeping and wouldn't stop, not even when the manager came back and hissed at her that the customers could hear and were asking questions.

Lihong had tried to help her. He had taken her to the sink and run cold water over the burn. Patted her shoulder awkwardly. Then whispered warnings to her that she had to be quiet.

Now another hoarse scream floated up.

"I wish she would just shut up," Feng muttered. "It's impossible to sleep with her wailing down there."

"She'd better be careful," Ping said from behind Lihong. "There's a lot worse things she could be doing than working in a restaurant."

"She's not pretty enough for that," Feng sneered.

"I hear that the men who come, they don't care so much about pretty." Ping bit her lip. "They could send her there as soon as her burn heals up."

Another shriek.

"That's it!" Feng balled his hands into fists. "If the neighbors hear, she'll bring the police down on us. All of us rotting in prison or sent back home."

"The freeway is so loud," Lihong offered, trying to placate Feng. He had found he could sleep better if he thought of it as a river. "It covers the sound."

Feng clenched his fists. "If she won't shut up on her own, I'll make her shut up."

"No, no," Lihong said hastily. "Let me talk to her."

Abandoning his place in line, he went back down the hall. When he ducked under the rope hung with drying laundry, a pair of damp pants slapped him in the face.

In the kitchen he washed out a glass and filled it with water. The basement stairs were next to the back door. On the door was posted a sign handwritten in Chinese. EMPLOYEES, PAY ATTENTION! TURN LIGHT OUT AT 12. PLEASE DON'T YELL, TALK LOUD, OR MAKE NOISE BECAUSE IT WILL DISTURB THE NEIGHBORS.

Lihong would be fine with disturbing the neighbors if he thought they might help. That was all he thought about now. How to get out of this place, this position he was in, before he was an old man. To make it so that the enforcers would leave him in peace— or at least not know his whereabouts.

He had thought of asking the people at the nearby businesses if they could help him get away. They came in to eat. It would not be hard to slip away and talk to them for a few minutes. But his English was very poor. And they were all friendly with the owner, and he bought them meals.

Lihong knew what would happen if he asked a policeman. Beaten, maybe killed. Or at best, jailed and then deported. The owner had explained it often. Just thinking about it made him long for a cigarette to calm his nerves. But he had smoked the last one from his pack today. Cigarettes were so expensive, costing nearly as much as the owner gave him in a day, but they blunted his hunger, tamped down his anxiety.

It was a cigarette that had led Lihong to his one hope, a man he called Mr. Scott. They weren't allowed breaks, but sometimes when it was slow he would slip out the back door and smoke for five minutes. A few months earlier, Lihong had gone outside with a cigarette already between his lips, but in the spot where he normally stood was a white American man. Smoking. Lihong had started to hurry back inside, but with gestures and smiles and words he didn't understand, Mr. Scott had indicated that he should stay. After exchanging names, they had smoked their cigarettes together. When Mr. Scott was finished, he had unwrapped a stick of gum that stank of chemicals and mint, then chewed it furiously. The whole time he talked, first asking Lihong questions that he could only answer with a smile and a shrug. Eventually it became a monologue that hadn't seemed to require anything from Lihong but an occasional nod.

Mr. Scott was well dressed, his clothes fitting him without a wrinkle, the stitching and the fabric very fine. And later, Lihong had seen him getting into his car. It was huge and shiny and raised high off the ground, without a single scratch or dent. Mr. Scott was like a vision of the America that Lihong had thought he was coming to. Maybe this was the sign he had been hoping for.

The next time Lihong saw him, Mr. Scott asked, with a combination of words and gestures, for a cigarette. Despite the cost, Lihong handed it over without hesitation.

Mr. Scott grimaced at the taste, and they had laughed, and somehow through the few words they had in common they started to become something like friends. Whenever he came to the restaurant, Mr. Scott would talk, long runs of words that flowed past Lihong like water. They were oddly soothing.

The fourth time he saw Mr. Scott, Lihong tried to ask for help, using words he had gleaned from TV.

But then Mr. Scott had so many questions. He had asked about "minimum wage." About "sick leave" and "health insurance." Words and concepts that Lihong didn't understand. You worked every day from ten in the morning to ten or eleven p.m. You worked if you were sick or hurt or exhausted. You would probably still work, they often joked, if you were dead.

And before Mr. Scott could help them, he had been killed in a car accident. A few months later, his wife had come to the restaurant. Lihong had been overjoyed. He thought she must be there to follow up on Mr. Scott's promise. But when he risked everything to ask her, she seemed not to understand. Later, she had come back with a magic phone that understood them both and translated from English to Chinese and back again. They hadn't gotten very far when the owner came out back and nearly caught them.

He hadn't seen the woman he called Mrs. Scott since. But he had seen the concern in her eyes, the caring. He was sure she would help if she knew what was happening.

Now Lihong's hand was slick on the stair rail. If the owner knew he was coming down here . . .

In the basement, Ying sat with her back against the wall. One arm was handcuffed to a pipe. The other had been roughly bandaged, although the once-white wrapping was now stiff and dirty. Her face was swollen, her eyes so puffy she could barely see.

Lihong put the glass of water in her free hand. She gulped it down greedily, and then he took the glass back. The last girl who had been put down here had tried to kill herself.

"You have to stop crying," he told her in a low but firm voice. "Stop shrieking, stop crying, apologize, and start working."

"My whole village saved up to send me here. This is not what I thought it would be."

Bitterness welled up in him. "Do you think it was for any of us? Besides, do you know what they'll do if you keep this up? You'll end up in a massage parlor or a nail shop."

She shook her head. "But I don't know how to give massages or do nails."

The girl was as stupid as she was stubborn. "That doesn't matter. You won't be doing either of those things. You'll be entertaining three or four men an hour, fourteen hours a day."

The one eye that wasn't quite as bruised widened. "Please. You have to help me. You have to save me." She raised the bandaged arm toward him, the one she had burned when he dropped the plate.

Lihong still had the small white cardboard rectangle that Mrs. Scott had given him. The printing on it seemed to be letters and numbers, and he was nearly certain it held her address. He would go there, he decided, with a sudden surge of fear and daring. He would go there and she would use her magic phone and they would understand each other.

And then she would help. Help free Ying from the dark basement. Help free Lihong from his days spent as a slave.

CHAPTER 2

Back home they had a saying. "Paper can't wrap up a fire."

And, thought the man who had brought Lihong here, Lihong was a fire. He could no longer paper over the problems Lihong kept causing.

If something wasn't done, he would burn everything down.

CHAPTER 3

TUESDAY, TEN DAYS LATER

Have you wondered what Dandan Yee's last thoughts were before she died?" asked King County prosecutor Mia Quinn. As she spoke, she was careful to make eye contact with each juror in turn. That morning she had pulled back her shoulder-length blond hair so that no strand would fall into her eyes. She wanted nothing to distract from the picture she was about to paint.

Mia had planned, she had prepared, but now she set that planning aside and let the words come from her heart. She needed the jury to see things through her eyes, and that wouldn't come from a rote presentation.

Sitting at the prosecution table behind her was the lead detective in the case, homicide detective Charlie Carlson. They had worked this murder together from the beginning. Now she could sense him willing her to get justice for Dandan Yee.

The case should have been open-and-shut, but two things were not in Mia's favor.

First was that the defendant, David Leacham, had used a good portion of the fortune he had made in the dry-cleaning business to hire one of Seattle's best criminal defense attorneys, James Wheeler. No crime, not even the murder of a teenage prostitute, was too low for Wheeler to take on. And Mia had to admit that he had done an excellent job, sowing confusion, countering every witness, and casting doubt and aspersions far and wide. Wheeler had even managed to get Leacham released on bail, despite Mia arguing that the man was a flight risk and could pose a threat to the community. Leacham had surrendered his passport, put up a million dollars bail, and walked out of jail with just an ankle monitor.

The second thing that had hurt the prosecution's case was that Mia and Charlie's key witness had been a no-show. She was a street kid and sometimes streetwalker with the unfortunate name of Sindy Sharp (and it was her real name, too, according to Charlie). But Sindy had disappeared from her new foster home before she could testify that Leacham had been one of her regular customers, and that he had liked it rough.

The massage parlor where Dandan worked turned out to have been rented under a false name. It never reopened after her death. The other girls gave the police fake names and addresses, claimed to have seen and heard nothing, and then disappeared.

To convict Leacham, Mia now had to nail her closing arguments and make the jurors face the hard truth: that a defenseless young woman had been purchased, used, and then brutally murdered by a rich businessman who thought himself above the law.

Mia continued, "Do you imagine that Dandan thought, *Why are you stabbing me? I have already done what you wanted. I have already given you my body.* Did she think, *My whole life I dreamed of coming to America to be reunited with my mother, and now I am being murdered by this man?*"

Several jurors cut their eyes to Bo Yee, Dandan's mother, who sat in her usual place in the front row, directly behind the prosecutor's table. She had been here every day, wearing a long, shapeless black dress and tinted glasses, clutching a neatly folded handkerchief that she never used. Sixteen years ago, when Dandan was three, Mrs. Yee had paid smugglers to spirit her out of China. She had been granted asylum in the United States, but had not been successful in getting her husband and daughter to join her.

A few weeks earlier, her daughter had gotten off a plane with a fake Indonesian passport, then promptly disappeared into Seattle's bustling Asian population. After she died, Bo Yee's name and address were found in Dandan's few belongings, but the two women had never reconnected. No one knew why. Had Dandan been unable to find her? Or had she been ashamed that the only job she had been able to find was as a prostitute?

All Mia and Charlie knew for sure was that less than two weeks after her arrival in America, Dandan had been stabbed to death by a client, David Leacham. Who then had the gall to claim self-defense.

Mia gave Bo a small nod before turning back to the jury. "Mr. Wheeler has tried to tell you that the whole thing was a terrible misunderstanding. That Mr. Leacham walked into a *massage parlor*"—she emphasized the last two words—"expecting to get a *massage* and nothing more."

A juror named Sandra, a secretary close to retirement, shook her head in disgust. Her caramel-colored hair didn't budge. Jim, a balding accountant, pressed his lips together.

Mia had the jury, she could feel it. When she took two steps to the right, their eyes followed her like magnets.

The only juror who avoided her gaze was Warren, a twenty-eight-year-old electrician with an unfortunate two-toned mullet. He had seemed checked out for the duration of the trial. Every time Mia tried to make eye contact, he was chewing his thumbnail or worrying at his cuticles. During jury selection he had been much more engaged. Now the only person he paid attention to was another juror, Naomi, a twenty-two-year-old student with a penchant for wearing three shades of iridescent eye shadow and tight sweaters.

"Mr. Leacham is forty-seven years old. Old enough to know that legitimate massage businesses do not have neon signs out front. Old enough to know that when you are given your pick between three pretty girls, what will be happening in that back room is a lot more than a back massage."

As she spoke, Mia briefly looked each juror in the eye. Naomi listened with a curled lip. As Mia had hoped during jury selection, she seemed to be relating to the victim.

"The defense has tried to cast this poor girl in an unflattering light, when it's a story as old as our country. A young girl arrives in America, the land of dreams, hoping to make a new life for herself, even though she is penniless, with no skills and nonexistent English. That's what happened to Dandan, at which point her dreams ran right into harsh reality. Mr. Wheeler tried to make you think that Dandan was a hardened criminal, but she wasn't. It's just that when she came here, she was so desperate that she was forced to sell the only thing of value she had—her body. And unfortunately for her, one of her clients turned out to be David Leacham."

Mia's mouth had gone dry. She turned back to the prosecution table, thinking to get a glass of water, but Charlie had already emptied the plastic pitcher. He gave her a guilty twist of a smile. She didn't let the pause break her stride.

Mia shifted her story into the present tense to help the jurors feel how immediate and urgent it was. "And it isn't enough for Mr. Leacham to have sex with this poor girl. It is far from enough. We will never know what his sick reasons are for stabbing Dandan, but we do know that's what he does and it is no accident and it is not self-defense.

"But after Mr. Leacham kills Dandan, he realizes he has gone too far. So he makes up a story and sets about trying to alter the facts to match it. He gives himself a few tiny cuts. Then he puts the knife in that poor dead girl's hand and hightails it out of there."

Mia spoke through gritted teeth. "If a witness hadn't noticed his car and the first few digits of the license plate number, he might never have been caught. But the story he made up doesn't make any sense. Mr. Wheeler expects you to believe that after their encounter, Dandan pressed a knife against David Meacham's throat and attempted to rob him."

The ridiculous theory had been picked up by a tabloid, which ran a photo of Dandan under the headline LETHAL BEAUTY?

"Why would Dandan do that? It defies logic. First of all, Dandan is five foot one and one hundred five pounds. Mister"—Mia gave the word a sarcastic spin—"Leacham is five foot eleven and two hundred fifteen pounds. And yet he is claiming that she is the one who attacked him, who threatened him." She raised a skeptical eyebrow and was rewarded with frowns from both Pete, the retired pharmacist, and Connor, the college student. *Yes!* The tension in her chest loosened.

"Mr. Wheeler would also have you believe that when this girl saw the money in Mr. Leacham's wallet as he paid one hundred for the use of her body, she decided to steal it. But why would someone who has risked everything to come to America jeopardize that for just $380? At a minimum, Dandan would have lost her job. She would have put her ability to stay in America undetected at huge risk. Even if she had taken those few hundred dollars, where would she have run to, with no English and knowing no one else in America besides her own mother? How far would she have gotten?" With her voice, Mia made her own answer clear. Not very far.

"As for those so-called defensive wounds, they are so shallow they barely amount to scratches. And you heard the testimony of our expert witness. Since the defendant was right-handed, any defensive wounds should have been on Mr. Leacham's right hand and forearm. But there weren't any, were there? These marks only make sense when you realize that it is *precisely* because Mr. Leacham is *right*-handed that he gives himself a single shallow cut on his *left* palm, as well as a scratch on his throat no deeper than a shaving nick. And then he sneaks off like a dog into the night.

"And you know what the defense boils down to? They want you to think that this man cannot be a killer. That everything that happened was Dandan's fault. Their argument is that you must have a reasonable doubt, because how can you believe that someone like Mr. Leacham"—she made her voice faintly mocking—"someone who's so successful, who's so nice-looking, who's so intelligent, who has such a wonderful family, how could you believe that someone like that could commit a murder like this? That's what they're really saying: that you have to have reasonable doubt because he doesn't *look* like a killer." Mia was in the zone now, the jurors' eyes riveted on her.

"But you don't have to look at the defense's theory very closely before you see even more flaws. A second problem with their story is something no one disputes: that before he stabs Dandan, Mr. Leacham has sex with her. This man, whom the defense claims to be happily married, has sex with a girl two years younger than his own daughter."

David Leacham's wife, Marci, was glaring at Mia from her seat in the courtroom directly behind her husband. Her face had been wiped of all expression, but her eyes still gave her away. If looks could kill, Mia knew she would be six feet under.

"And as the medical examiner has testified, Dandan had fresh bruises on her wrists. Now ask yourself, which is more logical—that she attacked him or that he attacked her?

"All the evidence and all the facts in this case point to one idea: that David Leacham deliberately murdered Dandan Yee." Mia made eye contact again with each juror. "We ask that you find him guilty."

CHAPTER 4

A different kind of person might have sat back and enjoyed the show James Wheeler was putting on as he gave the closing arguments for the defense, but Charlie Carlson was not that kind of person. Not when, at the end of the day, a man might get away with murder.

"Every living creature understands self-preservation," Wheeler was saying. His thick, silvery hair made him look leonine. "As human beings we go through life avoiding danger, hoping we will never be forced into a position where we must defend ourselves. But if we are threatened with death, our instincts take over and we do whatever we must in order to protect ourselves. And that is exactly what happened here."

By sinking his teeth into his tongue, Charlie managed to maintain a neutral expression.

"The evidence is clear: Ms. Yee was an illegal alien and a

prostitute who came very close to killing David Leacham in a botched robbery attempt."

When Mia talked about the dead girl, she was always Dandan or occasionally Miss Yee, but whenever her name came out of Wheeler's mouth, it was always "Ms. Yee." It was a tiny detail, but telling. Wheeler was trying to get the jury to think of the dead girl as older, more sophisticated, and the *Ms.* was just one more piece of that mosaic.

Charlie wondered how many of the jurors didn't like illegal aliens, or thought that a prostitute deserved whatever happened to her. Mia had tried to uncover any underlying prejudices while the prospective jurors were being questioned in her voir dire, but since most people know what the "right" answers are, they often give them.

"My client is not a worldly man. He works long hours at his dry-cleaning business, talking to customers, fixing machines, and even cleaning and pressing clothes."

Charlie wondered how much of that was true. He also wondered if Leacham was into fixing things other than machines. Since dry cleaning was often a cash business, it made the perfect front for money laundering.

Wheeler continued, "Mr. Leacham thought Ms. Yee was what she claimed to be, a massage therapist. He had a backache, and the pain became so intense he wondered if a massage might help. This is a man who has worked hard his whole life and who has built a successful business from scratch. A man who is still married to his high school sweetheart and who does not have a single criminal conviction."

While investigating the murder, Charlie had found Sindy Sharp, who painted a picture of a very different man. Then, just before the trial began, she left her foster home with nothing but her purse and never came back. The girl did have a long history of running away. Charlie just hoped that was what had happened.

"When Ms. Yee began to flirt with him," Wheeler said, "he was surprised and flattered. He lost his head."

Yeah, Charlie thought sourly, *at about the same time he lost his pants.*

At the defense table, David Leacham bit his lip and looked down at the table. His eyes shone with unshed tears. Just how hard had the man had to bite, Charlie wondered, to make those tears flow.

"Afterward, when he came out of the bathroom, Ms. Yee suddenly attacked him, demanding his wallet. She pressed the knife against his throat until she drew blood and said, 'Do it or die!'"

Charlie tried to imagine it, the tiny woman attacking the much bigger man who sat at the defense table. Judging by the expressions on the faces of the jurors, they were having a hard time as well.

"Mr. Leacham is not familiar with violence, with people who will steal and lie and cheat and even kill." Wheeler raised his chin and pressed the blade of his right palm against his neck as if it were a knife. "But after Ms. Yee cut him, he could feel the hot blood trickling down the skin of his neck." The fingers of Wheeler's other hand traced the contours of his throat. His eyes darted, as if he were panicking, then he dropped both hands and addressed the jury. "Mr. Leacham knew it would take only a little bit more pressure for her to cut his jugular vein. And he was also sure, deadly sure, that either way, she would still kill him. So he knocked her arm away. He did what we all would have done and tried to protect himself. To allow himself to get away to safety. But instead of backing away, his attacker became even more enraged. She came at him again, and they wrestled for the knife. Suddenly, David Leacham was fighting for his life."

Out of the corner of his eye, Charlie watched Mia's lips become a thin, white line as Wheeler piled on lie after lie.

"You've seen the photographs of the cut on his throat, the slice on his hand he suffered when he tried to defend himself. The cut on his throat is from her initial attack, when she told him that he was going to die if he didn't do what she said. The other cut is on his left hand because that hand was closest to the knife. Thankfully, he snatched it back as soon as he realized it was slicing into him, and it didn't sever blood vessels and tendons. Then he tried to grab her, to stop her from killing him, and their feet became entangled. That's when David Leacham got lucky. He got lucky because he did not sustain that third, killing wound this woman was determined to give him. Instead, they hit the ground, landing in such a way that the knife entered her body with his weight directly on top of it. Afraid that she would attack him again, he took that heaven-sent opportunity to escape."

Wheeler managed to proclaim this convoluted story with a straight face. Behind him, Leacham blinked, sending tears running down his red face. In the silence he took a loud, ragged breath.

"Because of chance or providence, Mr. Leacham was able to escape and he is still alive. And while it is very unfortunate that Ms. Yee lost her life, under these circumstances our laws recognize that Mr. Leacham did not commit a crime. Instead, this was a justifiable homicide."

Justifiable homicide was something Charlie had been forced to do a time or two. With a badge on his belt and a city-issued firearm. Not against a tiny woman who had been bought and paid for.

"You saw the prosecutor put these people on the stand who

claimed to be experts in their fields." Wheeler sighed. "I am just one man against the government. I don't have a vast army of employees and fancy equipment." It took a mighty effort for Charlie not to roll his eyes. "All I have"—Wheeler thumped his chest over his heart, or at least where his heart would be if he had one—"is the truth."

He walked back to the defense table and picked up a black leather Moleskine notebook. As Charlie watched him, his gaze snagged on Leacham's, who had turned in his chair. Not a muscle moved on the other man's face, but Charlie still felt his own shoulders tense as if he were getting ready to throw a punch.

"In Ms. Quinn's opening statement, which I wrote down"— Wheeler flourished the notebook dramatically—"she promised that you were going to hear from another prostitute who claimed she had evidence against Mr. Leacham. But that's not what happened, is it? The lady didn't even show up to testify." He mimed looking around the courtroom. "So where is she, this mysterious woman? Is she not here because she was seeking something—sympathy, money, fame—but then she got cold feet when it came time to come before you and lie about what happened?"

He nodded to himself. "Facts are stubborn things. An indictment is not a crime. Indictments mean nothing. Anyone can be indicted, and that should not affect your decision making in any way. Why do our courts have presumption of innocence? Why is our standard reasonable doubt? Because 'looking bad' and 'probably' are not standards of proof. That's the most important thing to remember. Human beings are naturally judgmental and critical of each other. But with presumption of innocence, we are forced to wait and weigh the evidence."

Charlie didn't think of himself as judgmental. He just called them as he saw them. And in his line of work, he saw a lot.

"The police botched this investigation from the start. I'm sure we all remember the officer who was in charge of logging people in and out of the scene, Officer Childs. While he was on the stand, I asked him for his notes, and he opened up a teeny tiny notebook. He did not have the names of anyone who was at the scene. At first he did not even recall if he was wearing gloves when he initially walked through the massage parlor. Then he remembered he wasn't." Wheeler shook his head. "Was there evidence that was never cataloged, perhaps even destroyed? We'll never know."

Wheeler went on, occasionally making a show of looking down at his notebook, casting doubt on every step of the investigation. Some of his points did not even make a lot of sense, but in aggregate they might leave the jurors confused enough that they would not be able to find Leacham guilty beyond a reasonable doubt.

But being found not guilty wasn't the same as being innocent. Even Wheeler would not go so far as to claim his client was innocent.

Finally, Wheeler summed it up. "The prosecutor has not proved her charges. Instead, she has dragged the name of an honorable man through the mud. I ask that you serve justice today. I ask that you find David Leacham not guilty. Because that is the truth."

CHAPTER 5

As she pushed back her chair and stood up from the prosecution table, Mia tried to take a deep breath. She had listened closely to Wheeler. Now was her chance to lay out her rebuttal. Her final chance to speak to the jury. Everything was riding on what she said next. She resisted the urge to wipe her sweaty palms on the skirt of her suit. As she walked to the jury box, Charlie gave her a subtle but encouraging nod.

"Ladies and gentleman of the jury, the Seattle Police Department, the crime lab, and the DA's office—we have done all that we can. There's nothing else we can add. Nothing else we can show you. And do you know why? Because we didn't make the facts. We didn't make the evidence. He did." She turned and pointed at David Leacham. He kept his face impassive, but she could see the hate hiding in his eyes.

The defense had called a dozen people to speak on his behalf, but Leacham himself had never taken the stand. Mia wished she could bring that up, could say to the jury, "Hey, what's Leacham so afraid of? Why can't he answer our questions? If his story is true, why won't he subject himself to cross-examination?" but she could not. The right to remain silent was guaranteed under the Fifth Amendment, and she could not comment at all.

Even though Mia knew, and Wheeler must know too, that if David Leacham had taken the stand, he would have cracked like a potato chip.

"When this trial is over, you will leave with questions that are never going to be answered. And for the rest of your life, when you think about your time as a juror, you're going to ask yourself: Why did he do that? Why did David Leacham take everything that girl had to give and then take even more?

"But having questions like that doesn't mean there's a meaningful doubt. What this trial boils down to is this: If you believe with all your heart and with all your gut that this defendant committed the murder, then you will find him guilty. And you, ladies and gentleman of the jury"—she swept her gaze from face to face—"better than anyone else in the world who wasn't in the room that night, know what really happened there. And I know you're not going to let David Leacham get away with it."

She lowered her voice, and the jurors leaned forward, as if she were letting them in on a secret. All the jurors, except Warren. He was staring down at the floor, as he had been ever since she began talking, his gaze vacant. Mia tried not to let the sight of his seeming indifference break her stride.

"The defense has tried to overwhelm you with trivial details. Yes, Officer Childs was not wearing gloves when he first walked through the massage parlor. He answered honestly about that.

He also answered honestly about not touching anything with his ungloved hands." She was relieved to see her words met by nods.

"As for our missing witness, we can only speculate as to what has happened to her. Unfortunately, we do not know." Out of the corner of her eye, Mia could see Wheeler readying himself to object if she did speculate. She decided to pivot to a stronger point rather than let him interrupt her flow.

"What you need to focus on is Mr. Leacham himself, and what kind of man he is. And to do that we need to look below the surface. We want to think that we know evil when we see it. We want to believe that evil is ugly. That it is friendless. That evil isn't a member of the Rotary Club, that it doesn't have a wife and kids and a successful business. We want to believe we can tell just by looking who is evil, because it makes us feel safer." Mia sighed, her mouth twisting. And was rewarded when the jurors seemed to sigh with her, a quiet echo.

"The defense has paraded people before you, people who are acquainted with Mr. Leacham from his church and from his business and from his volunteer work. They all thought they knew him. They all wanted to believe that there wasn't a secret, hidden, sick side to him. Can you imagine how you would feel if you thought you knew somebody and then you turned out to be so wrong? And meanwhile, you had perhaps let that person be around your family? Around your wife? Around your daughters? You would never want to believe you could be that wrong about anybody. But the simple truth is these people *were* that wrong, and they're still that wrong." Mia's voice strengthened with every word.

"Now it's time for the twelve of you to start deliberating, to sit down together and talk about what you have seen and heard. For you to reason together and come back with a verdict. It's time for this case to finally be resolved by you, the jury. Not by the media. Not by Mr. Leacham's acquaintances. But by you. It's time for justice to be served for Dandan Yee."

Her voice rang throughout the courtroom. "Because David Leacham is guilty of taking this vulnerable young woman's life. He is *guilty*. And I ask you to find him so."

CHAPTER 6

As he drove to the University of Washington law school, Eli Hall hummed an old Billy Joel song under his breath. Tuesday was the bright spot of his week. Wednesdays could sometimes be wonderful too.

Of course, judged objectively, neither day should be. Both started with ten or so hours at his job as a public defender. Both ended with a couple more at home, hunched over his laptop until he couldn't keep his eyes open.

But in between . . . ah, in between, that was a different story. Because Tuesdays and Wednesdays were the nights Eli was an adjunct professor.

It wasn't that the intelligence and enthusiasm of his law school students made Eli's long days worthwhile. These days the students mostly just made him feel old. He would be turning forty in a few months, older now than even the latest of bloomers in his class.

And while he could always use the money—he was a single

parent, and the worst-paid attorneys were public defenders—that wasn't what made those two days of the week stand out.

He had met Mia Quinn, another adjunct professor, at the beginning of the term and had fallen. Fallen hard. On Wednesdays they taught in adjoining classrooms. But on Tuesdays they were a team. First they demonstrated the given topic, then, along with the students, they listened to the lecture given by Titus Brown.

So in a few minutes Eli and Mia would be sitting just a few feet apart. With luck, they might even meet up in the parking lot beforehand and walk in together. And they would surely walk out together. They had fallen into a routine without having to discuss it. Walking and talking was just a given now.

They had a lot in common. As was true for Eli, one reason that Mia taught was because she needed the money. Like him, she had a teenager, although his Rachel was a couple of years older than her Gabe. But what drew Eli to her couldn't be summed up on paper, he thought as he pulled into the parking lot and felt a flash of disappointment at not seeing her.

It was her low laugh. How she tilted her head when she was listening intently. How she reached out to others. When she had learned that the mother of one of her son's friends was being treated for cancer and had lost her apartment, she had invited both mother and son into her own home.

Only once had Mia and Eli been on opposite sides, and he had seen then that she would never, ever give up. Not on her cases, not on her family.

Not like Lydia, who had taken off to "find herself" after endlessly complaining that she had gone from a child to being a mother. She learned she was pregnant her senior year of high school, and they married three months after her graduation.

After nearly seventeen years of marriage Lydia had left Eli and Rachel a year ago without a backward glance, a Skype visit, or even a letter.

Mia would never do that. He had seen how loyal she was to the victims she represented, to her co-workers, and to her friends.

Which was what Eli was. He wanted to be more. He had tried to drop hints, but he didn't have much practice.

Now his heart started beating a little faster as he pulled open the door to the classroom, which was modeled like a miniature courtroom. The students who had earlier been assigned to play jurors were already in the jury box. Mia was sitting at the prosecutor's table, deep in conversation with Titus. Tomorrow Eli and Mia would critique their own students as they put into practice what they learned tonight.

As Titus took the judge's chair, Eli shot Mia a smile. She nodded and smiled in return, but she seemed distracted.

After clearing his throat, Titus said, "Tonight Ms. Quinn and Mr. Hall will be modeling voir dire for you. The case for which they will be questioning prospective jurors concerns a forty-three-year-old black defendant who is charged with assaulting and raping a twenty-one-year-old white woman after they left a bar together."

Slipping into his role as judge, Titus asked the prospective jurors as a group if any of them knew the defendant, the victim, or the attorneys. By prearrangement they all said no, the same answer they gave when he asked if any of them doubted their ability to be fair and impartial during the trial.

Then he turned the jurors over to Mia and Eli. Just as in a real voir dire, they had been given the bare "facts" about each juror, such as name, age, and marital status. But Titus had gone one step further and slipped each of the pretend jurors an interesting fact to see if Eli or Mia would tease it out.

Mia was first up. "I want to begin this morning by telling you that you are all qualified jurors. When you came in, you had no idea whether it was to hear a case about a personal injury in a car crash, or about two partners who had a falling out over their company, or maybe it was a medical malpractice case or a criminal case. You had no idea, did you?"

Already caught up in Mia's spell, the pretend jurors bobbed their heads in agreement.

"And you ended up here, on a criminal case. Now, each of us has personal experiences that make the different cases the right case or the wrong case *for us*." She emphasized the last two words. "You may have personal feelings that make this an inappropriate trial for you, whereas you could listen to that partnership dissolution very easily. So the purpose of our questions is not to disqualify you. In fact, if you think about it, it's more like figuring out whether the *case* should be disqualified from *you*. Nothing is personal. And I think it's easier to answer the questions if you keep that in mind."

Eli resolved to borrow Mia's phrasing the next time he did voir dire. If you couldn't learn from the best, you didn't deserve to practice law.

"Have any of you been the victim of a crime?" Mia asked.

One of the pretend jurors raised his hand.

After checking her printout, Mia called out, "Juror Seventeen?"

Juror Seventeen, played by a young man, was supposedly a plumber in his forties. "Three years ago, I was the victim of an armed robbery and was pistol-whipped."

"Pistol-whipped?" Mia echoed. "So you were injured?"

"Yes."

"Were you satisfied with what the police did?"

Getting into his part, the young man jutted out his jaw. "They did nothing."

"So I would say that's a no."

About half the jurors smiled. Mia was already building rapport.

"No."

"And were you satisfied with anything the prosecutor did?" Mia raised one eyebrow.

"No. They never caught him."

"The police never did anything, so the prosecutor didn't do anything?"

"Exactly," the supposed victim said. "And now I have posttraumatic stress disorder."

"And in hearing the evidence about the alleged assault, do you think you would have a problem believing the police officer's testimony?"

He hesitated and then said, "Yes, I do."

Good job, Mia, Eli thought. Some people would feel a crime victim would naturally side with the prosecution, but in this case, the juror actually bore some animus toward law enforcement. And because of her careful questioning, she would be able to strike him for cause.

Mia looked back out over all the jurors again. "Now I'm going to ask you some questions that you may ask to respond to out of hearing of the other jurors, if you feel the questions are too personal. Have you, or has any family member or close friend, ever been the victim of any type of sexual assault?"

A juror raised her hand.

"Yes, Number Three?"

"My daughter was raped."

"And was her assailant caught?"

"She did not press charges."

"May I ask why not?" Mia said gently.

"She was afraid of how she might be treated."

"And what did you think?"

Suddenly vehement, the girl managed to channel a fifty-two-year-old mother. "If I had known about it at the time I would have told her that she had done nothing wrong, and that she needed to report him to the police so that creep couldn't hurt anyone else."

"Anyone else?" Mia asked, and then when no one answered, she went on to ask a handful of carefully chosen questions.

After Mia was finished, it was Eli's turn. After a few questions about what TV shows they liked to watch or magazines they liked to read—questions he always felt helped jurors let down their guards and still provide him with useful information—he asked them how they defined sexual assault. Some stammered and blushed while others answered forthrightly.

Eli then asked, "Does anyone know someone who falsely claimed to have been a victim of a sexual assault?"

A man slowly raised his hand.

"Number Sixteen? What were your feelings about that?"

"Well, since I was the one who was falsely accused, I had pretty strong feelings about it, as you can imagine."

"Do you think those feelings would make it hard for you to believe another woman claiming she had been assaulted?"

He paused, then said, "I don't think so."

"I sense some hesitation in your answer," Eli said. "It is absolutely okay to have some hesitations or reservations. I just need to know. When you say you don't think so, does that mean that it might?"

"I guess it might."

After Eli was finished, he and Mia both chose which jurors to strike for cause and with preemptory challenges. Then Titus began his lecture.

"*Voir dire* is a French term meaning 'to speak the truth.' It's when prosecutors and defense attorneys interview prospective jury members about their beliefs and life experiences. We say we want a fair and impartial jury, and maybe that's true for society, but it's not true for us as attorneys." Titus pointed his finger at his own chest. "I want a juror whose experiences make them biased in my favor."

His blunt words were greeted with nods and laughter.

"Voir dire is like going on a first date, something you ladies and gentlemen might have some experience with." He waggled an eyebrow. "When you go on a first date, you want to find out as much as you can about your date in a short amount of time so that you can figure out whether you want to see them again. You want to get your date to like you and have a sense of what you're about, but you also don't want to turn them off with a bunch of nosy questions."

Eli and Mia exchanged glances. He would have given anything to know what she was thinking. They'd gone out exactly that one time, for brunch. And even though it probably didn't count as a second date, he had once saved her life.

Titus continued, "Just as everything someone does on a first date is noticed, everything lawyers do and say during voir dire conveys a message. And just as lawyers are picking jurors, at the same time jurors are picking the lawyer they like and trust the most.

"Voir dire is the only time during a trial that you can talk directly with jurors. I'm not saying it is your chance to talk *at* them. No. It's your opportunity to find out who they are and how they feel. How you phrase things can make a difference. Ask people if they believe in racial profiling, and most will say no. But ask them if people from Muslim countries should get extra screening, and a lot of them will say yes. Jurors will shade their answers if they are afraid of being judged.

"You want to find out as much as you can about them, but without asking them endless questions. The trick is to ask open-ended questions so they'll say a lot more than just a yes or a no. So you don't ask, 'Do you believe in the death penalty?' Instead, you say, 'How do you feel about the death penalty?' In fact, once they answer, don't jump right in afterward. Give them a moment. A lot of times a juror will add something—something important." Titus nodded at his own words.

"And after you listen to the answer, base your follow-up questions on it. As you can see from Mia's line of questioning of the fellow who was pistol-whipped, those follow-up questions can provide you with a basis for cause strikes.

"Remember that this isn't a deposition. It's a *conversation.*" He stretched out the last word with the cadence of a preacher. "So you don't talk like an attorney. You talk like a person. You don't challenge. You don't criticize. You listen. And the more you listen, the more you learn.

"You can of course strike anyone for cause. It's only preemptory strikes that are limited. Each side has three. But trust me, you're going to need those three. Because there are times you are going to have to go with your gut." He turned to Mia. "So why did you choose to strike Juror Twelve?"

"I have found in rape cases that older women can sometimes be judgmental," Mia said. "That's just based on my experience. On the flip side, for this case I'd like to keep the older male jurors, because they might see the victim as their daughter or wife or sister."

Titus turned to Eli. "Why did you continue to question Juror Sixteen?"

Eli had used one of his preemptory challenges on that juror. "I always worry about prospective jurors who use the words *think* or *hope* or *try*. Because often they might be dropping hints that they aren't capable of being neutral. And I think that was the case here."

Titus nodded. "Nonverbal communication can tell you a lot. If a juror looks down or past you, it could mean they don't really care about what you have to say. On the flip side, someone who smiles or nods in agreement when you are speaking is obviously the kind of intelligent, thoughtful juror you want."

Eli and Mia laughed right along with the students. And looking at Mia, at her flashing eyes and her slightly crooked smile, Eli fell harder than ever.

CHAPTER 7

Gabe rubbed the steam away from the bathroom mirror. With his right hand he made a fist and then flexed his biceps. It looked like someone had slipped a softball under his skin. Along his forearm, veins popped. Nobody at school made fun of Gabe anymore. And lately girls had been looking at him. Talking to him. Sometimes, he thought, even flirting with him. He was no longer invisible.

If only he had been able to put on this weight before football season had ended. It would have been so much easier to push up and down the field if he'd weighed thirty pounds more. Except Coach Harper might have asked awkward questions, the way he sometimes quizzed the other football players about how exactly they had managed to bulk up. But now football season was over, and Gabe didn't have Coach Harper as a teacher.

"You've got to try to get bigger if you want to get any better," one of the seniors on the team had told him. Well, Gabe had tried.

He had done all that he could. Lifted weights until he felt like his arms would snap. Choked down protein powder drinks that were supposed to taste like chocolate but instead tasted more like chalk.

But nothing had helped. At least until now. Now he had the only thing that really could help.

These days his shirts strained across his pecs. He could bench forty more pounds than he'd ever done before. Yesterday, for the first time in his life, he had grabbed the ten-foot-high basketball rim while doing a layup. Soaring through the air, he had felt like he could fly. He had felt invincible.

Gabe's mom was sweet but clueless. She thought that if you worked hard, things eventually paid off.

But sometimes all that hard work needed a little extra help.

It was like diabetics whose bodies needed insulin because they didn't make enough. Or people who were depressed because their brains didn't make the right chemicals. Gabe was suffering from an imbalance. His body just didn't make hormones in the right proportions. Which was why he hadn't grown in the right proportions.

He had asked some of the guys on the team how they had managed to remake their bodies, and one had finally explained it to him—and eventually, as the season was ending, slipped him the number of this guy named Tyler who could hook him up.

They'd met at a restaurant near Gabe's school. Before Tyler showed up, Gabe ordered some food, but he was too nervous to eat it. Besides, it looked kind of greasy, and what if it sent the wrong message, like he wasn't serious about being fit? Gabe had been slowly shredding his paper napkin when a guy walked out of the kitchen area carrying a white takeout bag and slid into the seat across from him.

Even though it was nearly freezing outside, he was wearing a white sleeveless T-shirt and long navy-blue basketball shorts. The dude was seriously ripped. Not an ounce of fat on him, just pure corded muscle. He was like a walking advertisement for his product.

"Gabe?" It came out more like a grunt.

"Yeah." Gabe hoped his own voice didn't sound shaky.

Tyler nodded, but didn't offer his own name. "Did you come alone?"

"Yeah."

The guy kept his eyes on Gabe's face until Gabe grew uncomfortable, then slowly slid the bag across the table.

As he had been instructed, Gabe reached across the table and shook Tyler's hand. In his palm were ten twenty-dollar bills, folded in half. Birthday and chore money he had been saving for a mountain bike. Without counting them or acknowledging them in any way, Tyler pocketed them and then left with another nod.

Gabe made himself wait a few minutes before he put the white paper bag in his backpack. Then a few more minutes before he picked up his skateboard and left. He didn't even look inside the bag until he got back to his room.

Then Eldon had walked in, surprising him. After having his own room all his life, Gabe kept forgetting that he could no longer be sure of having any privacy. When Eldon came in, Gabe was still examining the bag's contents—a few syringes, a vial of clear liquid, and a bottle of pills. A two-week supply of two anabolic steroids.

Eldon stared. It was too late to hide everything or try to think of a cover story.

"Gabe, dude?" he said. "Is that what I think it is?"

Eldon and Kali, his mom, had moved in after Kali had been diagnosed with breast cancer, lost her job, and fallen behind on her rent. Before they came here, they had been living in their friend Danny's unheated garage. They were Samoan, both built like squares. If Gabe was downstairs and Eldon was upstairs, he could feel the whole house shake when Eldon walked down the hall. And even though Kali had lost a lot of weight because of the chemo, she was still a sagging mountain of a woman.

Eldon lowered his voice. "Are those steroids?"

The heat climbed Gabe's face all the way up to his hairline. "You can't tell anyone."

With a sigh, Eldon shook his head. "You know I won't. But I don't know, Gabe. Is it right?"

Eldon clearly didn't have an imbalance. He had no idea what it was like. "It's not like I'm going to be smoking dope or using heroin," Gabe said. "This is only so I can improve myself."

"Then why not do it, like, the natural way?" Eldon's voice was mild, but Gabe still felt irritated.

"Where have you been?" he said. "I have been doing nothing but lifting at school or going down to the basement to use my dad's old weights. I'm drinking protein or weight-gainer shakes three or four times a day. But it's not working. It's easy for you to say I should do things the natural way. You're built like a bulldozer. And I'm a toothpick."

Even after he got the steroids, it still took Gabe a week to work up the courage to push a needle into his skin. He found step-by-step advice on the Internet and read it over and over until he had it memorized. On Netflix he watched a really old football movie, *The Program*, to see how the players injected steroids.

Still, the first time he used a syringe to pull fluid from the vial, tilted it up, and squeezed out a drop to get rid of any air bubbles, and then jammed the needle into his hip, Gabe had been so afraid that he might die. His heart was racing, his palms were wet, and his head felt light. Would you even know you were dying? Or would you just suddenly wink out?

The next time it was a little easier. Same for the time after that. So every Tuesday and Friday for the past five weeks, Gabe had gone into his room and locked the door. He didn't need to hear any more comments from Eldon. And there, alone in his room, surrounded by Little League trophies, his homework, and posters of his favorite bands, Gabe jabbed a needle into his hip.

The steroids changed everything. He got bigger. He got faster. He got stronger. And girls noticed him now. They had never noticed before. Every day before he went to school, he rolled his shirt sleeves to precisely the right level to show off his new biceps. He brushed his teeth and even his tongue, gargled with mouthwash so minty it burned his mouth. He made sure his hair was perfectly mussed before he walked out the door.

He still had to work hard, of course he did, but the steroids had given him the base that had been lacking.

There was a knock on the bathroom door. "I need to go, Gabe." It was his little sister, Brooke.

Gabe gritted his teeth. The house was really too small for five people. Lately it just felt like he was never alone. Not even in the bathroom.

"Okay. Just a sec." He wrapped a towel around his waist. As he turned away from the mirror, he caught a glimpse of ugly, red acne speckling the tops of his shoulders. He had heard it was a side effect of steroids, but he had never thought it would affect him. He draped a second towel across his shoulders, hoping it would hide it.

"Gabe!" His little sister's voice was like a mosquito's, an annoying whine. "Now!"

"All right!" he shouted. "Can't you just give me a second?" He wrenched back the door. Brooke must have been leaning against it, because suddenly she tumbled in, her face scrunching up and her mouth opening as she gathered her breath to cry.

"Shut it!" he roared in her face, startling her so much she went completely silent.

Gabe stalked past her, his teeth still clenched.

CHAPTER 8

Gabe!" Mia yelled up the stairs when she heard her son bellowing at her daughter. She set down her purse and keys, then put her fisted hands on her hips. She hadn't even been home for a minute, and this was how it had to begin?

A beat. And then, "What?" Sullen, but not so sullen she could call him on it.

Realizing she was about to yell at Gabe that he shouldn't yell at his sister, Mia forced herself up the stairs. She barely had the energy to climb them, let alone lecture.

When had he gotten so big, she wondered as she took the last two steps to where he stood on the landing. Where had her little boy gone? Or her skinny teenager, for that matter? Now his shoulders were powerful, his chest broad. He had a towel around his waist and another across his shoulders. He looked like a man, not a boy. He looked, in a way that made her feel like someone had just slipped a knife in between her ribs and given it a good twist, so much like Scott.

Brooke's door was closed, and from behind it came the rhythmic sound of crying. There was an edge of theatricality about it, but a big part of it sounded real to Mia.

"What did you say to your sister?" she demanded.

"She wanted in the bathroom, and she wouldn't listen when I said she had to wait a sec. So I told her she had to give me a chance to get out."

"When you're Brooke's age, sometimes your body doesn't give you too much warning."

Gabe rolled his eyes. "But she obviously *didn't* have to go to the bathroom that bad or that's where she would be right now, not off in her room having a pity party."

Should Mia call him on the disrespect of the eye roll? But he would just deny it, and then the matter of how he had treated Brooke—which had clearly been inappropriate—would get lost. She worried, not for the first time, just how much, in addition to his looks, Gabe had inherited from his father.

"I need you to go in and apologize to your sister right now."

"She's making too big a deal out of it. She yelled at me, so I yelled at her just a little bit."

"You're ten years older than she is—and three times her size!"

He didn't answer, just stuck out his lower lip, making a face she had seen all too often from Brooke.

"Go apologize to her right now, Gabe. And I don't want any more arguing or eye rolling. If you don't stop right now, there *will* be consequences."

She hoped for both their sakes that he'd listen and she wouldn't have to choose a consequence. No matter what she chose, it wouldn't be simple. If she took away his phone, he would argue that he might need to call her in an emergency. If she took away his computer, he would surely need it for homework. If she grounded him, there would probably be a birthday party he had already promised to go to.

"Okay. I'll go apologize."

When he turned, she glimpsed an ugly rash of acne across his back. Next time she was at the store she would have to look for some kind of wash he could use in the shower. Stick it in the kid's bathroom without saying anything. He got embarrassed so easily.

She stood in the hall for a moment, but she couldn't really hear what he said to Brooke. At least it sounded gentle and more or less sincere. Lately, Gabe's mood could change so quickly. Hormones were no fun.

When he came out, she said quietly, "Thank you, Gabe."

He nodded, not making eye contact.

"Your working out is really paying off." He lifted weights every day after school and then came home and did more down in the basement with Scott's old set. "Good for you for sticking with it."

He flushed with pleasure, then shifted his grip on the towel to free one arm, which he flexed to show off his biceps. "Want to buy tickets to the gun show?"

Now it was Mia who rolled her eyes. Still smiling, she went back downstairs and past the family room, where Eldon was watching TV.

"Hey, Mrs. Q." He flopped one large hand at her in greeting. Eldon had always been a big kid, built like a tree trunk, but now Gabe didn't seem that much smaller. It had been good for him to have another male in the house, even if it was a boy, not a man.

"Where's your mom?"

Eldon's mouth twisted. "Sleeping. She's not feeling so good."

Some days it seemed like this latest round of chemo would kill Kali before it saved her. She had once been built like Eldon, but now her skin looked oddly loose, like she could push it all down to her ankles and step out of it.

"I'm sorry. Hopefully a nap will make her feel better."

Mia started to walk past the dining room, the one room that saw little use and thus the only room that was sort of clean. On impulse she went in and looked at the framed photo on the sideboard. It showed what had once been her family, the four of them on a beach in Kauai. Two weeks after that photo was taken, Scott had died in a single-car accident.

Mia had thought to compare Gabe's face to Scott's, but she had forgotten that in the photo Scott had been wearing sunglasses. If he hadn't, would she now be able to look at his expression and read all the secrets he had been keeping from her?

Scott kept smiling at her from the photo as if saying, *You'll never know, will you?* He had one arm around her waist and the other resting on Brooke's shoulder. Even back then, Gabe stood a bit to one side, as if already anxious to flee the family unit.

Mia just hoped she could make it through her kids' growing up with her sanity intact. Sometimes she looked around at her life and wondered what had happened. A year ago, it had been simple. She had been a stay-at-home mom. Scott had worked long hours, running his own accounting firm, trying to keep it afloat after the economy tanked.

After he died she eventually learned more than she had wanted to know about how Scott had failed. To keep his business going and his family fed during the lean years, he had run up thousands in credit card debt. Debt Mia was slowly chipping away at. Eventually he had decided that there was more money to be made as a dishonest accountant than as an honest one. And finally he had fallen in love with a twenty-two-year-old college student he had hired as an intern.

Then Scott had died, and Mia had gone back to work at King County. Tried to fit into the power suits she had left behind four years earlier when she had been pregnant with Brooke. Tried to be both mother and father to a preschooler and a teenager.

Even though ten years separated Brooke from Gabe, there were a lot of parallels. Both of them acted out. Both of them were determined to be independent while walking right into danger.

Mia gave herself a mental shake. She didn't have time to be reminiscing. Some days she didn't feel like she had time to think, period. She just had to act. She needed to start getting Brooke ready for bed, but first she needed to eat. Kali should have already fed the kids. Was there anything in the freezer worth nuking, or should she just make do with a bowl of cereal?

When she saw the state of the kitchen, she forgot all about dinner. The big blue mixing bowl sat on the white-powdered counter next to a bag of flour, a bag of sugar, an egg carton surrounded by scattered broken shells, and a half stick of butter that had been sitting out on the counter long enough that the edges were blurred.

The bowl was half full of chocolate chip cookie dough. And no baked cookies in sight. It wasn't too hard to guess where the rest of the dough had gone.

On the nights Mia wasn't home, the plan called for Kali to make dinner for the kids. And even Gabe knew how to take a blue box of mac and cheese off the shelf and pour the noodles into some boiling water. With all the effort they had put into making cookies, they could have made a halfway decent dinner.

The anxiety Mia had been feeling since the jury deliberations began now found an outlet. She grabbed the mixing bowl and opened the compost jar that sat on the kitchen counter. Scraping the dough into the coffee grounds and table scraps, she smashed the eggshells on top. There. Now none of them would be tempted to pick at it.

She went back into the hall. "Gabe, Eldon, Brooke! I need you down here."

When they lined up in front of her, it was clear they had totally forgotten about the evidence they had left behind.

"What is this?" she demanded, pointing into the kitchen.

After a pause, Eldon said, "Sorry about the mess. We forgot to clean up."

"We made cookies," Brooke said. "And I helped."

"And what about dinner?"

From the guilty looks they exchanged, it was clear there hadn't been any other than cookie dough. Mia stamped her foot, all her tiredness forgotten. "That's it. We're not doing this anymore. Things are going to change around here. No more junk food."

"But that's not junk food," Gabe protested. "It's homemade."

"It's still junk food, especially if you eat it for dinner." She walked over to the fridge, yanked off the menu from Pagliacci's, and stuck it in the recycling bag under the sink. "That's it. No more takeout pizza. No more fast food. From now on, we're going to eat salads! And if we want to have dessert, we'll have fruit."

"But I don't want fruit." Brooke pushed out her lower lip. "I want cookies."

Paying her no mind, Mia handed grocery bags to Gabe and

Eldon. She began opening cupboards and looking for things to get rid of. Sugary cereals, a bag of chips, crackers made from white flour. The contents went into the compost, the containers into recycling. Still-sealed containers went, with a few misgivings, into the grocery bags the boy held. She would take them to the food bank.

With each jar, box, or bag, Gabe's face got redder. Eldon looked like he wished his mom had never said yes when Mia had offered them a place to live. And Brooke was on the verge of tears.

"Okay," Mia finally said over her shoulder. "You guys can put your bags down and go upstairs. I'll finish up here."

"Do you need any more help?" Gabe asked.

She had seen his face when she put the new jar of Nutella into the bag. Maybe he was hoping to sneak it back to his room.

"No. I think you've done enough in here for one day."

At 1:12 a.m., Mia woke up to a growling stomach and realized she had completely forgotten to eat dinner. In her dreams she had been standing behind the prosecution table, waiting for the jury to announce their verdict. But something kept happening to delay it: an earthquake, a fire drill, a microphone that didn't work.

She lay in the dark, looking up at the ceiling. She had done the best she could. But was it good enough? Wheeler had done an excellent job. And Sindy was flown to the wind.

Finally she got up and went downstairs to make herself a bowl of cereal—one of the kinds she had deemed healthy enough to keep. But as she was opening the cupboard door, she remembered the secret stash of Kettle Brand chips she kept in one of the basement's Rubbermaid cabinets, hidden behind a twenty-five-pound bag of basmati rice from Costco. Those chips definitely had to go into the compost bin.

But when she opened the first package, and the smell of spice and grease hit her nose, Mia found herself sitting on the back step in her pajamas, barefoot in thirty-eight-degree weather, shoveling in the chips one handful after another.

CHAPTER 9

WEDNESDAY

When the blare of Mia's alarm woke her, her mouth tasted terrible. This must be comparable to how Scott had felt on the mornings when he'd had a hangover. Feeling low and ashamed, his mouth tasting like something had died in it. Only in Mia's case, what had died in her mouth was an entire bag of Kettle Brand Buffalo Bleu potato chips.

Eating all those chips hadn't done a darn thing to erase her anxiety about the jury deliberations. How many times must she learn the lesson that food didn't solve anything—and then promptly forget it? Plus, what kind of example was she setting? Thank goodness she had eaten the chips long after the kids were in bed.

With a groan Mia got up, pulled on a bathrobe, and padded into Brooke's room. "Brooke, honey, time to get up."

Brooke pulled the pillow over her head. "Go away. Brooke isn't here."

"Uh-oh. If you're not Brooke, then who am I talking to?"

Enchanted by this idea, Brooke threw off the pillow and sat up. "My name is . . . Break."

"Break? What kind of a name is Break?"

"It's because I break things." She jumped out of bed and started walking stiff-legged toward a pile of toys, her arms outstretched.

What was she picturing herself as—a giant rampaging lizard? A zombie? At four, you could almost convince yourself that you could be anything you wanted to be. Thirty or so years older than four, Mia sometimes felt she was barely capable of being herself.

She swept up her daughter just as an outstretched foot was about to crush a half-dressed Barbie. "Well, just for today, I think you have to be Brooke again. So let's go have breakfast."

Downstairs, Mia opened the kitchen cupboards, momentarily confused by their barrenness. "Cheerios or Raisin Bran?" she asked.

"I want the chocolate cereal!"

If memory served, that was the one with thirteen grams of sugar per serving. "We're not eating that one anymore." Luckily she had stashed the food bank bags in the hall closet. "Your choices are Cheerios or Raisin Bran."

"Then the one with marshmallows." Brooke seemed to have forgotten the events of the night before.

"No, remember, both those cereals have too much sugar. From now on, we're going to be eating healthy food."

"But I like sugar." Brooke's expression looked mulish.

"I know you have a sweet tooth, honey, but we're going to be eating less sugar from now on." Mia pulled a coffee filter from the pack.

"Do you want to see my sweet tooth?"

"Huh?" Mia stopped measuring coffee.

"My sweet tooth. Do you want to see it?" Brooke opened her mouth wide and pointed at one of her back molars on the left side. She spoke around her finger. "Tha my swee too."

Gabe and Eldon shambled into the kitchen, and suddenly it felt really small. They both seemed so . . . male.

At least they didn't complain about the newly truncated choices. Gabe had started eating hard-boiled eggs for breakfast, as well as juice and a big spoonful of peanut butter. He plunked four pre-cooked, pre-peeled eggs into a bowl, then took the now-empty plastic wrapper to the garbage can.

"What is this?" His foot was still on the pedal, and he was looking down. At the empty chip bag.

Mia started with the truth and ended with a lie. "Last night I remembered we had some chips, so I put them in the compost."

"Uh-huh." He tossed a dubious look at Eldon, who had the grace to look as if he believed her.

Brooke tugged at Mia's robe. "We have chips? I want chips!"

And that was pretty much how the morning went.

Before she went into the office, Mia stopped at Perk Up, a nearby coffee shop, and ordered a sixteen-ounce nonfat latte, even though she had already had coffee at home. The dairy was much-needed protein, she reasoned. And besides, she was exhausted.

"Name?" the barista asked her.

"What?"

"What name should I put on your order?" The girl was Asian American with bleached blond hair. A reverse skunk stripe marked her part.

"Mia."

"Mia?" The girl's gaze sharpened. "Hey, what's your last name?"

"Quinn."

"So did that Chinese guy ever find you?"

"What Chinese guy?" Mia was feeling lost, but then again she was not at her best this morning.

The girl looked up at the ceiling, remembering. "He came in like, what, two weeks ago? He was trying to speak in Mandarin to me, but I barely know enough to order in a restaurant. He had a business card with your name on it, but he was asking for a Mrs. Scott."

"My husband's name is Scott," Mia said. It was easier to use the present tense, to pretend for a moment that Scott hadn't died, than to explain to a stranger that he had been dead for months. "Did he tell you his name? Was it Lihong?"

"He didn't say much of anything past asking for you and pointing at your address. We had just opened. And then his friends came in and he left with them."

Before he died, Scott had befriended a young man named Lihong who worked at a restaurant called the Jade Kitchen. Mia had met Lihong a few weeks earlier. She was pretty sure he was an illegal immigrant, and it sounded like Scott had promised to help him, perhaps with his immigration status. It had been hard to understand Lihong, who only knew a few words of English. She had meant to follow up with him. She had meant to do a lot of things. Just one more item that had fallen off her plate. She made another mental note.

Once she reached work, it was a different kind of torment. She spent the morning aimlessly looking through files, wondering what was going on in the jury room. Every few minutes a well-intentioned co-worker would stop by.

"What time did the jury get the case?" Jesse asked.

A half hour later, Anne stuck her head in. "How long have they been out?"

Each time Mia answered in as few words as possible, hoping to cut off any further conversation. She knew they only meant to be supportive, or to strike up a conversation so they could discuss the case. But that was the last thing she wanted to talk about. She would rather talk about anything else—the stock market, the weather, the latest shenanigans of a movie star.

She told herself she had picked the best people for the jury that she could, based on her experience and intuition and the luck of the draw. That was all you could do. Then you just prayed they could play nice with each other and reach a decision.

When her phone rang, she pounced on it. But the voice on the other end of the line belonged to her father.

"How are things going, honey?"

It struck Mia with a spasm of sadness that the only people who called her "honey" these days were waitresses of a certain age and her dad.

"Fine." It was a relief to talk to someone who had no idea she was waiting on a verdict.

"I would love to see my favorite daughter for lunch today."

She laughed. "Dad, I'm your *only* daughter. You wasted your talents as a manager. You should have been in sales."

While Mia was growing up, her dad had dedicated most of his waking hours to his job at a packaging company. His retirement funds had been invested solely in company stock. When the company went bankrupt a year after he retired, the CEO got jail time and her dad had been left with nothing but Social Security. Nine months ago, he had started going to church. *Her* dad! Church! Mia wouldn't have been more surprised if he had taken up ballet.

"So will you come?"

"Of course." Half superstitiously, she hoped that if she left the office it would lead to a verdict. "There's a possibility I might need to come back here in a hurry so I'll just drive my car and meet you."

An hour later, she barely registered the other cars as she drove to the restaurant. A clock was ticking in the back of her head. The jury had been deliberating for over ten hours over the course of two days. Was that a good thing or a bad thing? There were various theories—that a quick verdict meant acquittal, or no, that a quick verdict meant conviction—but no one really knew.

She hurried into the restaurant her dad had chosen, then stopped short. Her father was already there. But so was a woman, and they were deep in conversation.

When he saw Mia, he gave her a grin and a wave, while the woman shot her a quick glance and an uncertain smile.

For years her father's world had had little to do with Mia's. Before her parents' divorce, he had spent most of his waking hours at work. After the divorce, when she was in seventh grade, she had barely seen him at all. Now that he had "gotten religion," he spent more time with Mia than he ever had before. She didn't know what to think of his transformation. Was he lonely, bored, just feeling mortal? Or was it real?

Now Mia wished she could turn back the clock to when her dad had called so that she could say no. Instead, she pasted on a smile and made her way over to the table. In the past there had been the occasional girlfriend, but her dad had had the good grace to keep them on the down low.

He stood up when she got to the table. "Mia, I'd like you to meet my friend Luciana. Luciana, this is my daughter, Mia."

Mia stretched out her hand and smiled, but part of her withdrew inside, like a snail in its shell.

Luciana was Hispanic-looking, and at least fifteen years younger than her dad. Maybe even twenty.

And she was beautiful. Her black shoulder-length hair was parted in the middle and tucked behind her ears, from which hung simple silver hoops about the diameter of a half dollar. Her black-framed glasses didn't fit her face at all. Both too narrow and too long, they just drew attention to her winged brows and high cheekbones. When she shook hands, she lightly grasped Mia's fingertips and then released them as quickly.

"So where did you two meet?" Mia asked brightly as they sat down.

Her dad shot her a glance, and she guessed she wasn't fooling him. "At church."

She was about to ask another question when the waitress appeared. "So does everyone know what they want to order?"

Thinking of her vow the night before, Mia ordered an egg white omelet and unbuttered toast, and subbed fruit for hash browns. Her dad raised an eyebrow but didn't comment. After the waitress left, Mia said, "So where do you work, Luciana?"

"Um, I am not working right now. I volunteer." Her dad patted Luciana's hand and then started asking questions about Gabe and Brooke, which Mia answered by rote. Luciana was quiet, keeping her eyes on her plate and picking at her food.

Meanwhile, Mia was asking herself the questions she really wanted to ask her dad and this woman. What did a beautiful young woman like Luciana see in her dad? Was she even in this country legally? Or was she what Mia had heard referred to as a "green digger"—a woman looking for greenbacks and a green card?

After about ten minutes, Luciana excused herself to go to the bathroom. As soon as she was a few feet away, Mia started in.

"Are you, like, dating her, Dad?"

"What are you really saying? What does she see in an old codger like me?" He grimaced. "We're not lovers, if that's what you are thinking."

Mia felt her face get hot. "Dad. Please. I did not ask you that. But what do you even know about her?"

"I know plenty. And you would too if you would listen with an open heart instead of acting like you're conducting an interrogation. Don't worry. Just because I'm spending time with her doesn't mean I don't want to spend time with you. So there's no need to be jealous."

"I'm not jealous. I'm just concerned."

The old version of her dad would have been yelling by now. Dad 2.0 just shook his head. "Sometimes I think your line of work has soured you on people. You're always looking for the worst."

"I think it's opened my eyes." Her phone began to vibrate on the table. "Sorry," she said, turning it over. It was Judge Ortega's clerk.

"Hello?"

"The jurors have sent a note to the judge."

It wouldn't be opened until they were all assembled. Mia's stomach clenched, and she wished she hadn't eaten anything at all.

"Okay. It will take me about fifteen minutes to get to the courthouse." She stood up. "Tell Luciana it was a pleasure to meet her. But I'm needed in court."

CHAPTER 10

As Mia drove back to the courthouse, her hands slid on the steering wheel and her stomach was in knots. She put her dad and his new whatever-that-woman-was into a box and closed it. She would think about them later. Right now she had to concentrate on finding out what the jury wanted, and then divining what it meant, if anything. A note from the jury could turn out to be anything from a simple request for a dry erase board to asking if they could view some of the evidence one more time.

When she entered the courtroom, James Wheeler and David Leacham were already sitting at the defense table. When Leacham turned and saw her, he lifted his chin. It felt like a challenge. Mia matched him stare for stare, keeping her face just as expressionless.

A few spectators were scattered on the benches. Bo Yee was in her customary place in the first row behind the prosecution table, looking as if she had never moved. She nodded at Mia, her expression unreadable behind her tinted glasses.

A hand touched her shoulder, and Mia started. It was Charlie.

"Sorry." He gave her a half smile. "I didn't mean to make you jump."

"Just a little anxious, I guess." For a second, her dad and Luciana peeped out of their box. "If I gave you a name, could you run it for me? It's personal."

Charlie raised one thick black eyebrow. "Who are you and what have you done to Mia Quinn?" More than once he had teased her for being such a straight arrow. When she started to stammer, he took her arm. "Don't answer that." He lowered his voice. "Just tell me the name."

Should she? Maybe she shouldn't. Guilt wrestled with worry. Worry won. "Luciana Sanchez," she said in a low voice. "I think she's my dad's new girlfriend. His way-younger girlfriend."

He nodded. Charlie had the ability to remember whole conversations without jotting down a note, so filing away a name was nothing.

When everyone was in their places, Judge Ortega took her place on the bench. After the courtroom had settled back down into their seats, the clerk handed the judge the note from the jury. Judge Ortega slipped on the black-framed reading glasses that hung on a chain around her neck, then opened the note and read it aloud.

"'We have reached a majority, but we are having difficulty reaching a unanimous decision. We keep going in circles. We are struggling with our next step. Please advise, as tension is getting thick.'"

Mia's heart thudded dully in her chest. This was not good news. The jury was hung, and the trial would not be over until they made a unanimous decision—or until it was clear they could not make one. She could not bear to think all their work had been for nothing.

The judge made a *tsk*-ing noise with her tongue. "I'm going to call the jury in and issue an Allen charge," she said.

An Allen charge took its name from a famous case when the judge had broken a deadlock by exhorting the jury. Because it was designed to dislodge jurors from entrenched positions, it was sometimes referred to as the "dynamite charge" or "hammer charge."

As the nine women and three men of the jury filed in and took their seats only a few feet away from her, Mia watched them closely, trying to figure out the lay of the land. She saw stiff legs, clenched fists, tight jaws, and furrowed brows. Sandra's cheeks were flushed, and judging by Naomi's red eyes and smeared makeup, she had recently been crying. Trapped in a small room with each other, jurors could quickly grow frustrated. They lacked the usual ways people had of dealing with conflict, such as leaving to get a beer or walk the dog or just going to another room. Mia knew of juries where insults had been thrown. Sometimes even chairs.

Judge Ortega was silent for a long moment before she addressed them. The silence served to give her words even more weight.

"Members of the jury, I know that each of you is dedicated to doing your duty and that you are being open-minded. And I know that all of you have been working hard to try to find a verdict in this case. It apparently has been impossible for you—*so far.*" She emphasized the last two words. "I'm going to ask that you continue your deliberations with the hope that you can reach agreement about a verdict and dispose of this case. I have a few comments I would like you to think about as you do so."

As she spoke, Jim, the accountant who was also the foreperson, scrubbed his face with his hands. He looked even paler, if that was possible, than he had looked during the trial.

"First of all, this trial has been expensive in all ways: time, effort, and money. If you should fail to agree, the case may well have to be tried again. But there is no reason to believe that it could be tried again any better than it has already been tried, or that any more or clearer evidence could be produced."

After pausing to let this sink in, Judge Ortega continued, "Any future jury would be selected in the same way and from the same pool as you were. I do not believe that the case could ever be submitted to twelve men and women who would be more conscientious, more impartial, or more competent to decide it than you."

Having offered a carrot in the form of a compliment, the judge now went for the stick. "Remember that you have a legal duty to discuss the evidence with each other. Your goal should be to reach a verdict. Of course, you must each decide this case for yourself, but you should also consider the views of the other jurors. If a substantial majority of you are in favor of a conviction, those who disagree should reconsider whether your doubt is a reasonable one."

Sandra, Naomi, and several other jurors turned to look at Warren, the young electrician with the two-toned mullet who had seemed uninterested when Mia gave her closing arguments. His expression vacant, he stared at his lap and gnawed on a nail.

Why hadn't Mia used one of her preemptory strikes on him? During voir dire Warren had seemed like a neutral choice, neither better nor worse than most of the other prospects. He had listened intently to both Wheeler and Mia, and answered their questions appropriately. Now any trace of alertness had vanished. He seemed lost in his own world.

Judge Ortega continued, "On the other hand, if a majority are in favor of an acquittal, the rest should ask yourselves whether you should continue to accept evidence that is failing to convince your fellow jurors. Do not hesitate to change your opinion if you become convinced that you are wrong." The judge was walking a fine line, asking jurors to change their minds. Showing her awareness of the danger, Judge Ortega added, "However, you should not change your mind just so that you can agree with the other jurors or just to return a verdict. At the same time, remember that it is your duty to agree upon a verdict if you can do so." She took a deep breath, which seemed to echo in the stillness of the courtroom.

"I have only one request of you. I want you to go back into the jury room. Then, taking turns, tell each of the other jurors about any weakness of your *own* position. You should not interrupt each other or comment on each other's views until each of you has had a chance to talk. After that, if you simply cannot reach a verdict, then return to the courtroom, and I will declare this case mistried and will discharge you with my sincere appreciation for your services." For a long moment, she looked from one face to the next. Even Warren gave her a flicker of a glance. "Please continue your deliberations."

As she walked out of the courtroom with Charlie a few minutes later, Mia asked him in a low voice, "So do you think it's Warren?"

"Either that or he's been farting in the jury room. I would also guess he's the only thing standing between you and a conviction."

"One vote might as well be a million if he won't change his mind."

Just as they reached the sidewalk, Charlie's phone buzzed and he pulled it free. "This is Carlson," he answered. Mia was about to turn away when she saw the expression on his face turn serious. He asked a few questions, then slid his phone back into its holster.

"A runner just pulled a body out of the Sound."

"So it's a murder victim?"

"They don't know yet." He looked up at the gray sky. "But it's not exactly the time of year when people go swimming."

CHAPTER 11

K enny Zhong sat in his office. On the desk in front of him were a white takeout box, his red-capped bottle of *baijiu* liquor, his calculator, a pen, and the small notebook he carried everywhere. Not only was it written in Chinese characters, it was also in a code he had invented himself, in case it should fall into someone else's hands.

Back when he was a little boy, when he was still called Kang, his grandmother used to tell him, "You can't catch a cub without going into the tiger's den." She was full of old sayings like that. Old, but true.

When he became an adult, Kenny realized he wouldn't be satisfied with just a single cub. He wanted the whole litter, and the tiger's skin as well. But in China that would never happen. Not in his province. Not with his provenance.

If you really desired to make a fortune, if you were really willing to take risks, then the place to be was America. Yes, you had to work hard, but your hard work would be rewarded. People said that American markets sold a thousand types of bread. That the very tap water tasted sweet. You could gain weight just by drinking it.

His family had paid the snakeheads to bring him here. It had taken all of them—every last auntie and cousin—to come up with the money. Despite how much it had cost, the trip to the United States had been hellish. He and twenty-three others had been smuggled in a forty-foot-long cargo container. The trip had taken five weeks. Each day they were given only a few mouthfuls of rice and some pickled vegetables. A single glass of water. If you wanted more than that, you had to buy it at twenty times the price it would cost on land.

Even though he had felt his stomach start to eat itself, Kenny had not spent a single extra yuan. He had curled up in the stinking, stifling space, laying his head on a tape recorder, half dozing, listening to tapes to help him learn English. He knew it would all be worth it: the sacrifice, the danger, the hunger and thirst, the seasickness and storms.

Thinking of food reminded Kenny of the fish in the tank behind him. It was time to feed them. There were seven of them, silver teardrops with red bellies, each about the size of his hand. Picking up the white takeout container, he took a pair of wooden chopsticks from his desk drawer.

He hadn't become acquainted with the English phrase "supply and demand" until his third year in America, but he had understood it on a visceral level even before he left China. If you had something someone wanted, wanted desperately, you could charge whatever people were willing to pay. Just as he had paid to come to America.

Like every other Chinese person on that cargo ship, once he was in Seattle, Kenny went immediately to work without one day of rest. Unlike the others, who could expect to work eight or ten years to pay off their debts, Kenny was making his own money from the start. First he had been a bus boy at a restaurant, then a waiter, then a manager, then the owner. All through a judicious combination of hard work, bribes, threats, and, when it was called for, unexpected violence. After buying the restaurant, he added three more.

As he slid the lid from the fish tank back, he could hear the din of customers out in the restaurant, crowding in for the lunch buffet. General Tso's chicken, stir-fried rice with pork, sweet-and-sour shrimp. None of it tasted anything like what he had eaten at home, but it was what the Americans liked.

Slowly he had adjusted to how different life was here. In China it was simple. If you had a business, you had to bribe everyone just to survive. You paid off the health department, the license bureau, and the tax office. You entertained the police and members of the neighborhood committees and did not charge them for their meals. Here, while you could do many of the same things, you had to be much more subtle. Still, they had a saying in America: "One hand washes the other."

About the time he bought his first restaurant, Kenny had hired his own snakeheads back home. They smuggled people into Mexico or Guatemala or Canada and then into the US, or created false passports and elaborate travel itineraries with "stopovers" in the United States, stopovers that became permanent once the traveler left the plane and never came back.

Everyone dreamed of coming to America, so much so that they were willing to pay the equivalent of $40,000 with just $1,500 down, the rest to be paid upon arrival. That meant that just twenty-five people were worth a million dollars. They looked at the cost the way an American parent might view taking out loans to pay for Harvard—expensive, but definitely worth it in the long run.

And if they had no relatives in the States—and many did not—they could borrow the balance once they arrived and work it off over time. As a result, Kenny's restaurant workers cost him next to nothing. Most of their wages went to repaying him for the privilege of being in America. And of course he charged them for food, rent, and transportation.

He even supplied workers to other businesses, where they did the kind of work that wouldn't require them to fill out a W-2 form. Menial laborers doing tasks that could be explained through gestures and maybe a few words of English. They sewed clothes, washed dishes, cooked, did domestic work, harvested crops, or worked in construction. But no matter where his people worked, Kenny's enforcers made sure that no one forgot about the money they still owed. The reminders came in the form of threats and, when necessary, something as persuasive as a lit cigarette. One especially valuable technique involved the enforcer striking the person's back with a hammer, just below the shoulder blades. The cracked ribs did not substantially affect the ability to work, but they were extremely painful, especially when a person tried to lie down to rest at night.

So debts to Kenny tended to get repaid.

He opened the takeout box. A single goldfish filled it from corner to corner, barely covered with water.

Kenny was a practical man. Just as a sly rabbit would have three openings to its den, he made money in as many ways as he could. If one source was briefly blocked, there were other avenues.

One of those avenues turned out to be steroids. Americans

were a strange people. Many of the men wanted to look like action hero manga characters with grotesquely bulging muscles. And they would do whatever they could to get them. Luckily for Kenny, hundreds of factories in China made steroid liquids or pills and were happy to ship to him. They came labeled as floral essences, packed inside bottles of Chinese herbs, mixed in with dried mushrooms, or stuffed in the hollow bodies of Buddha statues. The restaurants offered the perfect cover for sales. The red-topped vials and blue pills could be tucked in takeout orders, and the money he made could be rung up as food sales if he needed to launder it. His clientele included high school kids and security guards, gym rats and even a few cops. All of them sure they could avoid the side effects, that they could get something for nothing.

It was a customer who had given him the idea of expanding into girls. The man had asked to rent one of his prettier waitresses. It had started as a little joke and had ended with the man and the girl emerging from a back storeroom, her weeping and him grinning. Prostitution was illegal in Seattle, but nail salons and massage parlors were not, and they made the perfect fronts for both offering girls and laundering the money that resulted.

His girls had all left China of their own free will, sent off with the best wishes of their communities. They came over here with their ears filled with tales of wealth. No matter the reality, every immigrant who came back to China claimed that they had become rich in America, wanting to save face, to show that they had made their dreams come true, even if it was all a lie. Now that he lived here, Kenny knew that some of the big shots who had returned to Fuzhou for a visit actually worked as kitchen help, seventy-hour weeks for a thousand dollars a month, and lived in cellars.

Once they arrived, the girls felt duty bound to repay the debt they were told they owed. Besides, they could not bear to tell their families what they were being forced to do. To make sure, Kenny had his enforcers make videos of the girls at work. Any girl who protested was told the video could be sent to her parents.

As a result, none of his girls would consider turning witness against their controllers. Their heads were also filled with horror stories of how they would be raped by the police and thrown into prison, how their families back home could be killed. If a girl did attempt to run away, she was hunted down and abducted from wherever she had gone to ground, whether it was a hospital or a foster home. She was brought back, beaten, and raped. Locked up until she saw reason. And then set to work again.

The only time he let his girls go was if they were too damaged to work. Then they might be abandoned on a street corner, injured, sick, and/or pregnant. Still, they knew to keep their mouths shut.

With the chopsticks, he picked up the fish. He had learned the hard way that it wasn't a good idea to dangle food over the tank, not when fingers could also be thought of as food.

He held it over the tank. Below, the silver fish began to nose the water.

He opened the chopsticks and let the goldfish fall.

Kenny didn't know and he didn't care what had gone wrong with Dandan. All he knew was that he had spent perfectly good money on the girl and she had hardly earned him anything. Instead, he had had to clean up the mess she had left behind. He hadn't had time to make her body disappear, and so one of his best customers had been arrested.

The goldfish swam to a bottom corner of the tank, the other fish following close behind. He had heard that piranhas had an amazing sense of smell.

Leacham's wife had made it clear that if Leacham went to prison, Kenny would go down as well. He had sent someone to deal with Sindy, but even after she disappeared, the trial had still gone forward.

At first it looked like the piranhas were simply bumping the goldfish as it swam back and forth, more and more frantically. Then suddenly its tail was half gone, disappearing into a piranha mouth. In seconds, the other fish dismantled the goldfish piece by piece, until it was simply a floating lump of orange flesh.

Then even that was gone.

One of Kenny's people had found a juror who was willing to say no and stick to it. To never change his mind no matter how much anger or hostility or arguments were directed his way.

It seemed to be working. The jury had reported it was hung. The judge had instructed them to go back, try again, see things through each other's eyes. Kenny just hoped that the juror who had been more than happy to take a bribe could hold up to the pressure.

Because if this guy cracked, Kenny thought as he slid the cover back on the tank, he might just take his whole empire down with him.

CHAPTER 12

Golden Gardens Park hugged the shore of Puget Sound, not far from the Shilshole Bay Marina. The park's trails wound through the woods and past a pond. For the less able-bodied or adventurous, paved pathways offered easier access to nature. And then there was the beach. Out here, Seattle felt miles away, especially on a blustery day when the parking lot held only a few cars.

Gulls squawked overhead. The bright-blue tarp that lay next to the gently lapping water added a jarring note to the serene environment. So did the yellow crime scene tape that now blocked access to the beach.

"Whatcha got?" Charlie asked Carson Werther, who had been the first officer on the scene. The uniform didn't look old enough to shave, let alone to be dealing with a murder.

Werther nodded at the tarp. "A runner was going along the beach here when she spotted something in the water. It turned out to be a leg."

Charlie looked at the blue tarp with more interest. "So all you've got is the leg?" The lump looked bigger than that.

Red splotches of color appeared on Werther's cheeks. "No, no, it's the whole thing. She saw the leg first, but then she realized it was a body. She dragged it up on the beach, called 911, I was dispatched, and then I notified Homicide."

"Where's the runner?"

Werther pointed. Charlie turned and saw a woman in her forties clutching her elbows. She was pacing back and forth on a stretch of grass on the far side of the parking lot. She wore black running leggings, and her shoes and lightweight jacket were both neon green.

"The criminalists and the medical examiner will be here soon," Charlie told Werther. "You did a good job of setting up the perimeter. If anyone shows up, keep them well back. We're just lucky it's not a nice day." Six months from now there would be hundreds of people in this park.

He walked over to the witness and held out his hand. "Charlie Carlson. Seattle Homicide. I understand you're the one who found the body."

Although she had the twig-like body of a dedicated runner, the woman still had a firm handshake.

"Dee Sandoval." She mimicked his no-nonsense delivery. "Seattle runner." She had bright blue eyes. Her straight dark hair fell to her shoulders and was threaded with a few strands of gray. Now that he was closer to her, he could see that her shoes were sopping, her leggings wet to the thigh.

"Why don't you tell me what happened this afternoon?"

"I went for a run. Part of it was along the beach. I like it because it's such a good workout. The sand is always shifting under your weight. I saw something bobbing in the water, and I thought it might be a harbor seal. I've never seen one up close. Then when I came down to the water's edge, I couldn't figure out what it was. I was wondering if it was some kind of octopus." She colored. "I guess that was dumb."

"Why did you drag the body out of the water?" It would take a certain amount of courage.

"When I saw it was a person, I knew that whoever it was had a family. And that they deserved to know what had happened, even if the answer was terrible. I think he'd been in the water for a while."

"What makes you think that?"

Her shoulders hunched. "His skin was . . . loose. At first I thought it was his shirt. But then I realized he wasn't wearing one." She shivered and rewrapped her arms around herself.

The wind was picking up, slicing over the water like a cold knife.

"I'm glad you towed him in. Otherwise he might not ever have been found." Charlie took his notebook from his pocket. His memory was good enough that he didn't often take notes, but when it came to strings of numbers, he needed pen and paper. "About all I need from you right now is your name, address, and phone number."

After Dee reeled off the last digit of her cell phone number, she added, "It's been awhile since a man asked me for that." She tilted her head to one side, making her hair swing back and forth.

Charlie let out a startled laugh. The old Charlie might have taken Dee up on her hint. The new Charlie, well, he wasn't quite sure what the new Charlie was all about. Just that he had lost interest in any woman who wasn't Mia Quinn.

He still wasn't sure if that was a good thing or a bad thing.

It was getting dark and the fog was starting to roll in. "Do you need a ride home?"

"I'd love it, but I actually drove here." Her grin was mischievous. "But if you have any further questions about *anything* at all, Officer, you know where to find me."

"That I do," Charlie agreed. And just stopped himself from tipping her a wink.

Dee was getting into her car when the medical examiner drove up and parked a few spaces over. He got out and walked over to Charlie, pulling on purple vinyl gloves as he went.

"Hey, Doug," Charlie said with a nod. Doug's last name, Pietsch, was pronounced like the fruit. But with his bald head and stocky body, Doug looked a lot more like a fire hydrant.

"What have we got?"

"A floater. Runner spotted the body and dragged it onshore." They walked over to the tarp. Charlie tried to step lightly over the sand, but he could already feel grains trickling into his shoes.

Doug lifted a corner, and they regarded the corpse.

The man was naked, half sprawled on his back. His build was slight, his complexion dusky. The mottled skin was beginning to decompose. His thick black hair had fallen over his eyes.

"He's not Caucasian," Doug said, folding the tarp back all the way, "but I'm not sure of the ethnicity. Maybe Latino?"

"I'd bet he's Asian," Charlie said.

"You're on. A pint of the winner's choice?" Doug was something of a beer nut, always going on about ABVs and IBUs. Charlie just liked the taste and wasn't too picky.

"How long do you think he's been dead?" Charlie asked as the medical examiner continued to circle around the body, looking but not touching. Not yet.

"Ten days? In the Sound, it takes about that long for someone to come bobbing up, and he looks fairly fresh." He made a humming sound in the back of his throat.

"What?" Charlie asked.

"This guy has got contusions in various stages of healing. And it doesn't look like they're from running into things or being hit by objects." He pointed at some of the spots Charlie had thought were postmortem damage. "The edges are soft but the shapes are distinct. I think someone's put their hands on him. Multiple times, multiple ways. See on his upper arm, those are fingertip bruises. Someone grabbed him. Squeezed hard."

Charlie could see them now, oval dots.

Doug touched the ribs next to the spine. "I bet that one's from a fist."

"So given all those bruises, what do you think?" Charlie still hadn't seen any obviously fatal wounds. "Murder? Suicide? Accident?"

"With all those bruises I can see why he might want to depart this life, but naked suicide is pretty unusual, especially in water. Sometimes people who have decided to kill themselves get naked because they don't want to make a mess, but that's usually when they're using a gun or maybe a knife. Not the ocean. They'll strip and get in a tub or shower with a weapon, but that's just to contain the blood and such. I guess it's possible he was worried his clothes would add buoyancy and interfere with him drowning."

"And it's hard to imagine this was any kind of an accident," Charlie said. "Who's going to go swimming naked this time of year?" He pulled up his coat collar and tried to turn his back to the wind.

Doug didn't say anything, just nodded. He was still crouched down, lightly running his gloved hand back and forth over the man's ribs. Charlie guessed he was checking for broken bones. Then he reached out to the thick dark hair, brushed it off the face. Charlie wished he hadn't. The eyes were mostly gone, as were some bits of flesh.

"Do you think he was dead before he ended up in the water?"

Doug shrugged as he straightened up. "Probably. When I open him up, I'll look for water in the lungs. Then we'll know if it was a body dump or if it was the water that killed him." He stopped, his gaze riveted on something. He lifted one of the dead man's shoulders. "I think we just found our answer."

Charlie saw what Doug had spotted: the small, perfectly round hole in the man's upper back.

Charlie glanced from the wound to the hairless chest. As far as he could see, it was intact. "Where's the exit wound?"

Doug bent closer. "I think we're in luck, my friend. I think the bullet is still in there." He squinted at the wound. "And I don't see any muzzle print or laceration."

"So he wasn't shot at point-blank range?" Charlie had been wondering if they were looking at an execution.

"There's no stippling, but that doesn't mean much if he was originally wearing clothes." Stippling, or gunshot residue, occurred when power particles bruised or burned the victim's skin if the weapon had been discharged in close proximity. "But in my experience, people who are shot in the back are generally running away."

But why? A payback? Maybe a lover's quarrel? Or could the dead guy have been a kidnap victim? Was he a foreign national?

In his head, Charlie started making a to-do list. Get a dive team out in case the victim had been dumped in the water at this location and there was evidence on the floor of the Sound. Check missing person reports. Check with Harbor Patrol and the nearby marina to see if they had any reports of altercations in the past week or so. Check the shoreline in case the guy's clothes or any other evidence turned up. Check parked cars to see if any had been in the same place for a week or more.

Doug sat back on his heels. "I think the clothes are gone to make it harder to figure out who he is. Or maybe they were worried about trace evidence. They could have been thinking of the Sound as a gigantic bathtub. That by the time someone found him, he would be washed clean."

His gaze sharpened. "What's that?" He picked up a limp hand by a couple of fingers. Three angry parallel lines braceleted the inside of the man's right wrist. "Those look like burn marks."

"So they hit him and then they held him down and burned him? They must have really wanted to know something."

"I've seen marks like those before." Doug blew air out of pursed lips. "Just can't think of where."

Maybe it was some kind of gang thing. Or a drug deal gone bad. Had the victim kept something he wasn't supposed to keep and his killers had forced him to tell where it was?

What had the man's killers wanted, Charlie wondered. And had they gotten it?

CHAPTER 13

Is there anything else you feel I should know about you?" the red-haired woman asked the young man seated in the back left-hand corner of the jury box. He was wearing a faded green flannel shirt that was probably older than either of them.

"There is one thing, yes." For a second he pressed his lips together. "I am dying of cancer, so I might not be here for the whole trial."

The eyes of the pretend lawyer as well as the other pretend jurors widened.

"Very good, Samantha," Mia said. As Titus had the night before, she had given each of her students playing jurors an interesting fact to see if their classmates playing lawyers could suss them out during voir dire. "That question you asked is a great example of what some people call an oyster question. It's called that because you have to shuck a bunch of oysters before you find a pearl, but when you do, it's worth it. Some other oyster questions I like are, 'Is there any other reason why you might not be a totally fair and impartial juror in a case like this?' or 'Is anyone thinking, "You know, if the lawyer had only asked me this question, he really would have found out something important about me"?'"

As the students scribbled down her examples or typed them into their laptops, Mia tried to think back to the questions she had asked the potential jurors for Dandan's case. Was there anything she could have asked that would have revealed Warren's true nature? She was sure he was the holdout. The only question was, which way was the rest of the jury lined up? Was it possible Warren had voted to convict and the rest of them had wanted to let Leacham go free?

Mia realized the students were waiting for her to continue speaking. Between worrying about the trial and her dad's new friend, she was too easily distracted. She collected herself.

"I actually once got that answer Lincoln just gave from a prospective juror. Some of the other ones I've heard are, 'I was once accused of murder and acquitted,' and 'A cop beat me up when I was in college and now I don't believe any of them.' And my personal favorite has to be, 'We went out once in high school but you don't remember me.'"

Everyone laughed. Mia joined in, a little painfully. At the time it had been humiliating, casting her in an unflattering light. She had gone on to lose that case, and part of her had always wondered if the jurors were punishing her.

"One way to encourage the jury to be honest is, if you can, to reveal something about yourself before you ask anyone else to. During my first trial I was so scared that my legs were actually shaking during voir dire. So I didn't try to hide it. In fact, I told the jury pool something like, 'I have to confess that my knees are knocking because this is my first trial. But it is important that justice be done. I promise to deliver the evidence if you promise to listen to it.'" She let the more pleasant memory push aside the old one. "And you know what? We won!"

Lincoln, the student who had pretended to have cancer, raised his hand. "So how often do people lie to you?"

Maybe Mia was getting jaded, because there were days she thought everyone lied, at least to a degree. "I think it's pretty common. If people hold views they realize are not as popular, they'll often minimize them, if not outright lie. And you can all probably guess that potential jurors will also lie to get off a jury. They'll claim financial hardships or vacation plans that don't really exist. There are even times when people will lie to get *on* a case, especially if it's high profile. Take the Scott Peterson case, the one where the guy killed his pregnant wife and then stood in front of the TV cameras and begged for her safe return. Later, his attorney claimed that three people lied to get on that jury so they could try to turn their experiences into a book or at least media exposure. There are even times when people will try to get on the jury if they don't like the law. Before pot was legalized here, we used to see that all the time with marijuana cases. Some jurors would vote 'not guilty' even if they believed the person had smoked pot, simply because they didn't like the law."

Her thoughts snagged on the idea. Could Warren have angled to get on the jury because he didn't believe in the death penalty? But he had seemed equally checked out for both hers and Wheeler's arguments.

"So what do you do to make sure jurors are telling the truth?" another student asked.

Mia blew air out of pursed lips. "It's a balancing act. You've got to dig for the truth, but at the same time you have to be careful not to get to the point where you offend or embarrass people. Remember that some of your challenges for cause will be denied, and those folks could end up on the jury. Even if they don't, the other jurors are watching—and judging you. One way to help is to remember what Mr. Brown said last night. Ask lots of open-ended questions and don't jump in too quickly after they answer. Sometimes they'll add something that's very revealing. But at the end of the day, you might just have to go with your gut."

What had her gut told her about Warren? Nothing too bad. Compared to the people she had used up her preemptory challenges on, he hadn't made much of an impression one way or another. Mia had actually been more worried about Jim, the accountant who was now the foreperson of the jury.

Maybe she should still be. Accountants, and other people whose jobs required analytical thinking, such as engineers and computer programmers, tended to be very precise about the law and the facts. At times they could demand an almost unattainable level of proof to convict.

After class ended, Eli stuck his head in the classroom. "Do you have a verdict yet?"

So much for trying not to obsess about it. "Not only do we not have a verdict, but the jurors sent out a note saying they were hung. Judge Ortega gave them every good argument for continuing, but I don't know if it's going to work."

He grimaced. "All that work, and then you might just have to do it all over again."

Mia took her coat down from the hook. "The whole time I was watching the students practice voir dire, I was asking myself if there was something I could have done to avoid this mess."

"Sometimes it all seems nearly impossible." Eli took her coat and held it open for her. "First you're given just a couple of hours to decide if the people who got summoned are even capable of being unbiased. And then the jury system asks the resulting twelve people, these folks who are complete strangers, to decide the fate of a thirteenth. And then everyone wonders why it takes so long!"

"It's not the easiest system."

Eli sighed. "Sometimes every part of it seems pretty crazy. You know how big my caseload is right now? Close to three hundred."

Mia's mouth fell open. "That's impossible! How do you manage it?"

"The short answer is that I don't. The longer answer is that I sometimes worry I'll die trying. I've got clients charged with everything from juvenile delinquency to first-degree murder."

As they walked out to the parking lot, her phone buzzed. She checked the caller ID, knowing it was rude to do that in the middle of a conversation, but part of her always imagined it was Gabe facing some kind of emergency. And sometimes it was.

This time, however, it was Charlie. "Sorry," she said to Eli as she stopped walking. "It's Charlie Carlson."

His expression altered ever so slightly. Mia liked both Charlie and Eli. As friends. She didn't have time for anything more. At least that's what she told herself.

She pressed the button to answer. "What's up, Charlie?"

"Since I'm already at the office seeing if I can figure out who the floater was, I ran that Luciana for you."

"And?" She held her breath.

"She's forty-two. Born in El Salvador. Never married in the US. No criminal convictions. Valid Washington driver's license. She's lived in the same apartment for two years. And she's got a T visa."

The pieces clicked into place. "She was trafficked?" Mia felt her face get hot.

"It looks like she was freed from a brothel. She testified against her traffickers."

"Oh." For a second she imagined what it had been like for Luciana to see Mia's stare, her judgment. She tried to line up the reality of what Charlie had just told her with the quiet woman who had taken small bites and avoided eye contact, as if she was hoping to be invisible. "Thanks, Charlie."

"What was that about?" Eli asked after she hung up.

"Judge not lest ye be judged." Mia put her phone away.

"Hmm?" He tilted his head.

"My dad took me out to lunch today. I thought it was going to be just us. But it turned out he wanted me to meet his new lady friend. She's only a few years older than I am. She's obviously from another country. I was worried he was being taken advantage of by some illegal alien scam artist. But it turns out she was brought here and forced into prostitution. Now she's got a T visa."

"I've had clients who have been brought to the States like that. They come here thinking they're going to be working as maids or hostesses, and then they wind up in a cubicle servicing men ten hours a day." Eli sighed. "It's good that she's found a way to reclaim her life. A lot of those women wind up too broken to go on."

"I probably shouldn't have stuck my nose in my dad's business." It was a painful admission.

Eli didn't contradict her. "Your dad's been around the block a time or two. He probably knows what he's doing."

She crossed her arms. "Love can blind you." She thought of how Scott had lied and cheated and left her up to her neck in debt. "It can make you see only what you want to see."

"You sound like my wife." The words were out of Eli's mouth before he could call them back. He hadn't planned to say that. He hadn't planned to say anything at all. "Lydia thought love was basically just some kind of bait and switch."

Mia looked up at him, her eyes wide with surprise. "Don't you mean ex-wife?"

Heat climbed Eli's neck. If only he could relive the last thirty seconds, suck the words back into his mouth. "Not quite, to be honest," he said, knowing he hadn't been honest for far too long. "Lydia just took off, and I don't really know where she is. The last time I heard from her, she was in Vegas. Before that, Houston. And before that, I think it was St. Louis."

Mia stood frozen. "So you're not actually divorced?"

"No. Not really. Not yet." He knew it didn't count if it was only in his head. Only in his heart.

She took a step back from him and crossed her arms. "What about divorce by publication?"

Mia was talking about a procedure that had been drawn up for cases just like his. He would have to get permission from the court to publish a notice of the divorce in the newspaper. And to do that, he would have to show the judge that he had tried to find Lydia and tried hard. Asked her mother, her sister, her friends, the Portland middle school that had once employed her. Checked with the Teacher Standards and Practices Commission. Looked in online directories and phone books. Even prove that he had checked Facebook.

"I know I should." But for reasons he couldn't even articulate to himself, Eli hadn't yet done any of those things. Shame? Guilt? Inertia? "I just haven't yet. It's really just more of a formality."

"You know when a good time to tell me that would have been?" Mia demanded.

He held his breath, his heart beating in his ears. Was she going to say that a good time would have been before she had fallen in love with him?

"When?" he managed to ask.

"A long time ago!" And with that, Mia turned and walked away.

CHAPTER 14

THURSDAY

Charlie took another bite of his bear claw, savoring the sweetness of the icing, the flakiness of the pastry, and the crunch of the toasted almond slices.

He was sitting in the observation room that overlooked King County's autopsy suite. Below him was the corpse of the runner who had been fished from Puget Sound, lying faceup on a stainless steel autopsy table. Under the bright lights, the body looked vulnerable and small. Gathered around the table were a pathology assistant, a photographer from the forensics division, and Doug Pietsch.

Now Doug looked up. "Seriously, Charlie?" His surgical mask hid most of his expression, but Charlie could still see the raised eyebrows. "It's not like this is a double feature."

Charlie shrugged. "A guy's gotta eat." He took a sip of his twenty-four-ounce coffee, then raised it in Doug's direction. "And drink."

"You should just be glad you're up there and not down here and that there's a glass window between us. Because if you were down here you would be trying very hard to forget about the very concept of food. Being out of the water has not improved this guy's condition any."

"Don't come crying to me." Charlie spoke around another bite of pastry. "I've heard you say before that the smell of corpses is the smell of job security."

The criminalist and the assistant tried to hide their smiles.

Doug was undaunted. "Maybe today I wouldn't mind a little less job security. I'm just glad I printed him on scene. Time is definitely not improving things."

Charlie felt a surge of hope. "So did you get a match on the prints?"

"No. I would have told you first thing. But at least I know I have them and they're clear." Doug cleared his throat and looked at his team. "Okay, let's get this show on the road."

He pressed a pedal on the floor and began to dictate into the transcribing machine. "The body is that of a somewhat undernourished Asian or Hispanic male who appears to be in his early twenties. Decedent was found unclothed. The body weighs a hundred twenty-nine pounds and measures sixty-four inches from crown to sole. The hair on the scalp is black and straight. The eye color is unknown; the eyes are mostly absent due to predation from fish or crabs."

He peeled back what remained of the lips and peered into the mouth. "Both upper and lower teeth are natural. Several are missing, and there is evidence of untreated caries." He tapped the pedal again to turn off the transcriber and then looked closer. "It looks like I might just owe you a beer."

"What are you seeing?" Charlie asked.

"The upper incisors are shovel shaped, which means this guy's Asian. But the thing is, Charlie, he's got no dental work. Zero." He looked up. "Do you know how unusual that is?"

"Maybe he was too poor to see a dentist." Charlie swept his tongue over his back molars, dislodging an almond slice. Over the years, his teeth had been supplemented and buttressed with a variety of fillings and crowns. He was glad that the City of Seattle offered a decent dental plan.

"Yeah, but it's mostly adults that fall through the safety net, and this guy hasn't been an adult for that long. Minors can usually get dental care, unless their parents are totally negligent. I would expect to see at least an old filling or two, not missing teeth." Doug shook his head. "I'm starting to wonder if we're dealing with an undocumented immigrant. Someone poor enough that he wouldn't have had dental care in his home country. And then once he came here, he certainly wouldn't have been able to afford it."

"If that's true, we may never figure out who he is." This idea bothered Charlie far more than the prospect of watching Doug pick up the saw and open up the dead man. "We can't identify him by matching his prints. We can't identify him by matching dental work. And there's no point in running DNA if we don't have a missing person to match him to." He squinted at the man's thin face. "And so far I can't find a single report that comes close to sounding like this guy. Someone's going to have to tell us he's missing first."

But what if they never did?

"If we totally come up blank, there may be another way to narrow things down," Doug offered. "The water you drink deposits isotopes in your hair. So we could have his hair analyzed to see what part of the world he's from. It takes awhile, though, to get results."

"Let's hope it doesn't come to that," Charlie said.

The autopsy resumed. Doug carefully swabbed under the fingernails, in case there was still a fragment of the killer's skin under them. He examined the man's skin from head to toe, noting injuries that were both pre- and postmortem. Some might have come from the body scraping rough surfaces, others from fish. He took note of multiple blunt force traumas in varying sizes and varying stages of healing. Rows of oval-shaped fingertip bruises dotted the man's wrists and upper arms where someone had grabbed him, with slightly larger bruises marking the thumbs. Pinch-mark bruises marred the soft skin of his inner arms. And then there were the lines of burns on his wrists—three on the right and two on the left.

"I'm going to have to look at these under the microscope," Doug told Charlie. "But like the bruises, these burn marks also look like they may have been made at different times."

Charlie wondered if that ruled out torture. Or maybe it had been more a type of punishment, the burns doled out along with the bruises? He had seen more burns on bodies, living and dead, than he liked to remember. Burns from cigarettes and cigarette lighters. Burns from clothes irons and hair irons. Once from a blow torch. Usually the shape of the burn revealed something about its source. So what would leave a line like that?

As Charlie took the last bite of his Danish, Doug made the Y-incision in the chest, opened the guy up, and began the process of inspecting and weighing and measuring what he found inside. Midway through, he held out something on his red-streaked glove, offering it like a prize. Charlie leaned closer to the glass. It was a bullet.

"I think you're in luck, Charlie. It severed the aorta but it didn't hit any bone, so it didn't get too dinged up. Looks like it came from a .22. We'll get the crime lab to put it into NIBIN and see if they can get a match." NIBIN, the National Integrated Ballistics Information Network, was like a fingerprint database for bullets. It held scans of markings from bullets and cartridge cases found at crime scenes across the nation. With luck, there might be a match.

"Maybe we're finally catching a break." Charlie swallowed the rest of his coffee. "Because I'll tell you, Doug, this doesn't feel like a one-time thing."

On his way out to the parking lot, Charlie called Mia. Knowing she was anxious, he didn't ask about the jury's deliberations.

"Doug just finished the autopsy on that floater." He pulled his keys from his pocket. "It looks like wherever he was before he ended up in the water, someone got mad at him pretty regularly. There were lots of bruises, plus these weird burns shaped like lines on his wrists. At first I thought someone had tortured him, but Doug says they were made at different times, just like the bruises. So maybe he wasn't tortured. Maybe he was being punished."

"What was the cause of death?"

"Definitely a gunshot. He was dead before he even went into the water, which Doug thinks happened a week ago, maybe two. His fingerprints don't match anything on file. And he's never had any dental work, so Doug's wondering if he might be undocumented."

"What nationality did you say he was?" Mia asked.

"At first I said he was Asian and Doug thought he was Latino."

As he spoke, Charlie realized Doug hadn't actually made any plans for that promised beer. "But with the shape of the teeth and the skull and the eyelids, it looks like I was right."

Mia's voice sharpened. "Tell me some more about these marks on his wrists."

"Second-degree burns. About two inches long, but not very wide. Like lines. Doug says they're consistent with someone having brief contact with a very hot surface." He opened his car door and climbed in. "Why are you asking?"

"Do you remember that guy at the Jade Kitchen who talked to me about Scott helping him? The one who called me Mrs. Scott?"

"He worked in the back as a cook or a dishwasher? Yeah, what about him?" Charlie put his key in the ignition but didn't turn it.

"One of the baristas at a coffee place near work told me he came in super early one morning about ten days ago, asking for me. She could barely understand him, but he showed her my business card."

"But you never saw him after she talked to him?"

"No. She said he left with friends. But, Charlie—?"

"Yeah?"

"The last time I saw him, I noticed burn marks on his wrists. Like from the dishwasher or maybe an oven."

Charlie pulled his keys from the ignition. "Can you meet me down here? Now?"

CHAPTER 15

Could the man in the morgue be Lihong? Mia's stomach seized up as if someone had just kicked her. A bitter taste flooded her tongue. She dimly realized she was squeezing her cell phone so hard that it was hurting her fingers, but she still didn't loosen her grip.

"How long did Doug say that body had been in the water?" she asked Charlie.

"He said if you're fatter, you float sooner. But this guy was skinny. So a week, maybe two. No more than that."

And the barista had talked to Lihong about ten days ago. Still, the place where the body had been discovered was at least a mile from the coffee shop. But who knew exactly where it had gone into the water? The current could have carried it a long way.

Mia remembered how Lihong had tried to tell her something about Scott promising to help. But the communication between

Mia and the Chinese man had been so sketchy that she had never quite understood what Scott was supposed to have been doing.

Lihong had also said his boss was a bad person. Or at least that was how her five-dollar phone app had translated it. Judging by the mangled English it had given her when translating Lihong's other words, its accuracy was more than suspect. But the idea had been underlined when Mia secretly witnessed Kenny Zhong, the Jade Kitchen's owner, deliver a stinging slap to Lihong's face. Now the memory stung her as well. She had honestly planned to follow up with Lihong, but then life had gotten in the way.

Less than ten blocks separated the courthouse from the morgue. It hardly seemed worth it to pull her car out of the parking garage. Outside of Mia's window, the sky was the kind of pale gray that any Seattlite could tell you promised neither sun nor rain. At least no more than a sprinkle.

"I think I'm going to walk it," she told Charlie. "It probably won't take any longer than driving, and I need to clear my head. But if the jury comes back in while I'm there, could you drive me back?"

"I could drive you back either way if you wanted. See you soon."

Mia shrugged into her coat and picked up her purse. Before she even made it out the door, three colleagues asked her if the jury had returned a verdict. She just shook her head and didn't make eye contact, making it clear she didn't want to talk about it.

It was a relief to be out in the cold air and away from familiar faces. Away from sitting in her office, time moving so slowly the clock might as well be ticking backward.

Every time she was waiting on a verdict, Mia entered a fuzzy zone where she couldn't think about anything else. In another trial, when the deliberations had gone into their fourth day, she had gone to the grocery store, shopped, paid, walked out, gotten in her car, and driven back to the courthouse—leaving her bags behind at the store.

Knowing that the jury might be hung was like having a throbbing cavity in her mouth. No matter how much she tried to ignore it, her thoughts kept sneaking back to probe. Was the jury still hung? In whose favor? Why? Would Judge Ortega's instructions shake things loose?

The idea of having to go through all the work again was disheartening. And next time Wheeler would know every one of her arguments and fine-tune his counters. With the help of Leacham's deep pockets, he would bring in new and better experts. As for Mia, she couldn't change the evidence. She only had the truth, and lies came in a million flavors.

As she walked over I-5 she thought about Eli. She was still in shock that Eli Hall—someone who was so upstanding that he sometimes seemed rigid—was not officially divorced, despite the way he acted toward her. She thought of how his face lit up when he saw her and how he dawdled after classes so that they would walk out to the parking lot together. He always insisted on opening doors for her and helping her on with her coat. But maybe that was simply the way he treated women. And the time he had asked her to brunch? He had never actually said the word *date*. Maybe she was the only one who had seen it as one. She didn't know whether she was angry or disappointed—and if so, who those emotions were directed at.

And then there was Charlie. The two men didn't have much in common, except Mia. In fact, they were like some sort of reverse mirror image of one another. Eli had close-cropped blond hair; Charlie's was dark and worn as long as his bosses would let him get away with. Even more than a decade out of the service, Eli had kept his military bearing, while Charlie just switched from one slouch to another.

Both men were devoted to justice, but in very different ways. That military aura of Eli's was more than physical; it showed in his systematic approach to life. Charlie played by the rules only as far as he thought they made sense.

Both, she sometimes thought, wanted to be something more to her than a friend. But maybe she was as deluded about Charlie as she evidently had been about Eli. Maybe friendship was all either of them wanted. Or should want.

At the morgue, she showed her ID. Charlie came out to meet her and then brought her back to where Doug was waiting next to rows of galvanized-steel body refrigerators.

"I understand you might know the identity of our floater," Doug said.

Mia nodded. She only had eyes for the closed steel doors.

He pulled one open, releasing a wave of cold air and a smell so thick it was almost a taste. It was rotten and sweet and ultimately indescribable, furring her tongue. Doug slid out the top shelf, revealing the body of a young, skinny Asian man.

The Y-incision in his chest had been stitched closed with thick black stitches. Mia forced herself to focus on the young man's face, not to think about how he had been taken apart and reassembled. Even though the eyes were closed, the lids sagged over what seemed to be empty sockets. His face was not only scraped and battered, it was also starting to decompose.

She had only seen Lihong twice. At night. In the dark. When both of them were nervous, jumping at every sound. When they were focusing on trying to communicate, not on what the other person looked like. Focused on their lack of connection, their frustration.

Now they would never connect. But was this Lihong? She looked at the man's wreck of a face, tried to match it up with her memories—and found that she didn't know.

"These are the burn marks on his wrists." Doug lifted the dead man's wrists to show her.

"The thing is, I can't tell if it's him or not. It could be. Or it could be someone else. This guy's face is just too"—she sought a word besides *disintegrating*—"damaged." She looked from Charlie to Doug. "I'm sorry if I wasted your time."

With a shrug, Doug slid the body back and closed the door. "It's not a waste if it would have helped narrow things down. Because right now we don't have much to go on."

"I think our next step is to go back to the Jade Kitchen," Charlie said to Mia. "See if Lihong's there. And if he's not . . ." He let his words trail off. "So do you want a ride back to work, or do you want to walk it?"

She wasn't sure she wanted to be alone with her thoughts again. "How about a ride?"

After saying good-bye to Doug, they walked out to Charlie's car. "It's strange," she said, "to think that a couple of weeks ago that guy, whoever he was, was walking around, breathing, talking."

"Are you thinking about Scott too?" He clicked the fob to unlock both doors and climbed in.

She *was* thinking about Scott, she realized, as she waited for Charlie to lean over and relocate a half dozen discarded fast food wrappers scattered on the passenger's seat. With a sigh, she got in. "It's just hard to believe that you'll never see someone again, at least not in this world."

As she turned to buckle her seat belt, Charlie's eyes met hers. He was so close, she involuntarily caught her breath. He didn't move, his eyes studying her. She met his gaze for a second, then turned away.

Charlie broke the silence. "You didn't see Scott's body before it was cremated, did you?"

"Everyone told me it was a bad idea, with his face so broken." For a moment she pressed her fingers to her lips. "The problem is that you only get one choice, and you'll never know if it was the right one."

"That describes a lot of life," Charlie said as he started the car.

He was just pulling up to the courthouse when Mia's phone rang. It was the judge's clerk, telling her the jury had sent out another note. Her mouth went dry as chalk.

"That's it, Charlie. They're hung. I know it. They're hung. It's going to be a mistrial."

"You don't know that," he said reasonably. "It could be they're just asking for clarification on something."

But even Charlie didn't sound like he believed it.

CHAPTER 16

As Mia walked into the building, anxiety jockeyed with certainty. Her mind replayed key moments of the trial, imagining different actions and outcomes. What if she had used one of her preemptory strikes on Warren? Would the juror who replaced him have been any better? Or what if Sindy had stuck around long enough to testify? Would that have been enough to tip the balance?

As they went through security, Charlie joked with Bernard, one of the sheriff's deputies. "Pay no attention to Mia's twitching. It's just that we've been called back to the courtroom."

Bernard gave her a reassuring smile. She managed to lift the corners of her mouth in return. Her chest felt tight. She realized she was breathing shallowly, almost panting, and made a conscious effort to breathe from her abdomen.

Before she entered the courtroom, Mia lifted her head and tried to wipe all expression from her face. Behind her, Charlie lightly touched the small of her back.

Wheeler and Leacham were already at the defense table. Wheeler's expression betrayed nothing, but David Leacham was bouncing his curled index finger against his slightly parted lips, knocking his front teeth with his knuckle. He stopped when he saw her noticing.

Through her tinted glasses, Bo Yee was watching her, but she didn't look upset. Of course, she didn't know enough to be upset. Mia had tried to explain to Bo the day before that the jury was having trouble deciding, but Bo had seemed serene in her belief that justice would be done. Now Mia managed a nod as she took the last steps to the counsel table.

She and Charlie sat down. She knew they would be standing again in just a few moments. And deep in her gut she knew they would be hearing that these last few weeks had brought no justice for Dandan.

She caught a movement in the corner of her eye. Under the defense table, Leacham's leg was jigging.

"All rise!"

As they got to their feet, Mia exchanged a sideways glance with Charlie. He gave her a smile that was more a twist of the lips, as if he were thinking the same anxious thoughts she was.

After they were seated and Judge Ortega took the bench, she put on her reading glasses and unfolded the note. "We have received a communication from the jury, and it reads: 'Nothing has changed since your last charge. I am sorry, very sorry, that we cannot come to one accord. I have done the best I know how, but we are still deadlocked. Our discussions have ceased.'"

Behind her, a collective gasp rose from the onlookers. Even

though it wasn't a surprise, Mia slumped as if her strings had been cut. All that work—for nothing. It would just have to be done again. She turned toward the defense table. Wheeler was too much of a pro to let his feelings show, but Leacham was wearing a wide grin.

Somehow the defense had gotten at least one juror to agree with the ludicrous idea that a petite teenager had been the aggressor, to believe that her death could be construed as self-defense. To believe that Leacham had a right to use her and then take her life.

Mia tried again to take a deep breath, but it felt like it got stuck halfway. There was nothing up her sleeve now. She had given it her best shot. And what was to say that the next jury wouldn't hang, or even vote for acquittal?

Judge Ortega took off her reading glasses and let them fall on their chain. She pinched the bridge of her nose. "I propose to bring the jury out and briefly question them." No one objected.

Wheeler leaned over and whispered in Leacham's ear. Mia didn't know what was said, but she could guess, as she watched his expression change so that now he looked serious, even contrite. While they waited for the jury to be brought in, the room quickly filled with reporters, as well as David Leacham's friends and family. Somehow word had spread. Dandan was represented only by her mother.

Bo looked confused. Mia caught her eye, shook her head, and mouthed, "I'm sorry." How could she explain it to her? She could barely understand it herself.

When the jurors filed in, they looked even more upset than they had yesterday. Several of the women were clutching sodden tissues.

"Will the foreperson of the jury please stand and state his name for the record?" Judge Ortega said.

Jim unfolded his lanky form. Even when he was on his feet his shoulders stayed bowed. "It's Jim Fratelli."

"Mr. Fratelli, has the jury been able to reach a verdict in this case?"

"No, Your Honor." He sighed. "We have not."

"If the court were to give you more time to deliberate, could the jury reach a unanimous verdict?"

It was obvious that Jim wished he could give a different answer. "No."

The judge looked at each of the jurors in turn. "If any of you disagree with Mr. Fratelli's answer, please tell me now."

The jurors cut their eyes sideways, but no one raised their hands. Instead, they pressed their lips together, shook their heads, crossed their arms. Connor looked like he wanted to spit out something rotten. Naomi knuckled away tears. As Sandra looked from Mia to Bo, she started to cry in earnest.

And the one person they all looked at, or looked away from, was Warren. He sat with his head hanging, seemingly engrossed in worrying a tiny bit of skin next to his thumbnail.

Mia took a quick look behind her. Dandan's mother still looked confused. She was leaning forward, her elbows on her knees, turning her head to look at Mia, then the jurors, then the judge, then back to Mia.

"All right," Judge Ortega said to Jim. "Please be seated." She turned toward the jurors. "Ladies and gentleman, I want to thank you very much. Because you cannot reach a unanimous verdict, I'm going to declare there is a manifest necessity for the declaration of a mistrial. I realize this has been a long road. So I'm going to excuse you back into the jury room, where I'd like to step inside just to express my appreciation. And you are now excused."

The clerk was saying, "All rise for the jury" when a woman's scream tore through the room.

"No!" It was Bo. "What is happening? No! You killed her!" With bared teeth, she launched herself at Leacham, her hands outstretched as if to strangle him. "You're a murderer! A murderer! You killed her! You killed my daughter. You must pay!"

The deputies were on either side of her in seconds as the crowd around her gasped and murmured and backed away. She sagged between the two burly men and would have fallen if it weren't for their arms. Her cries turned to wordless screams while the judge banged her gavel.

Every shriek was like a dagger to Mia's heart. If she had done a better job, would Dandan and her mother have justice by now?

CHAPTER 17

It was clear that Bo Yee would never rest. Kenny saw that now. It didn't matter if David Leacham walked free. She would still haunt him. Hunt him.

In America and China both, they had the same saying: "An attack is the best defense."

He picked up the phone and dialed a number.

"I need to talk to you. I have a business proposition."

He would wait until they were together to spell out the deal. As they said back home, on the other side of the wall, there are always ears.

CHAPTER 18

An hour later, Mia was sitting in Frank D'Amato's office, fighting a headache. Fighting and losing. It felt as if someone were pushing a stainless steel knitting needle through her temple.

Everything that had happened after Bo went for Leacham and then collapsed was a blur. The poor woman had been taken to a hospital for evaluation. The only good news was that she had harmed no one and was not facing charges for her outburst.

After Bo had been escorted out, Judge Ortega had set a hearing in two weeks to discuss how to proceed. Leacham had walked out of the courtroom and into the arms of his supporters, all of them laughing and hugging and high-fiving as if he had been acquitted. Now Mia was meeting with Frank, her boss and the district attorney, to tell him about her plans to refile.

Years ago, when Mia had first started working at King County, Frank had been just another co-worker, albeit one with five more years' experience. But Frank had always wanted to be more. When he ran for district attorney, to the surprise of everyone but himself he beat his more experienced opponent.

As the years passed, his external image caught up with his self-perception. He had traded in his Dockers for tailored suits, his passion for careful calibration. Now his thick black hair was touched with silver at the temples. When he wasn't at the office, he was out in the community visiting victims of violence in the hospital, speaking to civic groups, and attending fund-raisers for various charitable causes. Was he doing it because he truly cared or because he knew it would eventually help him get reelected? Mia figured the answer to both questions was probably yes.

As the years had passed, Frank's life had become his job, and vice versa. Although framed photos of his children were displayed on his credenza, rumor had it that was about as close as he ever actually got to them.

While he had been busy climbing the ladder, Mia had jumped off it. She had left the office after Brooke was born and only returned after Scott's death.

A few weeks ago, Frank had narrowly won reelection. The close-ness of the race seemed to have left him off balance. Instead of basking in his win, he often seemed irritated and impatient.

As he was now.

"There's a certain energy, a certain momentum that went into this trial," Frank said. "You can't recreate that or put it back in the bottle. It's gone. You and I both know that the second time is not the charm. Your case became immeasurably weaker without that girl testifying that Leacham had previously held a knife to her throat. A retrial without that Sydney—"

"Sindy," Mia corrected.

Frank waved a hand. "It doesn't matter what her name is if you don't have her. Because without her, this case will just get worse. Wheeler will be going over the court transcripts like he's cramming for a final exam. He's going to know exactly what your witnesses are going to say. He'll know what you're going to ask on cross. He's going to go through the witness testimony line by line, looking for any inconsistencies. He'll have twenty-twenty hindsight that will let him use whatever weaknesses or flaws he didn't exploit the first time. And knowing Wheeler, he'll find them."

Mia pressed her finger into her temple, trying to get the pain to stop or at least recede. "The same's true for me." She knew it wasn't, not really, but she could not let this go. "I can learn from what Wheeler did. I can change things up."

"I don't see how that's possible, Mia. The defense will know every word you're going to say, but you won't have anything new to add. The evidence is unchanged. Meanwhile, Wheeler will bring in even more people who will airbrush Leacham's image, and this time he won't put on the stand the ones you were able to pick apart. He'll be sure that all the jury hears about is how devoted Leacham is to his family, how he gives to widows and orphans and helps the poor." He heaved a theatrical sigh. "Et cetera, et cetera, et cetera."

What had happened to the old Frank, the one who gathered with them around takeout pizza in the break room on late nights, the one who was part of the team instead of the man who had his secretary summon her to his office? Mia was pressing her temple so hard she could feel her pulse under the pad of her finger.

"Leacham's story is impossible to believe."

"I will grant you that it is improbable." Frank shrugged. "But it's *not* impossible. Wheeler got at least one person to believe it. For all you know, he got eleven."

"I'm almost positive it was just the one juror who hung it, Frank. One. One juror who was incompetent or stupid or crazy, and who was also stubborn. It was just bad luck that he ended up on our jury."

Mia had walked into this meeting expecting Frank to be upset at the jury's inexplicable inability to decide, but also certain he would agree with her about the next steps. Now she felt like she had been sucker-punched. Did he really think she could let David Leacham get away with murder?

Frank said, "You know the saying that defense attorneys have. 'It only takes one.' They don't need twelve, like we do. All they have to do is convince one juror. And in this case they've done it once, and they could easily do it again. It's nearly impossible to get twelve people to agree on anything." He made a sour face. "Meanwhile, what are you going to do? You've got the same old witnesses, except you haven't even got the most damning one, the one you *promised* this jury."

"What if Sindy didn't disappear on her own?" Mia blurted out.

"What?" Frank's gaze sharpened. "Do you know something you haven't shared with me?"

"No," she said reluctantly. "It's just a gut feeling."

He blew air through pursed lips. "Right now I only want to hear about facts. And the fact is you're not going to develop more evidence or better witnesses. You fought the good fight, Mia, but you lost." He steepled his fingers, carefully matching fingertip to fingertip, then looked up at her. "I don't see the point in refiling."

A flash of anger jolted from her head to her heels. She took her finger away from her temple and jabbed it his direction. "The point is that a young woman died."

"I'm not denying that. Unfortunately, she's also not the most sympathetic of victims. An illegal immigrant? A prostitute?" He tilted his head.

"What?" Mia thought of Luciana. "Are you saying she should have known what she was getting into?"

"I'm just saying it's hard to get jurors to identify with her."

"Are you asking me to forget that she was also a teenager who died choking on her own blood? I want this conviction, Frank. I want justice for Dandan."

"Everyone involved wants to bring this to a close," Frank said, which wasn't exactly Mia's stance. "I say we go to Wheeler. Offer him a plea deal."

Inside, Mia went cold and still. "For what?"

"Second-degree manslaughter. Two years."

"Two years?" She wanted to scream. "A girl is dead, Frank. Dead."

"And she'll still be dead no matter what we do. At least this way there will be some recompense."

"Leacham deserves at least twenty years. And we can get it. I know we can. Two years is a slap on the wrist. And a slap on the wrist is not closure. It is not justice."

Frank had run on the office's winning record. But key to that record was taking on cases you couldn't lose and then pleading out the rest. And he clearly thought Dandan's murder now fell into that territory.

"It may not be justice, Mia, but it might be the best we can do at this juncture. Just because the state is automatically entitled to re-try this case does not mean we are obligated to. You already put on your best case, and you still didn't get a conviction."

"I can't let this go, Frank." Why couldn't he see this the way she did? What had happened to the old Frank, the one who saw that there were times when black was black, certainly not white, not even a shade of gray. Mia thought of an explanation for his behavior, shied away, and then circled back to it.

Frank tapped on his computer keyboard, obviously having already mentally dismissed her. "Then you have until the day before you're due back in front of Judge Ortega to bring me something new. If not, then we offer the plea agreement."

"Let me ask you something, Frank." Even as Mia gave voice to her suspicions, another voice inside her was telling her to shut up. She ignored it. "Is it possible that one of the reasons you're taking this tack is because David Leacham has deep pockets and lots of politically connected friends?"

Frank reared back as if she had slapped him. He stared at her with narrowed eyes, shaking his head slowly, his lips pursed. "You're not the only one who can ask questions, Mia. How many years have we known each other? You know what I'm all about, or at least you should by now. But instead, you impugn me to my face. When I'm the one who offered you a position back here when you needed one. Offered it even when you hadn't been in a courtroom for four years. And this is the thanks I get?"

Mia heard the subtext. Frank had given—and Frank could take it all away.

CHAPTER 19

Judy Rallison caught Mia's eye as she closed Frank's door behind her with a shaking hand. On paper, Judy was just the department's secretary, but she was really the one who kept all the moving parts lubricated and in motion.

"Someone's here to see you." Judy cut her eyes sideways at the figure sitting slumped on the couch. At the sight of Bo Yee, a fresh wave of guilt washed over Mia. She had failed Bo and Dandan. And now she had put her job—and her chance to persuade Frank to refile—at risk by speaking with her gut and not her head.

She sank onto the cushions beside the other woman. "How are you doing?"

Bo lifted her head. Despite her shadowed eyes, you could see where Dandan had gotten her beauty from. "David Leacham bought my daughter." Her voice was bitter. "And now he has bought his freedom."

Mia kept her voice low. "That's not exactly what happened." How was she going to explain that Frank would probably not let her refile? "Here, let's go into my office, where we can talk privately." She helped the other woman to her feet. She thought they were about the same age, but today Bo moved like an old woman, with her head curled over her shuffling feet. In the hall they passed DeShauna and Jesse, who looked at them and looked away. Were they second-guessing how she had handled the trial?

When they reached her office, Mia wished it offered something as comfortable as the lobby's couch, but all it held was her desk and a round conference table with three chairs, only two of which matched. Mia pulled one out for Bo, then grabbed the box of Kleenex she kept on her desk for victims and their families and plopped it in the middle of the table.

When Mia took her own seat, Bo raised her head. Her black eyes looked straight into Mia's. "Do you know how I came to this country?"

"No." Mia didn't know where this was going, just that it was a relief not to be trying to explain the inexplicable. A brief reprieve before she had to tell Bo of Frank's decision.

"It was because I got pregnant."

Mia wasn't following. "With Dandan?"

"No. I already had Dandan. This was my second pregnancy. You have heard what happens in China, right? One-child policy. At least for the poor." Bo's lips pressed together. "You can have a second child or even more—if you pay the fine. For us, it would have been one hundred thousand yuan. That is like thousands of US dollars. Only the rich can pay that."

Mia nodded.

"But I became pregnant. And I wanted that child. So I tried

to hide my belly. Someone must have told. We heard later that the officials wanted to make an example of me. When I was seven months along, they came for us. Many men. And they took me and my husband and Dandan to the city's family planning bureau."

Mia said nothing. She knew what must be coming, but that didn't lessen the horror. If anything, sitting knee to knee with Bo, seeing her hands twist on the table, hearing her breath go shallow as she remembered, made it worse.

"They yelled at me," Bo continued. "They beat me. They hit my belly." She laid her hands on either side of her flat abdomen. "I was on the floor, trying to curl up. They kicked out this tooth. Later, I tried to push it back in, but it didn't work." Pulling her lips back, she pointed at the hole where one of her bottom eye teeth was gone.

"My husband tried to protect me, but they beat him, too, and dragged him away. They took his camera. The guards were in the hall holding him. They hit him in the head and tore his shirt. They said they would call the police and have my husband put in jail for obstructing their official duties. I could hear my daughter crying. She was only three."

Mia nodded, her eyes never leaving Bo's face. Dandan had been only a little younger than Brooke. How terrified she must have been to see her mother and father beaten.

"I was worried that Dandan would have no parents, so I begged the officials to let my husband go. They said they would only do that if I took the shot to make the baby come."

Mia felt a sudden jolt of nausea and tried to swallow it back down. This was it. The dark heart of Bo's story.

"So I said yes." Bo's face twisted with pain. "I hoped that after they let my husband go I could somehow stop what they were going to do. But then they wanted me to sign that it was okay to do it, and I said no. So one of them, she signed for me. Then they said I had to put my thumbprint next to the signature. I still said I would not. They tried to pry my hands open, but I held them tight, like this." She lifted her fists, the fingers curled over to hide the thumbs, and showed them to Mia. "One man held my wrist and one hit me in the head and one pulled my fingers apart until they could put my thumb on the ink and then on the paper."

Bo was nearly panting now. It came to Mia that it was as if she were giving birth to the terrible story, laboring to bring forth a monster.

"After that they dragged me into the operating room. Four women held me down. The doctor came with a huge needle. When I felt it go in, I cried and cried." Her words became so soft that even sitting next to her, Mia could barely hear them. "I could feel the baby dying inside me. It had been kicking, but the kicks got weaker and weaker." Bo took a deep, shuddering breath. "And then they stopped."

Mia blinked and felt tears run down her cheeks.

"It was another day before the baby came. A perfect little boy." She looked at Mia with red, brimming eyes. "It hurt so, so much. Death would have been better. If I had not already had another child, I would have let go and died."

"I am so sorry." Mia's words felt so inadequate she might as well have not said them. But she had to say something.

"After that, the authorities found ways to make an example of me so that no one would try to do what I did. So my relatives helped pay for me to come here, to America."

Bo had gotten asylum here, but was that really a happy ending? She had had to leave her family behind.

"But now I know that America is no different from China. If you have money, you have justice." She shook her head. Her eyes were flat, unfocused. "No money, no justice."

"That's not true," Mia said. "What happened wasn't because Leacham is rich. It was because at least one of the jurors was not convinced he was guilty. For better or worse, that's how our system works."

"It was the man with the ugly hair." Bo put her hand up to her own hair, black and shiny as a crow's wing, caught up in a thick bun.

She meant Warren's two-toned mullet. If the circumstances hadn't been so tragic, Mia might have smiled. Instead, she simply said, "Yes, I think it was that man."

Bo nodded. "Because he was paid to do that."

"What? No. That's not how it works, Bo. In this country it is illegal to bribe jurors."

"There is the law that is written, and there is what really happens." Bo's tone was fatalistic. "The same as in China."

"What are you saying?"

"Just before the trial started, I saw the man with the ugly hair talking to another man in the hallway. Talking very quietly. As if they had a secret. When they saw me noticing, the other man walked away."

"So?" Mia said. "That doesn't prove he bribed him. Did you see money changing hands?"

"No. But two days later, I went to a restaurant to get something to eat. I saw Leacham's wife. She was talking to this same man."

Mia's headache came surging back. "Are you sure?" She could hear Frank's voice in her head. *Don't bring me speculation. Bring me proof!* "Who else saw this man talking to that juror?"

"I do not know if anyone did. The hallway was nearly empty."

"What did he look like? Tall, short, fat, thin?"

"A short, white man with a thick body. And with a round face, like the moon."

It was nothing. Mia knew it was nothing. The man Bo had seen could have been Warren's old co-worker or neighbor. Someone who just happened to also know Marci. He could have just been asking directions to the nearest restroom.

But what if Bo was right? What if someone had bribed Warren, bribed him so that Leacham's jury would hang?

She needed more than a distraught woman's imaginings to go on.

"It's not like you saw money exchanging hands. You saw two men talking. There's no law against that," she said. "We need to be able to prove that's what happened."

And how much good would Leacham have thought a hung jury would really do him? If the end result was a retrial, there was no guarantee that another jury might find him not guilty. Leacham would have had no idea that Frank would balk at the idea of a retrial.

Mia froze. At least, he *should* have had no idea that Frank would balk. But what if her suspicions in Frank's office hadn't been too far off the mark? What if Leacham had paid a juror to hang the case— and then found a way to persuade Frank not to refile?

Maybe Frank hadn't been angry at her because he felt betrayed. Maybe he had been angry because she had connected the dots.

CHAPTER 20

FRIDAY

THE SEATTLE TIMES
HUNG JURY IN CASE OF MURDERED PROSTITUTE

The case of Dandan Yee, a prostitute who authorities charge was murdered by her client David Leacham, has ended in a hung jury that split eleven to one. Leacham claimed that Yee's death occurred during a struggle after she held a knife to his throat and tried to rob him. The trial has been dubbed The Lethal Beauty Case.

The jury of nine women and three men deliberated more than a total of sixteen hours over the course of three days before finally declaring that they had reached an impasse that could not be broken. Under Washington state law, all twelve jurors must find a defendant guilty in order to convict him. When it was over, eleven angry jurors—some of them in tears—pointed to a lone holdout who wouldn't vote to convict.

Jim Fratelli was the foreman of the jury. "It was a tough case. It was long and it was hard and it was grueling," an emotional Fratelli said afterward. "We gave it our best shot. It is what it is, I guess."

According to juror Samantha Streeter, "The atmosphere in the jury room was positively poison. One juror refused to listen. People were yelling, even threatening him. But he didn't let it get to him."

Another juror, Naomi Jennings, said, "It seemed like he tuned us out, just like he tuned out the whole trial. Anyone could see that David Leacham was guilty. But he wouldn't even talk about it."

Warren Paczkowski confirmed to the *Times* that he was the lone dissenter but declined to comment further as he left the courthouse by himself.

Leacham, who has been out on a million dollars bail since he was first charged, told the press, "I continue to have faith. Faith in God and faith in the jury system."

On the steps of the courthouse, Leacham's attorney James Wheeler said, "The State, with all its might, had the simple task of convincing twelve—just twelve—people of the guilt of an individual beyond a reasonable doubt. And they failed. The jurors in Mr. Leacham's case heard every word of the evidence. Why should the government get another bite at the apple when they couldn't prove their case the first time? Mia Quinn's relentless pursuit of Mr. Leacham, an innocent man, has already cost the county tens of thousands of dollars. And now she wants to do it all again?"

Reached by telephone, King County prosecutor Mia Quinn said, "While the defense can spin the facts of this case any way they want to, it was my job as the prosecutor to present those facts. And we think the facts overwhelmingly indicate the guilt of the defendant." She added that a final decision hasn't yet been made about trying Leacham again.

CHAPTER 21

"Oh, hello, Mr. Carlson."

Emily Barlow, Sindy Sharp's foster mom, did not look surprised to see Charlie standing at her door. She stepped back and motioned him in. She was about sixty, with straight, blond hair cut in a style Charlie remembered from his childhood, like a bowl had been placed on top of her head and the hair cut to match. "I'm afraid I haven't seen or heard anything from Sindy. I would have called you if I had."

"I know you would have. But we really need to find her." Charlie followed Emily inside.

The last time Sindy had posted anything on her Facebook page was the day before she disappeared. The phone number she had used to set up "dates" had been disconnected. Charlie had checked homeless shelters and cheap motels. A BOLO—be on the lookout for—had been issued to all law enforcement agencies. And with her shocking pink hair, she certainly stood out. Still, a girl like Sindy had learned at her mother's knee how to fly under the radar. At least that's what Charlie told himself. When he wasn't picturing her body left in a shallow grave scratched out in the woods somewhere.

"Could I make you some coffee? Tea?"

Charlie waved a hand. "No thanks. I'm good. Did you hear about what happened at the trial?"

Emily settled on a green velvet recliner, and he took the plaid couch. The living room was surprisingly neat for a house where a half dozen teenage girls lived.

"No, I'm afraid I haven't been following it, but it's been busy here. We just got a new girl a couple of days ago. She came with only the clothes on her back."

"Does that happen often?"

Emily gave him a pained smile. "More times than I can count. If you had asked me years ago, when we first started to foster kids, I would have said it was enough just to give them the things they need and try to love them. But just *trying* will not take care of their problems. You can buy them a whole new wardrobe, you can buy them everything, but if you do not love them unconditionally, then in the end it means nothing. Of course, we let them know there will always be food available, there will always be a clean bed to sleep in and clean clothes to wear to school. We show them that it's possible to disagree without screaming and yelling and hitting each other. But what's key to making this work is that I do not criticize, I do not condemn, and I accept them for who they are."

Charlie thought of Sindy, with her pink hair, her defiant eyes ringed with black liner. "That must be harder with some than others."

"I'm not saying it's not a challenge. But all children need a family. At eighteen, when they age out of foster care, where do they go? When Thanksgiving or Christmas rolls around, who do they eat with? My husband and I will always be here for them, they know that even if they know nothing else. If they get a good job or things are going well, they always know they can pick up a phone and say, 'Hi, Mom.'" Her sigh was heavy. "And when things are not going so good, they know I'll tell them, 'I'm sorry.'"

"Have you thought any more about where Sindy might have gone?"

Emily's mouth twisted. "She didn't trust me yet. With some of these kids that can take years, and she was only here for a few weeks."

"It really hurt our case that she wasn't there to testify. The jury hung. If we're going to have any hope of convicting David Leacham of that girl's murder, we need her."

"Her old life may have come calling for her. These kids, most of them have never known love. They don't know what to do with it and they don't trust it. And according to Sindy, she didn't need anything or anyone else. She thought she was perfectly capable of looking after herself."

"She's only seventeen," Charlie said. But maybe all seventeen-year-olds thought that way.

"If she went back to what she was doing, it's true that she could make enough money to support herself physically." She smiled sadly. "David Leacham's not the only one who likes girls that young."

"Could she have gone back to her mom?"

"I heard her mother's back in jail now for soliciting." Emily grimaced. "I try not to be judgmental about the parents. Maybe they didn't have good role models themselves. But what she let happen to Sindy . . ." Her words trailed off.

"I'm worried Sindy might not have left of her own free will," Charlie said.

"Do you think she's come to harm?" Emily's gaze never wavered.

He didn't sugarcoat it. "It's possible. It's a little too convenient that she disappeared the day before the trial began." At first Charlie had chalked it up to stage fright or the girl's general skittishness, her unwillingness to do anything she was supposed to do. "Or someone might have paid her to get out of town."

"Sindy? All she knows is Seattle. We took the girls to Leavenworth the first weekend she got here. She was almost"—Emily hunted for the right word—"frightened. Lost. She looked like the little girl she is."

Leavenworth was about three hours away—a bit of a tourist trap, in Charlie's opinion—and billed itself as a faithful reproduction of a Bavarian village. Even the McDonald's was fashioned to look like a chalet, albeit one made of brown plastic.

"Can you think of any place she might be? Anyone she might be with? Anyone it might be worth reaching out to?"

"One of the girls she shared a room with is home sick today. You could try talking to her."

Emily led him down a long carpeted hallway, then knocked on a door. "Teal, a policeman would like to talk to you about Sindy."

"Okay," a girl's voice called.

Before Emily opened the door, Charlie said, "Would you mind if it was just us? She might tell me more if she doesn't have *two* adults staring at her."

"That's fine. I'll be in the living room."

Teal was on her feet next to the bottom bunk she had clearly just vacated. She had dyed black hair that fell to her shoulders and two tiny gold rings in her left nostril. Looking at her, Charlie realized he didn't need to worry about catching the sickness that was keeping her home from school. Teal looked like she was about five months pregnant, her belly high and tight on her thin frame.

She couldn't have been more than fourteen.

She saw him noticing and crossed her arms over her abdomen, carefully not making eye contact. She took the only chair in the room, a wooden one in front of a small matching desk. There was another bunk bed in the room, both beds neatly made. Charlie didn't want to perch like a hunchback on the other lower bunk, and he didn't want to loom over the girl either. There was only one other place to sit, an orange beanbag chair. He crossed his ankles and managed to sit down without plopping too much. He just hoped he could get back out of the darn thing without looking like a fool.

Behind her hand, Teal hid a smile.

"So Sindy shares this room with you?"

She guessed what he was thinking. "Mother Emily already went through her things. She didn't leave any clues about where she went." After a moment's hesitation, she added, "You're not the only one who's come looking for her. There was a man who asked me about her when I was walking to the bus stop. I told him the same as I'm telling you: I don't know where she went."

"Can you tell me about this guy?"

"He was old."

"Old as me?" Charlie asked.

"No, you're way older."

He tried to let that one slide off. "When was this?"

"A few days ago?" Teal said. "Maybe a week?"

"What did he look like?"

"I don't know. A white guy. Really big. Like . . . hulking."

The word *hulking* sounded almost exotic coming out of Teal's mouth. "What did you tell him?"

"Just that no one knew where she was." She raised her shoulders and shivered. "Something about him was creepy. I didn't let him get too close, and I was ready to scream if I had to."

Charlie was glad for her sake that she hadn't had to find out if anyone would actually respond. "Did Sindy say anything to you before she left?"

Teal rolled her eyes. "Sindy was always talking. She thought she was all that and a bag of chips. She said she didn't need a pimp. She was so proud of herself because she said she didn't need to share her money with anyone. But she wasn't as smart as she thought. When she showed up here she had bruises on her throat and her arms. She said some guys like to tie her up before they had sex, even pretend they were going to kill her. I was like, 'What's to stop them from just *doing* it?' but she was so sure she knew what she was doing." Teal snorted. "Guess she didn't." Her face belied her harsh words. She looked frightened. "Right before she left here, she starting saying she was going to get rich."

"Rich?" Charlie sat up straighter, which was not easy to do in a beanbag chair. "What did she tell you about getting rich?"

"Not that much. She just started talking about how her life was going to change. That she was going to come into a whole lot of money."

Had someone representing David Leacham offered Sindy money not to testify?

Or, Charlie wondered bleakly, had it been a bait and switch?

Had they offered her money—and taken her life?

CHAPTER 22

"And what are we doing today?" The hair stylist swirled a black plastic cape around Bo's neck and then snapped it into place.

Bo pulled the pins out of her bun and shook her head. A black river of hair tumbled down, falling past her shoulders, past the arms of the chair, and finally ending only a foot from the floor. For a moment, everyone in the shop went silent, just looking at it.

"Chop it all off," she said bluntly. "Cut it to here." Bo put the blade of her hand against her neck, right below her ears.

"Are you sure?" Looking reverent, the stylist gathered the weight of it in his hands. His own yellow-tipped black hair stood up in short gelled spikes. "It must have taken you a really long time to grow your hair this long."

She lifted her chin. "All my life."

His brows drew together. "Then why do you want to cut it off?"

The answer she gave was doubly true. "I don't want to be me anymore."

In the mirror his eyes met hers, and she saw a muted understanding. "Okay, then. Let's make you *not* you." From a drawer he took a black hair elastic and made a low ponytail. It took a long time for him to pull the yard of hair through. "If you want, I could donate your hair to Locks of Love. It's a charity that makes wigs for children who are sick and have lost their hair. They could really use hair that's this long."

Bo imagined a girl who looked like a younger Dandan, the Dandan she had only seen in a few snapshots. She pictured her with a drawn face and a vulnerable, naked head. Imagined how the warmth and the weight of the wig would cradle her. As if someone had laid their two hands on top of her head, like a blessing. For a moment, the thought comforted Bo. But only for a moment.

She nodded. The stylist picked up his scissors in one hand and the ponytail in the other. He began to cut just above the hair elastic. A few minutes later, the hank dropped into his hand. Freed from her, it looked like a horse's tail. Bo's head suddenly felt weightless, like it might float up to the ceiling. She closed her eyes.

She was doing this for Dandan, she thought as the hairdresser began to comb and snip and ruffle. She would do anything for her. When she had seen her daughter's body in the funeral home, seen her daughter for the first time in sixteen years, she had promised her justice. But the courts had failed her.

She had thought of trying to get to David Leacham. Sneaking up behind him as he pressed the fob on his keychain to unlock his car on some dark street. Imagined saying Dandan's name so that he turned. Imagined plunging a knife into his chest, just as he had done with her daughter. And then she would whisper her daughter's name in his ear again as he died. She would erase him from the world, and he would die knowing why.

Or if Bo were to dress a certain way, make up her face, she was sure she could catch his eye. And then all it would take would be a few moments alone.

But after watching the trial, she guessed his attorney and his wife would keep him on a short leash. They would never let him get close to another Asian woman.

So what did that leave? Leacham had thought he could buy justice by bribing that juror with the ugly hair. The paper had identified him as Warren Paczkowski. Mia Quinn had said that without any proof of what had happened, there was nothing she could do.

But if Bo could expose what Paczkowski had done, then Leacham would be punished for both things: killing Dandan and bribing Paczkowski. And Bo had seen the hungry way that Paczkowski looked at one of the other jurors, a young women dressed in clothing that was too revealing, heels that were too high, makeup that looked like a clown's. He had ogled her like a starving man outside a mansion, staring at a feast with his nose pressed against the window glass. With his two-toned hair, it was no wonder the girl had clearly not returned his interest.

In the phone book, Bo had found Paczkowski's address. He lived in an apartment not that far from her, in a little neighborhood filled with restaurants, coffee shops, and pubs.

Bo had already talked to the people at her job and at her church. Everyone understood, their voices soft with sadness. Of course, if she needed some extra time to recover, she should take it. It wasn't fair, they told her, what had happened. They had reassured her that in the next trial, Leacham would surely be convicted. They didn't know that Mia Quinn's boss had said there would be no next time. Not without more evidence.

So it was true that Bo needed extra time away from work and her duties at the church. But it wasn't to come to terms with what had happened. It was to get the proof of what she knew to be true.

Forty-five minutes later, she had bangs cut straight across, just above her eyebrows. The stylist offered her a mirror, and when she took it from him, her hair swung back and forth. He had cut it into a short, slanted bob that ended in points on either side of her chin. Slowly he spun her chair so she could see how he had layered it in the back so that it followed the curve of her skull, angling down to the shaved nape of her neck.

"Wow, that's quite a change," the woman in the next chair said. "No one would even recognize you."

Bo allowed herself something that was not quite a smile.

At Macy's she bought a padded push-up bra, two low-cut sweaters, high-heeled shoes, large hoop earrings, a fake leather jacket, and a pair of jeans so tight she could barely pull them over her feet. She regarded herself in the mirror.

She looked nothing like what she was: a mother, an immigrant, a woman who worked on an assembly line at a tea factory wearing a smock and a hairnet and blue rubber gloves. Too many Chinese who came over eventually "ate American," ate food that came from cans, went to McDonald's, and it showed. Bo still kept to the old ways. It took time to prepare good food, and you did not eat too much of it.

Her skin was unlined. Her figure slender. She looked like a college student. A fresh-faced college student.

Too fresh-faced for Paczkowski.

Carrying her bags, she went back down to the first floor and looked at the various white-coated women selling makeup. She chose the one who looked the most colorful.

"I'd like a makeover," Bo said. She never wore makeup.

The saleswoman began, "So do you want smoky, colorful—"

Bo interrupted her. "Both. Everything. I want it to be dramatic."

She nodded. "And what feature would you like to emphasize? Lips, eyes, cheeks . . . ?"

"No, you don't understand," Bo said patiently. "I want lots of makeup on every part of my face. I want people to look at me and notice my makeup."

The girl clapped her hands. "A woman after my own heart! Dramatic, mysterious, adventurous." She had Bo sit in a black swivel chair and then set to work.

Thirty minutes later, thick strokes of black eyeliner emphasized Bo's tip-tilted eyes. Purple and green eye shadow shimmered on her lids. Her lips were a scarlet slash.

"Wow." The girl stepped back to admire her own work. "You don't even look like yourself. If I hadn't been the one who did it, I would say you were not the same person who walked in here."

Bo smiled. That was the point. She looked garish, like the picture on the first TV set she had owned, where the colors had all been too bright and slightly wrong.

"Show me again how to make those rings around my eyes."

The girl picked up the black pencil and pulled down her own eyelid as she leaned toward the mirror. "When my mom used to get all dolled up before going out to dinner, she would say she was putting on her war paint."

"War paint?"

"Like Indians do? Um, Native Americans?" She held her palm

out flat and then tapped the insides of her fingers against her lips, making the faintest ululation. "They would paint their faces before they went to war."

Bo nodded. She liked the idea. War paint.

CHAPTER 23

It was after five, and Charlie was driving Mia to the Jade Kitchen to see if they could track down Lihong. Driving in theory, anyway. On this stretch of I-5, nobody was doing any driving, just sitting. Seattle rush hour traffic was notoriously bad, and on a Friday night it was even worse. They hadn't moved more than a couple of car lengths in the last ten minutes. Times like this it was pretty tempting to use the lights hidden in his grill. But this wasn't exactly official business. It was a hunch.

"Even though it's clear Warren was the only holdout," Mia said with a frown, "Frank still doesn't seem persuaded that we should refile."

"Let me guess," Charlie said. "Did he tell you that you need to look at the big picture? Because I hear that all the time. *Finite resources, need to prioritize, if this were a perfect world,* blah, blah, blah. Meanwhile, we're the ones dealing with the victims' families.

We're the ones trying to explain that justice is sometimes just too expensive. That sometimes you have to forget it and walk away."

Charlie never forgot, though. If you pulled the pencil drawer in his desk all the way out, tucked in the back you would find photos families had given him of victims, photos from cases that were so far unsolved. And every four or five years or so, he was able to close a case that everyone else had long ago written off.

"Reading between the lines of the *Seattle Times* story," Mia said, "it's clear that Warren simply refused to participate. But based on the voir dire, I would never have guessed that he was going to be the lone crazy holdout."

"Don't second-guess yourself, Mia." Charlie feathered the accelerator. Traffic was finally moving again, if you called thirty miles an hour on a freeway moving. "I didn't hear anything that made me doubt him. Maybe the power of being able to have the final word went to his head. Maybe he secretly has something against capital punishment."

"The thing is, Bo Yee thinks he was tampered with."

Charlie stiffened. If that was true, this was a whole different ball game. "What makes her say that?"

"Bo says she saw Warren talking in a low voice to some guy in the hall the day the trial began. And a few days later, she saw that same guy with Leacham's wife, Marci."

"Did she hear what they said? Did she see them shaking hands, exchanging a package, anything like that?"

"No, the guy took off after she noticed him."

Charlie settled back into his seat. "There could be a million explanations. And it's not like I could get a warrant to go trolling through Warren's bank accounts, see if he's picked up a new life for himself. Not unless there was a lot more proof."

"That's what I told Bo." One hand briefly covered her eyes. "I talked to her a long time. Bo told me that when Dandan was three, Bo got pregnant with a second child, but the Chinese government forced her to get an abortion when she was seven months along."

"Seven months?" Every part of him recoiled.

"And now both her children are dead. I look at her and try to put myself in her shoes, but I can't stand even to think about it."

By the time they finally reached the Jade Kitchen, it was bustling. But they weren't going into the restaurant. At least not yet. Instead, they were lurking behind the Dumpsters, trying to spot Lihong.

"And I thought the dead guy smelled bad," Charlie complained. The reek of rancid cooking oil, rotting shrimp, moldy rice, and a few other smells he was pretty sure he did not even want to identify filled the air.

A middle-aged man came out with a white bucket full of shrimp shells. Charlie looked over at Mia, but she shook her head.

Even though Charlie would have said it was impossible, when the man lifted the lid of the Dumpster, the stench got stronger. Beside him, Mia was shielding her mouth with her cupped hand, breathing shallowly.

Five minutes later, a younger man came out, this time with a bulging black plastic garbage bag. Again Mia shook her head. But this time when the man was done, he leaned against the wall, pulled a hand-rolled cigarette from his pocket, and lit it. The flare of his lighter showed a thin, tired face. And something else. Mia nudged Charlie at the same time that he noticed it. On one wrist, two dark lines. He couldn't be sure, but he thought they looked like the burn marks on the floater.

They waited another fifteen minutes, but no one else came out. Time for Plan B. They walked around the corner and in the front door. Inside the restaurant smelled of ginger and garlic and red chiles. Charlie took deep appreciative breaths, trying to scour the old fetid air out of his nasal passages.

"It's kind of disconcerting that it smells so good in here and so bad out back," Mia whispered.

"Yeah, but have you ever smelled a potato when it goes bad? That's got to be one of the worst smells in the world. And I still love potatoes."

At the host stand, Charlie gave his name to the manager, a Chinese guy sporting a clip-on bow tie. They waited in the small entryway along with a family of seven, a couple who appeared to be on their first date, and two tired parents who couldn't keep their eyes off their sleeping newborn.

A few minutes later, a couple of muscle-bound teenage boys swaggered in to pick up a takeout order. When one of the kids caught sight of Charlie, he froze for a half second. Even dressed in plain clothes and with his hair touching his collar, Charlie was identifiable as a cop to some people. They seemed to have a sixth sense about it. He was willing to bet there was beer in the kid's car or a joint in his pocket, or maybe both. They were minors, but they also didn't seem inebriated, so he figured he didn't have a dog in this fight. After picking up their food, they hurried out.

Seated near the waiting area was a family with two kids, an older boy and a younger girl. The dad reached for a dish of string beans just as the teenage son, grinning mischievously, put out his hand and spun the lazy Susan built into the middle of the table, rotating the beans out of reach. Smiling, the dad lifted the serving spoon mock-threateningly.

When Charlie looked over to see if Mia had caught the scene, she wasn't smiling. Instead, she looked on the verge of tears.

"How's Gabe?" Charlie asked, guessing she was thinking of the family she used to have. The family she might still have if Scott hadn't decided to cheat her and the government.

"I definitely know I'm living with a teenager. He's gotten so moody. I never quite know what's going to upset him."

"I can remember being so embarrassed by my mom when I was his age. Once she took me shopping for school clothes, and I insisted she stay a minimum of fifty feet away from me at all times." His face got hot, remembering. Poor woman had complied too.

Mia shook her head. "I don't know if that would be easier or harder to take, but that's not it. He just gets angry over the littlest things. He's definitely going through puberty. Suddenly he's got all these muscles. And acne. He must be a stew of hormones."

"Testosterone can make guys do some crazy things." Not that he knew anything about that.

"Table for two for Charlie?" the manager called out in accented English. When they nodded, he took them to a booth and set down two menus and two sets of silver wrapped in salmon-colored cloth napkins.

Charlie and Mia had eaten here once before, when they were trying to unravel what Scott, who had been Kenny Zhong's accountant, might have done to get himself killed. Today Charlie observed again that all the workers, from the waitresses to the bus boys, looked Chinese. Kenny Zhong had talked about how supportive the Chinese community was of each other. Maybe only hiring other Chinese immigrants was Kenny's way of giving back.

Charlie looked over the menu. Lo mien, spare ribs, pork-fried rice, beef with broccoli, General Tso's chicken. All of it, according to Kenny, modified for American tastes. He had spoken enthusiastically of the rat and snake they served back home, which had made Charlie glad the dishes here were something less than authentic.

"What do you think the healthiest thing on the menu is?" Mia asked with a frown.

Charlie rolled his eyes. "A—we're in a Chinese restaurant where every dish has been tweaked to appeal to American tastes, which probably means more salt, more fat, and more breading. And B— you're seriously asking me? You've seen me eat." Life was too short to diet, Charlie figured. And while he did have a gym membership, he had not seen the inside of the place for several months.

When the waitress came back, he ordered sweet-and-sour chicken while Mia got egg flower soup and a vegetable stir-fry.

"What's your name?" Charlie asked the waitress.

"Chun."

"Your accent is beautiful. Where are you from?"

She looked down. "China," she murmured shyly.

"And how do you like Seattle?"

"It is hard to say." She shrugged one slender shoulder. "I work many hours."

"What about Lihong?" Mia asked. Charlie wished she had been a little more subtle, hadn't jumped in with both feet. "Is he working tonight?"

An expression crossed the girl's face at the sound of Lihong's name, there and gone so fast that Charlie couldn't identify it. Confusion? Anxiety? Or had it been something more primitive, like fear?

She shook her head without saying anything. Underneath her black bangs, her face was once again impassive. But Charlie could tell that Mia's words had rocked her.

"Lihong." Mia pointed. "He works in the back? As a dishwasher or a cook? He smokes?" She put an imaginary cigarette to her lips and took a drag.

"Sorry!"

As Chun started to turn away, Mia reached out and caught her wrist. The girl winced and Mia quickly pulled her hand back.

Charlie saw why she had grimaced. An oval bruise, the size of the thumbprint, had been been pressed onto the inside of her wrist. When she saw Charlie noticing, the girl pushed the sleeve of her silver blouse down, but not before he saw a line of oval bruises less than an inch away from the bigger bruise.

Someone had grabbed her. Hard. Just like they had grabbed Lihong.

CHAPTER 24

From across the room, the manager barked something in Chinese at Chun.

She flinched and then nodded rapidly. "I will request your food now." Before Mia could say another word, the girl hurried back to the kitchen. She was sure Chun had not only understood what she was asking but that the mention of Lihong's name had startled her.

"Did you see the bruises on her arm?" Charlie asked.

Mia nodded, feeling grim.

"The body you looked at yesterday had bruises like that too. But I guess that doesn't prove anything. They both got grabbed, but human beings like to grab each other's arms. It could be whoever killed our floater grabbed him before shooting him. It could be that our waitress is in a domestic violence situation. She could even have gotten the bruises from practicing wrist grabs in kung fu. Bruises don't tell you how they came to be there."

When a young man came to pour tea, Mia tried again. "Is Lihong working tonight? In the back?"

His eyes widened at the mention of Lihong's name, but she wasn't sure if he understood more than that. He shook his head and left, not making eye contact.

When Chun brought their food, Mia looked over her shoulder for the guy with the bow tie. He had his back to them, talking to some diners on the other side of the room, but she still kept her voice low. "Could we talk to you during your break?"

The girl hesitated and then finally said, "No break."

Mia would not be deterred. "How about after work?"

"Too late."

Her eyes cut to one side. She stiffened. The manager had turned back around and was now watching them, his face stony.

"Here is your order," she said in a louder voice. "Sweet-and-sour chicken and vegetable stir-fry with egg flower soup. Please to enjoy."

Even when Chun had left, the manager was still eyeing them. Mia picked up her fork. The food, which had smelled so delicious before, now just reminded her of the rotting reek behind the restaurant. Which was true and which was illusion? Or was it all just a matter of perception?

"Do you think they don't understand or they don't want to say?" she asked Charlie.

Charlie's mouth twisted. "If you don't want to talk about something, pretending not to understand goes a long way. Either way, it's clear they're not comfortable talking about Lihong."

They were just finishing their food—Charlie appeared to be having no trouble polishing off his—when a small Chinese man came in the front door.

Kenny Zhong. Charlie and Mia exchanged a look.

Kenny came up to their table. "Mia, Charlie," he said, inclining his head. "How nice to see you here again."

"The food's always good," Charlie said, putting the last forkful into his mouth.

"I understand you have been asking questions about one of my employees," he said with disconcerting directness. "Or should I say, my ex-employee. Would you like to speak in my office?"

Ex-employee. Mia exchanged a look with Charlie as they both got to their feet. As Charlie reached for his wallet, Kenny waved his hand. "No, no, it is my pleasure."

"I insist." Charlie's voice had enough steel in it that Kenny didn't persist.

Mia caught a glimpse of the bills as Charlie laid them on the table. It was enough to pay for their meal twice over. Maybe it would be a start on helping Chun get out of whatever situation she was in.

Kenny took Mia's elbow and steered her through a narrow hallway, with Charlie following. They went past a kitchen where cooks tended woks nestled in flames, down a short hall, and into his small office. Mia and Charlie sat in two chairs that looked like they had been retired from the dining room after they had gotten too battered. The only thing that wasn't utilitarian was the large fish tank behind him, filled with a half dozen silver fish that swam in sync with one another.

"So why were you asking about Lihong?"

Kenny's expression was mild, but she remembered the way he had yelled at the young man, not knowing he was being observed, and then dealt him a stinging slap.

Mia had spoken with Lihong twice. He had called her Mrs.

Scott. And he had tried to tell her something about Scott, saying, "He help."

His words had lit a tiny wavering flame of hope in Mia. Sure, Scott had cheated on her, and he had helped many of his clients avoid taxes, but he had also drawn the line at assisting a drug dealer with money laundering—a decision that had ultimately cost him his life. However Scott had helped Lihong, it had made it possible for Mia not to be so angry at him.

Mia answered Kenny Zhong's question with a question. "You said Lihong no longer works here?" She did not want to get him into trouble.

Kenny shook his head. "I had to let him go two weeks ago."

"The last time I was here, I happened to talk to him. He said that Scott had been helping him."

Kenny's brows drew together. "Helping him? Did Scott tell you about it?"

"No," Mia admitted. But by that time Scott hadn't really been talking to her. Not about anything that mattered. "And then Lihong asked if I could help him."

"But help him with what?"

"That's just the thing. He seemed to know only a few words of English. And he seemed frightened. He left before I could figure out what he wanted." She skipped over the part about how Kenny had yelled at him and then slapped him.

Kenny's face smoothed out. "I am too soft. People come to me with very low-level language skills. They do not realize that in America you must speak English to get a job. But I still try to help out people from my homeland. Lihong was one of those people." He shook his head, his expression changing to one of disgust. "And how did he repay me? Every time I came looking for him, he was out in the back taking a cigarette break. We have a saying. 'When a lazy donkey is turning a grindstone, it will take a lot of breaks to pee and poop.' I told him again and again that it wasn't acceptable, but he wouldn't listen."

Mia nodded, remembering the flare of Lihong's lighter, how it had revealed how thin his face was, how drawn.

"But it turns out he had taken advantage of me in other ways as well," Kenny continued. "And that was probably how he wanted Scott to help him. With something illegal."

Mia blinked. "Illegal?"

"Two weeks ago, I learned that Lihong's papers were false. Of course I fired him on the spot. He may have asked Scott to help him get a better set of documents."

It felt like she had swallowed a boulder. She hadn't even considered that possibility when Lihong had said Scott was helping him. To Lihong, a better set of false papers would have been a good thing, allowing him the flexibility to find employment somewhere else without the risk of being deported.

"Do you look at the papers for all your restaurant workers?" Charlie asked.

"Certainly. But I'm not an expert. If it looks right to me, how am I to know it's wrong?"

"Then how did you figure out it was wrong?"

Did Kenny hesitate? "Another worker told me."

And what had Lihong said to her, at least what had her phone translation app said he said? *He pay, so they will look the other way. Your husband is trying to help.* Was Kenny bribing someone to look the other way about people's immigration status? Maybe he had decided, for whatever reason, that it wasn't worth keeping Lihong.

"Why didn't you report his immigration status to the authorities?" Mia asked.

He leaned across his desk. "We all have problems within our family." He looked at her for a long moment. "But we don't talk about them outside our family."

Mia heard the subtext. As far as the wider world was concerned, Scott had died in an accident. Scott's mistakes had died along with him. They hadn't been paraded before the public.

"Do you have an address for Lihong?" Charlie asked.

Kenny shrugged. "I do not know where he is."

"Are any of the staff here friends with him?" Mia asked.

"No." A decisive shake of the head. "He worked here for less than a year and he kept to himself."

"A man's body was found in Puget Sound two days ago," Charlie said. "Mia thought it looked like Lihong. I have a photo of the man's face on my cell phone. Would you mind looking at it?"

He stiffened. "I am not sure I could be of help, but of course I will look."

Mia didn't say anything. Officially, Charlie should be showing Kenny a sketch made by a forensic artist, not a snapshot of an actual corpse, especially one that wasn't in the best shape. But Charlie had never been one to play by the rules, and clearly there had been no love lost between Kenny and Lihong.

Charlie pulled his cell phone from his pocket, found the photo, and handed it over.

Kenny looked at it for a long moment. He pressed his lips together. Then he handed it back. "It could be him. But with the condition of his face, I am not certain. I am sorry." He tilted his head. "Did this man kill himself?" The thought did not seem to particularly bother him.

"The cause of death is still being determined." Charlie scrolled forward. "Let me show you another photo. There were some marks on his wrists. They looked like burns."

When he saw the second photo, Kenny nodded. "Those are burns from the edge of a wok. I do not know if it is Lihong, but I believe whoever it is worked at a Chinese restaurant."

CHAPTER 25

Mia sat slumped in the car, the side of her forehead resting against the cold window. Charlie had moved the car down the block, where it was half hidden by a Dumpster. She squinted at the clock on Charlie's dash. "I can't believe it's after eleven and they're all still working."

Charlie was watching the Jade Kitchen with a small pair of binoculars he had taken from his glove compartment. Kenny had driven away hours ago. When Chun finally left, their plan was to follow her home to see if she would be more willing to talk when she wasn't surrounded by witnesses.

With a sigh, Mia pulled out her cell phone and called home.

"Hey, Kali," she said after the other woman answered. "I hope I didn't wake you up."

"I was still awake."

"I'm afraid I'm not going to get home until pretty late. Probably not until well after midnight."

"Oh. Okay." Kali's voice was flat. She sounded exhausted.

"Is everything all right? Are you having problems?"

Kali had had chemo two days before, as she did every Wednesday. It seemed like each treatment left her weaker. She had lost all interest in food, and there were days Mia feared she had lost interest in life as well.

Now she sounded like even the simple act of talking required too much of an effort. Had she been throwing up again? Was she dehydrated? She had had to go to the emergency room once before for IV fluids.

Mia calculated how long it would take her to get home. Her car was still at the parking structure, but if it was really bad, Charlie could just drop her off and she would take Kali's car.

Charlie had taken his binoculars away from his face and was now watching Mia.

"No, no, I'm fine." Kali's tone was unconvincing.

"Well, something's wrong. I can tell."

"Eldon and Gabe got into a little bit of a fight."

"A fight?" Mia thoughts flashed to Eldon's fists, as big as hams. "Was anyone hurt?"

"Not really, expect maybe bruised feelings. There was some shoving and name calling. I'm not sure who started it, but I sent Eldon to my room. I didn't feel right disciplining Gabe so I didn't tell him to do anything. He went to his room anyway." The two women had talked about how Kali could deal with Brooke if Mia wasn't there, but Mia had assumed Gabe was too big to be concerned about. Obviously erroneously.

"Could you do me a favor and give the phone to him?"

Kali's breathing grew labored as she climbed the stairs. "Gabe," she called, "your mom's on the phone and she wants to talk to you."

After a moment Gabe said, "Yeah?"

Just the way he grunted that one word made Mia grit her teeth. "Kali says you and Eldon got into a fight. What the heck happened, young man?"

"I just lost my temper." A long pause, as if he were calculating what he could get away with. "Sorry. And I already said sorry to Eldon."

Probably with the same lack of enthusiasm. "You've been losing your temper a lot lately."

An exasperated sigh. Mia didn't need a video feed to know that Gabe was rolling his eyes.

"Please don't start talking to me about puberty. Because if you do, I'm going to hang up right now."

"Gabe!" She fisted her free hand and knocked it against her lips. What should she do? What was her priority? Her kid? Her job?

She remembered something Anne, who worked down the hall, had once told her.

"My rule is, wherever my feet are, that's where my heart is," Anne had said, looking down at her flats. "So now when my feet are at work, my heart stays at work. And when I'm at home, my heart stays at home. I don't split my attention anymore."

Easy enough for Anne to say. While she did have four kids, she also had a husband who could backstop her. Still, Mia decided to put her advice into practice. Her feet were in Charlie's car, so that's where her attention would be.

"We're going to have to talk about this more tomorrow morning. For right now, I expect you to behave yourself. Don't start any arguments and don't respond to any. When I come home, I don't want to hear there were any more problems tonight. Okay?"

"Okay."

He still sounded sullen. But she would deal with him when her feet were in the same room as he was. She tapped the button to disconnect.

"Everything all right?" Charlie asked. He must have figured it wasn't too bad because he had put the binoculars back up to his eyes.

"You probably heard the high points. Eldon and Gabe got in a fight. Nobody was hurt. I don't even know what it was about. Maybe it's partly my fault. I didn't ask Gabe before I moved another kid into his room. And not just any kid. You've seen Eldon. He must weigh like two hundred twenty, two hundred forty pounds? He takes up a lot of space."

"He's two forty, easy," Charlie agreed. "But he's also so mellow he always looks half asleep."

"I wish some of that would rub off on Gabe. It seems like lately he's got a hair-trigger temper. Last week I had to ground him because he threw his glass against the wall." Mia remembered how they had all stared at the milk trickling down the wall, the curved pieces of glass gleaming on the floor. Even Gabe had looked surprised.

She remembered her feet and where they were. "I guess I'll worry about it when I get home." Bringing herself back to the matter at hand, Mia asked, "Do you think Kenny was telling the truth?"

"About what? Since Scott was his accountant, it's pretty likely there's a lot Kenny doesn't tell the truth about, starting with the IRS and probably moving out from there."

Mia had found a note to Kenny that Scott had written shortly before he died. He had warned him that, when compared to his credit transactions, Kenny seemed to be underreporting his cash and that the IRS was going to notice. Scott hadn't spelled out any remedy. At least not in writing. But she had since learned that he had helped other clients hide money from the IRS.

"I think Scott probably helped him get better at hiding things."

"And didn't you tell me Scott had to warn Kenny about—what was that term?"

"Guan-xi." Mia pronounced it *gwan-she*. "I guess in China they say, 'No guan xi? No good!' Kenny tried to spin it as being all about building relationships."

"In America, otherwise known as bribes and kickbacks." Charlie shook his head. "I think the guy in the morgue is Lihong, and I think Kenny knows it. He probably figured it was safer to hedge his bets. And you also can't tell me he believes that all his workers are here legally. Financially, it probably makes more sense for him to look the other way. That way you can pay people below the market rate, because where else are they going to go? But maybe Lihong's papers were so bad he decided he had to turn him loose. Or I guess it could even be like he said—that Lihong spent all his time out back smoking."

"Or maybe Kenny fired him because he was complaining about the way they were being treated. Remember what Lihong told me? He said something about Kenny hurting them. In fact, I saw Kenny hit him." Mia remembered the shock of it, Lihong cowering, his hand raised. Kenny hadn't known he had a witness.

"Was he physically hurt?"

Mia didn't know. "It was an open-handed slap."

Charlie's mouth twisted. "That would certainly sting, but would it leave a permanent mark? There were plenty of bruises on that body. Even if it does belong to Lihong, who's to say the bruises were from Kenny? Maybe he got them after he was fired."

"Didn't you say they were in different stages of healing? Maybe they were accidental, like those wok burns." Thinking of what Kenny had said, she asked, "Do you think Lihong *could* have killed himself? No job, no money, no papers, no English. He must have felt pretty hopeless."

Charlie made a raspberry sound. "So how would that have worked? He stood naked in the Sound, fired the gun at his own back at what would have to be near point-blank range, yet somehow managed to make it so that the bullet didn't punch through him *and* it didn't leave any powder burns on his skin? I don't think so. So please stop beating yourself up."

Mia remembered Lihong's face, the desperation warring with hope as he beckoned to her. "He was looking at me like I was going to save him. And instead, I just forgot about him."

"You were in the middle of a big case, remember? In fact, you almost got killed. And it's not like Lihong gave you a lot to go on. Besides, if Kenny's right, and he was looking for help with illegal papers, there's no way you could have helped him."

"He got fired, he came looking for me, and he didn't find me. Maybe he wasn't desperate enough to commit suicide, but he could have been desperate enough to do something illegal. He wouldn't have had a lot of other options for making money."

It was irrational—she hadn't even known Lihong had been looking for her—but Mia couldn't help feeling she had let him down. Twice.

As Mia was speaking, Charlie lifted his head to stare at the restaurant. The back door had opened and the bow-tied manager walked out. He got into a small, dark Honda just as a white fifteen-passenger van pulled up at the back door. The rest of the restaurant workers—and certainly there were more than the fifteen the van should hold—shuffled out of the restaurant and started filing on.

Even from this distance, their slumped shoulders and dragging footsteps made it clear just how tired everyone was.

Charlie started the car. "I'm starting to get the feeling Chun doesn't live alone," he said.

CHAPTER 26

Charlie followed the white van, hanging far enough back not to arouse suspicion but not so far that he might lose it. When it turned to get on the freeway, he got closer, leaving only one car in between. Even so he almost missed the van when it suddenly took an exit without signaling.

Was the driver trying to lose him? But as they started driving through a run-down area that paralleled the freeway, the van didn't take any more evasive maneuvers. Used car lots and small, worn-out-looking houses were interspersed with strip clubs and restaurants offering pho or tacos. A car pulled up to a girl standing on the corner, and she leaned in to bargain.

Finally the van stopped in front of a shabby two-story house that had once been white. To the right was a windowless tavern. To the left stood a house with boarded-up windows and a listing For Rent sign in the yard.

"Home sweet home," Mia said as Charlie drove past the workers who were beginning to climb out of the van. He circled the block and pulled into the trash-strewn 7-Eleven parking lot kitty-corner from the house.

"You still want to try to talk to Chun?" he asked. Thin seams of light showed on the edges of the windows, which appeared to be covered with newspapers. "'Cause there's gonna be an audience."

"At least the manager won't be there." She waved one slender hand at their surroundings: the cracked asphalt, the shabby buildings, the tags on any blank surface. "I'm sure when people dream about coming to America, this is not what they picture."

"Maybe living in this neighborhood gives them the incentive to work hard so they can climb the ladder and get to someplace better." Charlie didn't really believe that, and judging by the look Mia gave him, she didn't either.

The white van passed, empty now except for the driver. That meant a minimum of fifteen people were living in what looked like a two- or three-bedroom house.

Mia was tapping on her phone. "This is the app I was telling you about." She held it out in landscape mode. On one side it said *English* and on the other *Chinese*. In the middle was the illustration of a button. "You press that before you start talking and then again when you're done. It listens to you, figures out whether you're speaking English or Chinese, and then translates it into the other language."

Charlie was impressed. "How the heck does it work? Are there real people sitting in a room someplace on the other side of the world, translating away?"

"Not for a five-dollar app. I think it just uses some database to make its best guess. And sometimes what it guesses doesn't make much sense."

They got out of the car and walked up the now-empty drive-way. The lawn was nothing but calf-high weeds. As they went up the chipped concrete of the front steps, Charlie could hear people moving inside, a few quiet conversations. Then he knocked on the door, and all sound ceased.

He knocked again. "Chun?" Mia called out.

On the far side of the house, a door banged open. A figure bar-reled through the side yard and then down the street. It was a man, shirtless and barefoot. And flat-out panicked.

"We're not with ICE. Not ICE! Tell them." Charlie turned to Mia. "Have your phone tell them we're not ICE." ICE was US Immigration and Customs Enforcement.

She hit the speaker button on her phone. "We're not with immi-gration. We just want to speak with Chun. We are friends of Lihong."

After she pressed the button to translate, a mechanical-sounding voice began to speak, presumably repeating her words in Chinese while Mia held the phone up toward the door.

Finally it creaked open an inch. Two. A frightened eye peeked out.

"What do you want?" A young woman's voice. Charlie thought it sounded like Chun.

"We don't care about your status, or anyone's status," he said. "We just want to talk to Chun. We want to talk about Lihong."

Farther back in the house, people were arguing. They sounded panicked, angry. Charlie didn't have to understand Chinese to guess what they were arguing about. Their voices were overlaid by a steady chirping. It was the sound of a smoke detector with a dying battery.

Finally the girl opened the door. It was Chun. She was biting her lip.

Charlie went in first and almost fell. Mia grabbed his elbow. He had tripped on one of several dozen pairs of shoes parked next to the front door.

The carpeting was a dirty gray, worn to the backing in places. Laundry hung from a rope strung on their right. To their left was what should have been the living room. Instead, it held a set of bunk beds and an air mattress.

The people they had seen working at the restaurant tonight—plus several more who must have been laboring out of sight—were huddled together at the edge of the kitchen, staring at them. One middle-aged woman was weeping silently, tears sliding down her face. A skinny old man was drinking something from a bowl, his face impassive. His yellow T-shirt said *Sarah Goldberg's Big Fat Bat Mitzvah!* None of them paid the slightest attention to the beeps of the smoke alarm.

Charlie took Mia's phone from her and spoke into it. "Don't worry. I'm not with immigration. I'm with the police." He pressed the button to translate. After a few seconds, characters showed up on the Chinese side and the phone began to speak.

Their expressions changed, but not in the way he had thought. At the news that he was a cop, they wailed and hid their faces, or cowered with their arms wrapped around their heads. They looked, Charlie realized, like they thought he was going to hurt them. It was one thing to be feared because someone felt guilty when they looked at you because of something they had done. This was something else entirely.

He tried again. "I don't care about your immigration status. We just want to ask you some questions about Lihong."

"No!" said a man in English. Charlie recognized him as one of the waiters. He shook his finger at Chun. "They should not be here. You should not have let them in."

"But, Feng—" she started to say.

He cut her off with a wave of his hand and stomped out of the room.

"So Lihong talk to you?" Chun's expression trembled between hope and fear. "You help us?"

"Help with what?" Mia asked.

"We work every day. But no money. The boss, he takes our tips."

"You be quiet," the older man said. He had burn marks on his wrists and hands that looked like the ones on the body. "The bosses will know you talked."

The girl lifted her chin. "They come here because of Lihong. They help us."

Charlie was counting in his head. With the addition of the guy who had run out and the waiter who had stormed out, nineteen people were living in this small house. Split that many ways, the rent on this dump of a place had to be next to nothing.

"Can we talk to you alone for a minute?" Mia asked Chun.

After a moment, she nodded. "We can go up." She started up the narrow stairs, and they followed.

At the top there was a short hall with four doors, two on either side. Three were padlocked. The fourth belonged to a small bathroom with a peeling linoleum floor. Chun hooked a string from around her neck. At the end was a key, which she put into the nearest door on the right-hand side.

The room was crammed with two sets of bunk beds as well as clothing, food, battered suitcases, and old shopping bags now stuffed with belongings. A white ten-gallon Kikkoman soy sauce bucket had been balanced on one top bunk to catch water that was leaking through the ceiling.

"This place is a death trap," Charlie whispered in Mia's ear. The sole outlet bristled with cords, and old smoke marks streaked the wallpaper above it. The window looked like it had been painted shut.

Since there wasn't really any place to sit, they all stayed on their feet.

"So Lihong told you?" Chun asked again. This close, Charlie could see her lips were trembling. "You help us?"

"Kenny told us he fired Lihong," Mia said. "Why did he do that?"

"Kenny always say Lihong *lo sow*." Her face scrunched up as she sought the English word, smoothed out when she found it. "Trouble."

"What kind of trouble?"

"He talk back to the bosses. He break things."

"When was the last time you saw him?"

"Maybe . . . ten days? No one hear him go, but we know why. To get help. He always saying we not treated right. That this is America."

"Not treated right," Charlie repeated. "Are you paid minimum wage?"

Her eyebrows drew together. "What is this?"

"You should be making something like ten dollars an hour."

Chun looked at him for a long second and then laughed as if he had told a joke. Charlie realized she hadn't been asking him for the amount she should be paid. Instead, she was unfamiliar with the idea of minimum wage altogether.

Charlie and Mia exchanged a glance, then she said softly, "Are any of you in this house legal immigrants?"

Chun didn't answer. She didn't have to. Her expression was answer enough.

It was clear that Kenny could pay them whatever he wanted. After all, who were they going to complain to?

"What about the bruises on your wrist, Chun?" Mia asked. "Where did those come from?"

She looked from Mia to Charlie. "My skin is tender."

Did she mean she was an easy bruiser, or was she saying her skin was sore from being bruised? Meanwhile, Chun clearly had other things on her mind.

"So Lihong talk to you? You help us?" she asked again. "We need help. Help to be legal. Help to be free."

Mia sighed. "I talked with Lihong at the restaurant once, but it wasn't for very long. Then about two weeks ago, I guess he tried to come to my office. But I never saw him."

Her eyes went wide. "Then where is he?"

"The thing is, Chun, a body has been found," Mia said softly. "It might be Lihong's."

"You mean he is dead?" The girl put her hand to her mouth.

"We don't know whose body it is for sure," Charlie said.

"How is he dead?"

"A gunshot wound."

"A gun?" Her eyes darted around the room as if she were trapped and seeking an exit. Her whole body was shaking now.

"Yes," Mia said. "If it was Lihong, do you know anyone who would want to kill him?"

She clamped her lips together and stiffened her body, as if trying to force herself to be still. She stared at her hands, which were squeezing each other so tightly that her knuckles had turned white. "We do not know America well. He must have met the wrong people."

Charlie said, "Does Lihong have any family here?" If he did, maybe they could identify his body.

Chun shook her head.

"Is there a hairbrush or comb of his here? A toothbrush? Clothes, even?" With luck, they could match DNA. But Chun just shook her head again.

"Who is his closest friend?"

"No friends." Seeing their expressions, she hastened to explain. "In China, we did not know one another. And here we just work. Work and sleep. No time for friends."

Mia's expression softened. "Didn't you come here wanting more than that? Didn't you come here with a dream?"

"We have no dreams now." She lifted her head to look at them. Her face was drawn, her eyes empty of hope. "Now we know what we are. We are so low."

And when he showed her the picture of the dead man's face, she said she did not recognize it.

The thing was, Charlie was pretty sure she was lying.

CHAPTER 27

SATURDAY

Kenny fisted his fingers in the hair on top of Chun's head. He yanked up until she was looking into his dark, dead eyes. Then he raised his free hand and drew it back over his shoulder. The movement was slow and deliberate. Almost theatrical. As if he were enjoying himself. And judging by his smile, he was.

Chun twisted her head to one side, ignoring the sharp pain as her hair began to rip free from her scalp. There was no way she could run or hide or even protect her face because she was hand-cuffed to a pipe. The same pipe Ying had been shackled to before she had finally been taken away.

Chun knew that Ying's fate would soon be her own.

No matter how much she tried to tuck her head, to turn her face away, she couldn't avoid Kenny's slap. She had lost count of how many times he had hit her. This blow was so hard that for a moment she saw sparkling white dots of light floating through the air. Her mouth filled with a sharp, salty taste of blood. Her tongue probed the sharpest source of pain. One of her teeth was loose.

The rest of her housemates were watching in silence, clustered on the stairs or standing farther back in the basement. Kenny had insisted they gather around, serve as the audience for her punishment. She was the lesson they were supposed to learn. This was what happened when you talked to outsiders.

Through the one eye that could still see, Chun looked from one face to the next. Feng pressed his lips together and slowly shook his head as if to say, *I told you so.* Most of the others adjusted their heads a few millimeters so they would not meet her gaze. A few were biting their lips or twisting their hands, but she knew none of them would interfere.

At this moment, all they wanted was to not be her. They would do whatever was required to avoid her fate. The only one who might have been willing to stand up to Kenny was Lihong. And now he was a cold body in a metal refrigerator drawer in a country far from home.

"You knew the rules," Kenny said. "But you talked to the police. You talked to that woman." He used the term that meant old barbarian or foreign Westerner.

"I did not tell them anything," Chun said. "They asked about Lihong and I told them he left. That's all." When the cop and the woman had shown her the photo and told her Lihong was dead, she had realized that they could offer her no protection. That the hope that had led her to open the door to them had been a false one. But by then it was too late to undo what she had done. "They showed me a photo of his dead face and I said I had no idea who it was."

"Lihong is dead because he defied me." Kenny looked at the ring of faces. "But there are things worse than death." He turned back to Chun. "You are a fool." His tone was conversational. "You will soon know how good your life was here, but it will be too late to get it back." With his free hand, he grabbed one of her ears and twisted, squeezing it like a lemon. It felt like it was ripping right off her head.

She screamed then. Blood flew from her open mouth and freckled his face. Letting her head drop, he stepped back, his features drawing together in disgust.

"Look at her! Let this be a lesson to you all. If you try something stupid, you'll be punished."

Chun saw that there was no point in trying to placate him. She might as well tell the truth. Maybe one of the others would take her words to heart and find a way to get free. "We are not slaves," she said with her broken mouth.

"Ha! Don't tell me what you are and what you are not. I brought you here. I treated you like my own daughter. But no more. No more. You are a fool. You know the saying. 'Wait to butcher the donkey until after it has finished its job on the mill.'" Kenny let out a sound that was somewhere between a grunt and a laugh. "Now you are the donkey. And you haven't finished your job. You still owe me money, and you'll still be paying me back. Just in different ways from before." He voiced another Chinese proverb: "You'll be like the freshly bought horse. The only way to break it in is by constantly mounting it and continually beating it."

He took a deep breath. "And I promise you this: you *will* be broken in."

He turned to the rest of them. "Let Chun be a lesson to you. You take what I give you and you are grateful for it. And you pay what you owe."

CHAPTER 28

Bo's feet ached. How did so many women manage to spend entire days walking around on their tiptoes? The saleswoman had told her that the high-heeled shoes she had bought were specially engineered to be more comfortable. More comfortable than what, was the question. Instruments of torture? Bo lived in sneakers, both on the floor of the tea factory and off it.

Now she shifted from foot to throbbing foot, a cement wall cold against her back. For over an hour she had been stationed across the street from Warren Paczkowski's apartment building. She was pretending to check her phone, randomly scrolling up and down. Not making eye contact with the men who walked by and took second and sometimes even third glances. Her new glasses with the thick black frames made her look studious, or at least like someone trying to look studious. She had purchased the clear-lensed glasses at the Spy Shop. Their thick side pieces hid a video/audio recorder. But it was her clothes that drew men's eyes. This morning she had pulled on the tight jeans, the padded bra, and the low-cut sweater. The heels made her stand with her bottom back and her chest forward. Her coat was styled to look like a snug-fitting motorcycle jacket, only it was made of black vinyl, not leather. It was not nearly warm enough, but she hadn't wanted to bundle up. Her body was the lure.

And Paczkowski was the fly.

She had prayed and prayed for justice, and she had been rewarded with nothing. Maybe eventually there would be justice in heaven, but she could not wait. Dandan deserved justice on this earth. And it wasn't like Bo was going behind God's back. He could watch for all she cared.

She was willing to do whatever it took to get this man with the unpronounceable name to admit the truth. To admit that even in America, justice had gone to the highest bidder. How different were things here, really? In China, the authorities had beaten Bo and killed her baby. In America, the authorities had let the killer of her firstborn walk free.

She closed her eyes for a second, remembering how Charlie Carlson had brought her the terrible news, knocking on her door just before nine on a Tuesday evening.

"Are you Bo Yee?" he had asked when she peeped out.

"Yes?" Even though she was here legally, her heart still sped up.

"I'm with the Seattle Police Department. May I come in?"

As he took a seat on the edge of her gold brocade chair, she realized she had never before had a man visit her apartment. She was still married, even if she had been separated from her husband for sixteen years. China would not let Bo's family leave, and there was no more money for smugglers. It had all been spent on Bo.

The policeman looked around her apartment, furnished with other people's castoffs. Even her electronic keyboard, her most prized possession, had once belonged to someone else in her church.

When Bo was lonely (and she was often, so achingly lonely), music soothed her soul. It connected her to something bigger, to something beyond words. She had found the connection by accident, when she had bought a cassette player and a half dozen tapes of classical music at a garage sale.

Eventually she had also found a church here, one where a good number of the congregants were Chinese. Back home she had not been religious, but just like music, the sermons and the fellowship had filled some of the empty spaces inside her. She had made a few friends, people who told her about places to eat, grocery stores that sold food she recognized.

On Sundays she had started slipping into a front pew early just so she could hear the pianist, Abigail Endicott. Watch her fingers dance over the keys, her feet move on the pedals. When Abigail saw her interest, she had offered to teach her, taken her on as a private student for free. Since Bo couldn't afford to buy a piano, she practiced at home on the electronic keyboard Abigail gave her. After the older woman began to find it too tiring to play for both services, Bo took her seat at the piano for Sunday's second service. Her life was a quiet round of work and church and work again.

Now the detective asked, "Do you have a daughter named Dandan?"

"Yes?" A tiny seed of hope sprouted within her. For a moment, she thought he was here to tell her that the Chinese government had relented, that they could be reunited.

His expression didn't change. "When was the last time you saw her?"

"Sixteen years ago." A gulf of time. An eternity.

"In China?"

She nodded. It was impossible to find words, to form them with her tongue.

"Any chance she could be here in Seattle?"

Bo started to smile, but then something about his unsmiling face and shadowed eyes made the smile fall from her face like a plate from the shelf.

"The thing is, the body of a young Asian woman has been found. And she had your address and this photo in her possession." He took the tattered photo from his jacket pocket. It had been slipped inside a plastic sleeve. It was Bo's family, the three of them, in a park, all of them smiling. All of them young. Taken when Bo was pregnant, although she hadn't known it then. She held the photo and her fingertip touched her old self's belly, then her daughter's tiny face. Everything inside her was still. Holding its breath.

"Could I show you a drawing of the girl's face?"

Bo didn't think she had moved, but she must have nodded, because he was handing her a second plastic sleeve. Over the years her husband had managed to send her a few letters. About a year ago, the letter had been accompanied by a photo of the two of them. Even without that photo, Bo would have known her only living child's face. In the drawing the girl's eyes were closed, her cheekbones high, her face slim and somehow elfin.

"That is my daughter," she said. The words felt like she was hearing someone else say them. "That is Dandan." This couldn't be real. It must be a dream. Or a mistake. A terrible mistake. "How can my daughter be here? She is in China." The words sounded as if someone else were saying them.

"Somehow she made it over here, but we don't think she's

been here long. She was working in a massage parlor when a client stabbed her."

In China her daughter worked in a roadside stand that sold soup. "But she doesn't know how to give massages," Bo said. A pulse of hope raced through her.

"I'm afraid it wasn't that kind of place. Only men went there. Do you understand what I am talking about?"

She understood then. Through church, Bo had met other women from China, women who had been forced to pay back the human smugglers who had brought them here, pay with the only thing they had of value.

At the funeral home, Bo asked the man who worked there if she could have some time with her daughter. He looked at her, his pouchy eyes sad and tired, and finally nodded.

Then he opened the door to a small room where her daughter lay on a metal table. A white sheet had been pulled up to her chin. After the man left, Bo clambered up and tried to gather Dandan in her arms. Her daughter's body was as cold and firm as the table. Like a doll. A perfect, life-sized doll, clumsily stitched in places. Bo had howled then, pressing one hand against her mouth so that only the faintest sounds leaked out.

After she composed herself, she had cleaned her daughter's body with a damp towel she had brought with her. She had dressed her body in the new white clothes she had purchased for her, including a long white dress. She had slipped shoes on her feet. They were too big, and for a moment she had caught herself worrying that they would blister her daughter's feet. As if Dandan would again walk on this earth.

Several months later, she had sat in the courtroom only a few feet from the man who had killed her daughter. Behind her tinted glasses, she had stared at him. Sweaty and red-faced and over-weight. Older even than Bo. She had imagined Dandan under his weight. Listened to the lies told about her daughter and that pig of a man. Watched as Warren Paczkowski chose to ignore all the evidence of Leacham's guilt. Paczkowski and Paczkowski alone.

And here he was. Stepping out of his apartment building. Bo unzipped her jacket until it flapped open, pushed it back. Then she started walking, too fast, her face still tilted toward her phone, her thumbs moving as if she were texting, her hands slick on the plastic. Watching Paczkowski out of the top of her vision.

Running into him so hard her face bounced off his chest. Her hand flew up to pin her glasses in place. She needed them for this to work.

"Hey, watch it!" Instinctively he reached out to grab her as she teetered on her heels and started to fall.

"Sorry." She thrust her chest toward him. This was the man. The man who had chosen to let the killer go free. Freed the killer who felt her daughter's life was worth less than a tissue.

"You almost knocked me over." The anger left his face as he looked down at her. Not at her face, but at her cleavage.

"Sorry!" She smiled up at him through the thick layer of lashes she had painstakingly glued on top of her own this morning. It had been much harder than when the girl at the makeup counter had done it.

He snorted a laugh. "For a little thing, you pack a pretty powerful punch."

"Sorry!" she repeated, toying with her hair. "It was an accident."

"That's okay. I know you didn't mean to."

She tilted her head. "Can I buy you a cup of coffee to apologize for my carelessness?"

"Oh." He blinked. "Um, I guess so."

"My name is Song," she said. She put out her hand, but instead of fully shaking his, she just briefly pressed his fingertips.

"Song," he repeated. "That's a pretty name. My name is Warren." He gestured. "There's a coffee shop down the street?"

They started walking. She was freezing. She rubbed her hands up and down her arms. "I guess I didn't dress right for the weather." She made no move to zip her jacket.

Bo had hoped for his arm, but instead he shrugged out of his own coat and put it around her shoulders, his hands lingering for a moment.

"Thank you," she said as it sagged heavily across her shoulders, smelling of cigarettes and sweat. It came down to her knees.

Now Paczkowski was the one who walked with his arms folded against the cold. "You're a tiny little thing, aren't you? If you took off those shoes, you wouldn't even come up to my chin."

"I'm little, but I'm strong." Stronger than he knew.

At the entrance he held the door for her, and she rewarded him with a smile.

As they reached the counter, he said, "Even though I know you're the one who almost knocked me over, why don't you let me buy you a coffee? After all, it's not every day I'm lucky enough to literally run into a beautiful woman."

She forced a smile while she looked down at her toes. "Thank you." She ordered a house coffee, even when he encouraged her to order whatever elaborate drink she wanted. Bo normally only drank tea, but for now, she wasn't Bo. She was Song. The former juror— she had to think of him as Warren now, instead of Paczkowski—got a mocha for himself.

"Sorry if I was kind of rude back there," he said as they waited for his mocha. "I work with just all guys. I forget what it means to be polite."

"No problem!" Bo giggled, trying to ignore how it stuck in her throat. The last time she had flirted had been before Dandan was born. "Here, let me give you back your coat."

"Are you sure you're warm enough?"

"I am now." She gave the word *now* a special emphasis, as if offering him credit.

After they got their drinks, he sat down at a booth. When she sat on the same side, his eyes widened. Bo kept her face blankly smiling, her face turned toward him.

"So what do you do that you work with all guys? I'm a student." She had prepared an entire back story if he asked her which college, what she was majoring in, etc. But he didn't.

"I'm an electrician. But I haven't been at work recently. In fact"— he took a deep breath, his chest rising—"I might not go back."

"Why not?" She moved a little closer.

"I came into some money." Warren shrugged, but his face was proud.

"An inheritance?"

"In a way. Now I'm thinking of getting my own business."

"Really? How will you do that?" She kept her face—and her glasses—turned toward him like she was a flower and he was the sun.

Under the table, she adjusted her shirt, pulling it a little tighter, then leaned even closer to him. Weaving her web.

CHAPTER 29

The thought of how Lihong had tried again and again to turn to her for help haunted Mia. In the headlong tumble that was her life, she had forgotten him, but he had not forgotten her.

Was his the body in the morgue? Or was it possible that he still might be out there someplace?

Even though it was a Saturday morning, Mia and Charlie were trying again to find out by going to the last place they knew for sure Lihong had been: Perk Up.

"No rest for the wicked," Charlie said as Mia got into his car. They pulled away from her house, where everyone was still sleeping.

"Weekends are for the weak," Mia answered in her best imitation of Charlie's growl.

At the coffee shop there was just one girl at the counter, a blue-eyed blonde with a diamond stud in her nose that Mia presumed was fake. A family was already ahead of them: a mom and dad and a daughter. The girl looked ten or eleven. Her brown hair straggled down her back in long wet snakes. She was sagging against her mom.

"We need a twenty-ounce coffee," the mom told the barista.

"Room for cream?"

The mom looked down at her daughter. "Do you want any milk in it, honey?"

The girl nodded, and the mom turned back to the barista. "Yeah, leave an inch or two at the top. Sophie had a swim meet this morning, and we don't want her to be too tired for her basketball game this afternoon."

Mia bit her lip to stop herself from saying anything. Were the parents even thinking about the kind of message they were sending little Sophie? That you should ignore what your body was telling you loud and clear? That you did whatever you could to win the meet, be awarded the scholarship, get on the news highlights reel? Lance Armstrong hadn't come out of nowhere.

When it was their turn, Mia said, "I'm looking for another barista who works the early-morning shift during the week. I talked to her a few days ago. She's Asian American and has blond hair."

"Laura," the girl said. "She's on break. Should I get her?"

"Maybe I need my coffee first," Charlie said. "I'll have a twenty-four-ounce Mindsweeper to go. With an extra shot and whipped cream."

"That already comes with four shots," the girl told him.

"I know."

Maybe wrinkled, rumpled Charlie should be the cautionary example for the parents, Mia thought, not Lance Armstrong. *Look, Sophie, if you drink all your coffee like a good girl, maybe you can grow up to be a homicide detective who doesn't know the meaning of the term* day off.

"I'll just have a sixteen-ounce nonfat latte." Next to Charlie, Mia felt a little prim and proper. After the girl went to the espresso machine to make their drinks, she turned to Charlie. "Don't you ever worry about your heart exploding?"

"I'm just training it to work harder and faster." He thumped a fist over his chest. "Besides, if I'm going to be working on a Saturday, I need a boost."

Sophie and her parents had just left, so Mia said, "At least you have a hundred pounds on that poor girl. Those parents were basically blood-doping their kid."

He shrugged. "We live in a quick-fix culture."

She pressed her lips together. "Maybe not everything needs to be fixed."

After the barista handed over their drinks, she went in search of the girl Mia had talked to earlier in the week. Laura was tying her apron when she came out but stopped when she saw Mia. "Are you here about that guy who was asking for you?"

Mia nodded, and Charlie stuck out his hand. "I'm Charlie Carlson, Seattle Homicide."

Her face stilled. "Homicide? You mean like murder?"

"I'm afraid so. A body washed up on the shore of Puget Sound. We're wondering if it's the same guy you talked to."

Laura's mouth twisted and her eyes narrowed until her expression became a combination of fascination and fear. "So do you want me to go down to the morgue?"

"That won't be necessary. I've got a photo on my phone of his face." Charlie scrolled back, then handed it over. "Tell me if it's the same guy."

"Okay." Cradling Charlie's phone in her palms, she sucked in a breath. "Oh no!" She shook her head.

Mia's heart sank. "Is it him?"

"It's hard to say for sure because his face isn't in the best shape, but I think it is." Laura pressed her fingers to her lips for a moment.

Why had Kenny—who had known Lihong well—not been able to identify him? Had he been hedging his bets, hoping the body would stay unidentified? Hoping that no one would show up asking awkward questions about Lihong's papers, his provenance?

Or was it that they had primed Laura so well that she was already well on her way to "identifying" Lihong before Charlie even handed over his phone?

"Got any surveillance cameras in this place?" Charlie asked, scanning the walls.

Laura shook her head.

"I know you already told the story to Mia, but could you tell me everything you remember, starting from when you first noticed him?"

"He came in before we get really busy. It was still full dark outside." Laura looked up, remembering. "He was walking toward me, but he kept turning and looking behind him. I thought maybe he was meeting a friend here. Then, when he focused on my face, his face lit up, and he started rattling off a bunch of stuff in Mandarin. Even if I knew how to speak it, I think he would have been hard to understand, he was talking so fast. I told him the only phrase I really know, other than food words, which is 'I don't speak Mandarin.'" She bit her lip. "Then he said something like, 'You know Mrs. Scott?' and I said I had no idea who he was talking about. I said that in English. That's not that complicated of a sentence, but he didn't even understand that. So I simplified it and just said no. He took out your business card"—she pointed at Mia with her chin—"put it down on the counter, and started trying to ask me about you. I think he wanted directions to your office. I don't think he understood that you wouldn't even be there at that time of day."

"And his friends came in while you were talking?" Charlie asked.

"Yeah. One white and one Chinese."

Mia saw this story in a new light. Where had Lihong made these so-called friends? According to Kenny and Chun, he didn't have friends. "Why did you think they were his friends?" she asked.

"The Chinese one was talking to him in Mandarin. The white guy slung his arm around his shoulders. I thought they were buddies, like maybe they had been out all night drinking." She rolled her eyes. "You see that a lot when you work the opening shift. Sometimes it's people who didn't even know each other but just spent six hours together at a strip club or something. Then the Chinese guy said something to me in Chinese, but I told him I only spoke English. Then all three of them walked out the door. And after that the morning rush started and I stopped thinking about them."

"There wasn't one word of Chinese they said that you understood?" Mia asked.

"The second Chinese guy did say one thing to the guy who was looking for you that I understood, because my mom used to say it to me when she was really mad. It was 'Don't be so troublesome!' *Lo sow*—that's troublesome. And the guy who's dead now, he did say this other word I knew. A couple of times. It was *bù*. Basically, it means no."

Charlie and Mia exchanged a look.

"What was his expression like?" Mia asked. "Did he look happy to see them?"

"He was kind of, I don't know, grinning. But looking back, it was a weird grin." She stretched her mouth wide, baring her teeth. More rictus than smile.

Any hope Mia had had died. "What did these men look like?" she asked.

"Like I said, one was white, one Chinese. The white guy, he had a shaved head, and I'd say he was in his thirties. He was built like a square. About my height, but really muscular. The Chinese guy was skinny and younger." She looked from Mia to Charlie. "I guess they really weren't his friends, were they?"

"Probably not." Mia felt queasy. She wished she hadn't ordered coffee.

"I should have noticed that." Laura bit her lip. "I should have done something. Asked him if he was okay."

"It sounds like you were all alone here when it happened," Charlie said. "If you had said anything, it could have been both of you dead. They would have opened your till, made it look like a robbery gone bad."

"What about my business card?" Mia asked suddenly. "You said it was lying on the counter. Did either of the men notice that?"

"I sure hope not." Laura put her hand to her mouth. "Only the thing is, I don't remember what happened to it afterward. I could have put it in the recycling, but I don't remember picking it up. It's possible—it's possible that one of them took it."

CHAPTER 30

Charlie pulled up at Mia's house, put his foot on the brake, and waited for her to get out.

Only she didn't.

"Do you want to come in?" she said, surprising him. "Maybe we can keep brainstorming."

Was there a hidden message in what she was saying? Mia played her cards close to her vest, and Charlie never knew quite what she was thinking.

He liked that.

"Sure." He threw the car into park and told himself not to get his hopes up. They were working on a case together, that was all.

When they came in, Kali and Brooke were in the living room, around which were scattered dozens of pink toys, from a doll's convertible to a shopping cart that was the right size for Brooke. Kali was sitting on the couch, but she was fast asleep. In her lap was a plate and in her loose hand was a bagel with a bite gone. Sitting inches from the TV and wearing a pink tutu, Brooke was engrossed in some kind of cartoon about superheroes.

Mia turned off the TV, then swung Brooke up on her hip. "Hey, baby girl, where're your brother and Eldon?"

"Gabe took the bus to the mall . . . but he wouldn't take me with him. Eldon"—she screwed up her face, remembering—"Eldon is at Danny's house."

With a snort, Kali woke up. When she saw Charlie her expression changed to one of embarrassment. "Oh, uh, hello."

"Hey." Charlie nodded, suddenly wondering what he was doing here in a room filled with females and pink plastic toys.

"I guess I'd better go officially lie down." Kali levered herself off the couch. She was still a big woman, but she had lost a lot of weight. She gave them a nod and left the room.

Brooke pushed Mia's nose and made a beeping sound, then laughed, delighted with herself.

Mia set her down. "Brooke, honey, could you go upstairs to your room for a little while so I can talk to Mr. Carlson?"

She tilted her head. "Can't I stay down here with you?"

"It's grown-up talk."

Charlie braced himself for an argument, but instead Brooke just said, "Okay."

He sat on the couch and something jabbed his thigh. A naked Barbie was stuck between the cushions. A shoestring was tied around her middle. Maybe he had been in his line of work too long, because looking at the doll made him think of a crime scene.

"I think Brooke's been twirling her Barbie around, pretending she can fly," Mia said by way of explanation.

"Naked?"

"Maybe it's more aerodynamic." Mia shrugged, then went to a desk in the corner and started digging through it. "I know you don't need to make notes, but I do." She took out a pen and then kept digging. Every piece of paper she pulled out had already been enthusiastically scribbled on with crayon. "We've got to have some paper in this house," she said in an exasperated tone, straightening up and scanning the room. She walked over to a backpack that had been shrugged off next to the TV.

She opened it up. "Why does Gabe have a Dopp kit?" she said to herself. She took out the small brown leather bag and pulled the zipper. And then went so silent, so still, that Charlie knew she had found something terrible.

He got up and looked over her shoulder. Inside the bag were a bottle of pills and three small glass vials. And two needles.

"It's heroin, isn't it?" She grabbed Charlie's arm so tightly that her fingernails were poking holes in his skin.

Charlie picked it up. The label read *Decagen*. "It's not heroin, Mia. It's steroids."

He watched as the emotions washed across her face. First she went pale with relief. Then red with anger.

A voice from behind them made them both jump. "What are you doing in my stuff?"

For a long beat, Mia was quiet. "I don't think that's the real question, Gabe." She turned around. In one hand was the Dopp kit and in the other, one of the needles.

The last time Charlie had seen Gabe, a month or two earlier, he'd still looked like a kid. Scrawny, gangly. Now his shirt strained across his thick arms and wide chest. Football season was over, but if Gabe was going to suit up today for a game, he would probably need a new, bigger uniform.

"It's like a supplement—" he started, but Mia cut him off.

"It's not a supplement, Gabe. It's steroids. That's an illegal drug."

"But it's not like cocaine or anything like that. It's not like heroin." Gabe glared at them. "I'm not an idiot. I researched it pretty good before I started." He looked from Mia's face to Charlie's. "Two months ago, I could still wear T-shirts I've had since sixth grade. I was doing everything they say to do. I lifted weights all the time. I tried all those stupid shakes, the protein shakes, the weight-gainer shakes. I ate eggs and peanut butter. I tried. You saw how I tried. But I still didn't have any more muscles than Brooke. I still looked like a little kid, not a man. There's something biologically wrong with me." He nodded at the vials. "And that fixes it."

Kids these days were expected to look like models and play like all-stars. There were certain areas in Seattle, awash in Boeing and Microsoft and Amazon money, that were hypercompetitive. Snobbish. Charlie was pretty certain this was one of them. Areas where both parents and kids tried to one-up each other with their expensive houses, cars, and clothes. And now, he guessed, their chiseled physiques.

Charlie had always been only an observer of that world. On a homicide detective's pay, there was no way he could compete. So he drove a car with stains on the seats and his shoes were down at the heels and he needed a haircut—and he didn't care.

And maybe Gabe's family had once been part of that world, but then Scott had died and the house of cards, or rather credit cards, had tumbled down. The expensive Suburban had turned out to be leased. And from what Mia had told him, she was just barely hanging on to the house.

So if Gabe couldn't compete by boasting about going helicopter skiing in Canada or snorkeling off Kauii's North Coast, then he had to have something. And Charlie guessed that something was his body.

"What about Eldon?" Mia asked. "Does he use steroids too?"

"No, he's big because he's Samoan." Gabe's voice was bitter. "You guys really don't understand. It's not like bad kids take this stuff. It's for kids who want to do better. Kids who want to improve themselves. It's for the good kids. And older guys on the team told me I needed to get bigger, faster, stronger."

Mia shook her head. "You are way more than what you look like on the outside."

The kid rolled his eyes. Charlie tried to repress his irritation at his insolence.

"People can't see my insides," Gabe said. "They can only see what's outside." He flicked a hand from his biceps to his flat belly. "And judge me on that."

"If that's all people judge on," Charlie said, "then you don't need them as friends. You think just because you work out with weights and now thanks to steroids you've got big muscles, that makes you a man? That you're an adult now? You know what makes you a man?" He tapped his thick index finger right between his own eyebrows. "It's what's up here. It's how you think. How you act. What you decide is important."

"You're not my dad!" Gabe shouted. He turned to Mia. "He's not my dad! Why is he even here?"

"Can I talk to Gabe alone for a minute, Mia?" Charlie asked in a reasonable tone of voice.

"Why?" mother and son asked at the same time.

"Because part of what I want to say to him is a conversation that should really be between guys."

She looked from Gabe to Charlie. "Okay."

"But, Mom—" Gabe started.

She leaned forward until she was only an inch or two from his face. "Don't start with me, young man. You are on thin ice right now." Her face was a mask of anger, but Charlie guessed that inside she was close to crumbling.

"So you decided to take a shortcut," Charlie said mildly after Mia had left the room.

The kid puffed out his chest. "It's not a shortcut. I was doing everything right but I wasn't getting any bigger."

"That's because you're only fifteen. It takes awhile for guys to reach their full height and weight. And you don't want to mess around with Mother Nature."

Gabe shrugged, still glowering.

How could Charlie get through to this kid? It might be twenty-five years ago, but he still remembered what had worried him as a teen. He had wanted to be accepted. He had wanted to look his best. Had wanted to get the girls. He had wanted the other guys to admire him.

"Gabe," he started, but then stopped, uncertain of what direction to go. Kids' desires hadn't changed since Charlie was fifteen. Only everyone wanted things *right now*. Charlie was no better than anyone else, impatiently waiting for the microwave to *bing* because three minutes was too long to wait.

The difference was that in today's instant gratification world, kids had access to drugs that could make things happen now. Steroids could build your self-esteem at the same time as they built your muscles. The problem was, all that growth came at a price.

After a long silence, Gabe said, "What." Not making it a question. Still, Charlie chalked it up as progress.

"Steroids aren't like taking baby aspirin. These are freakin' hormones. And at some point your body will start thinking it has plenty of testosterone and it doesn't need to bother making it any-more. So that makes your"—Charlie had to pause for a minute before he came up with the polite word—"your testicles shrink. Maybe makes them decide to stop working all together. It does other stuff too. Do you really not want to be any taller than you are now? Do you really want to end up with breasts? To go bald? You could be damaging your liver. Screwing up your blood pressure."

Gabe didn't answer. His expression was blank.

Charlie could imagine what was going through the kid's mind. In his eyes, any problems were a long way away. When you were fifteen, all that mattered was *now*. And right now, Gabe had the muscles he had always dreamed of.

"Look, man, I understand. Who doesn't want to be big? But these drugs can affect your mind, not just your muscles. They can make you depressed. There're guys your age who have killed them-selves after they started taking steroids. Sometimes they hurt other people. Just snap for no real reason." He thought of what Mia had told him in the car last night about how Gabe had been acting lately. "It's call 'roid rage. I'll bet there've been times lately when you've gotten really angry at something and then later you couldn't even think of why."

"I can control my temper."

"You don't even know how pure this stuff is. It could be cut with just about anything. This kind of thing gets made in someone's bath-tub or in a Chinese factory someplace, and they don't care what they put in it. All they care about is making money. It could not even have any anabolic steroid in it. It could have poison. Your dealer doesn't care if you get muscles. They don't even care if you die. Not when there are other customers lining up right behind you."

"I don't have a *dealer*!" Gabe spit out the word like he was swearing. "It's just some guy. When I first called him, he was in an SAT prep class. We meet at a restaurant."

"Well, you're not going to be meeting anymore. Because as of right now, you're done. Your mom's going to be watching you like a hawk and so am I."

Gabe kicked the coffee table so hard it skidded forward two feet. "Great. Everything sucks. I'm going to shrink down to nothing again. My dad's dead, and now you seem to think you get to take his place. I don't even have my own room anymore."

Everything the kid said was true. So what was Charlie supposed to say?

In the end, he just said nothing.

CHAPTER 31

As he stood half dressed in front of the bathroom mirror, Warren generously sprayed Axe cologne over his chest. But what if he put his arm around Song tonight? She was so petite that her nose would be right next to his armpit. Just to be safe, he sprayed his pits as well. Then fanned his hands in front of his chest to make sure it was completely dry before he put on his shirt. He had last worn it to a wedding, and for the past six months it had hung in his closet, white and pristine and shrouded in plastic.

Now maybe he would have the kind of life where he wore dry-cleaned cotton shirts every day. Instead of a polyester blue shirt with his name embroidered over the breast pocket.

Thinking about the money made him a little anxious. He had been warned not to put it in a bank, that the IRS kept track of deposits over ten thousand dollars. He had split it up and hidden it in various places in his apartment: inside a DVD case, in a plastic bag in the freezer, in a water bottle in the toilet tank, in an envelope taped to the bottom of a drawer, and inside an old sock in his sock drawer. Now he was afraid he would forget where it all was.

Still, he was beyond lucky. He had more money than he had ever seen in his life and tonight he would have a beautiful woman by his side. And it wasn't like Song had come onto him because she knew about the money. No, it was because she had genuinely been attracted to him. For a second he imagined how he would tell their kids someday, "Yeah, your mom and I met when she literally ran into me!"

Tonight they were going to go out dancing. He wasn't even sure how that had happened. They had been talking at the coffee shop, and she had asked him what he liked to do in his free time. He had started to stutter, trying to think of something besides "play video games," and then he had remembered that tonight there was going to be a band in the bar down the block. And then somehow Song was agreeing to meet him there without his being exactly sure how it had happened.

Always he had watched and wondered how other guys did it. How did they get dates? How did they get girlfriends? And lately, how did other guys get wives? Everyone else had gotten the girl, gone to college, taken exciting jobs.

Even though she didn't know about the money, Song must have picked up on the confidence it had given him. His life was finally beginning to change.

And tonight it wouldn't be like the other times he went to bars. Always standing on the edge with a beer, bobbing his head in time to the music, trying to look like he was having fun. Going home by himself at the end of the night. The only time he didn't feel totally alone was when he went outside for a cig break. At least when you had a cigarette you could nod companionably to your fellow smokers. You could ask for a light. You could complain about the jerks who glared at you. You could let people who claimed they were quitting bum a smoke.

Sometimes a local band was playing at one of the neighborhood bars, usually with guys his own age, only they actually knew how to play a guitar. They probably knew how to read music, even. Warren could read a blueprint, but music had always been beyond him. In sixth grade he had struggled through weekly lessons, trying to learn how to play the guitar his mom had bought at Sears, until finally he gave up, both he and the teacher relieved when it was over.

Song would never know that he had failed even at that.

There was one thing that bothered Warren. That made him feel a little guilty when he thought about Song. It was that she looked a little like the dead girl. Like Dandan. Could they have known each other?

But Song had said she had come over here when she was a baby, and Dandan had only been in the US for a few weeks before she was killed.

His last day at work—which he hadn't known was going to be his last day at work—had been like any other. He had gone to the main office. Drunk coffee with the guys. Finished up paperwork from the day before. Got in the service van to go out on calls. Spent his day installing outlets, switches, and garbage disposals. He had solved one customer's problem in ten minutes. But because Stirling Electric billed by the hour, she had insisted on getting her money's worth. She had actually handed him a broom and made him sweep the dining room and kitchen before she let him leave. And he had done it!

The last call was for some people who wanted a light fixture moved from one side of the front door to the other. It was already a complicated job, but this home was made of brick, a rarity in Seattle. He spent a big chunk of the afternoon figuring out which bit of Romex wire went to the front-door light fixture, then finding the breaker and disconnecting the wire, cutting the wire in the attic, jumpering to new wiring inside a junction box, securing it to the rafters, then running the new wire for the new fixture down. Hammer drilling and then chiseling out the bricks and then installing the new metal box. Figuring out there was a bit of dead space, scooping away insulation, and fishing down his new Romex cable.

Being happy with how everything had gone until it turned out that the owner expected Warren to not only have on hand some mortar and bricks, but also to have bricks that exactly matched the ones used in the house, like he was a brick mason as well as an electrician. The owner had ended up cursing Warren out in the driveway.

The next day it had been a relief to go to jury duty, even though he knew it was just trading one kind of hassle for another.

After he had been picked for a jury, he had gone out to lunch. He had been sitting at a table by himself in the corner, looking at his phone, when this guy appeared at his table. Just materialized, like a ghost or something.

"Warren?"

He jumped, then tried to cover it. "Yeah?"

If he was a ghost, he was a very solid-looking ghost. No more than five foot nine, but two hundred twenty pounds. Easy. A shaved head, a round face, a big neck, heavily muscled shoulders.

There was no one else around, but even so, the guy sat down and leaned close, pitched his voice low, just for Warren's ears. "Warren

Paczkowski? The electrician who is twenty-eight years old? Who lives at 4927 Terrace Drive, apartment 15?"

Warren's eyes had widened at that.

"Yes?"

"We have a deal we want to talk to you about."

"I don't work off the books." Well, he did, occasionally, but not for some guy who just came up to him in a restaurant.

"It's not about your electrical skills."

"Oh?"

"It's about your jury duty."

"What about it?" Warren was suddenly aware of how close the guy was. Too close.

"We want to make you a deal. We want you to vote not guilty."

"But the case hasn't even started yet. And you want me to vote that the guy is innocent?"

"I didn't say that." The man's voice was calm, but with a flick of menace. "I said *not guilty.*"

"Why should I do that?" Warren wasn't fishing. He genuinely wanted to know.

"Because we can make it worth your while." A pause. A smile. "Very much worth your while."

Sometimes being an electrician was like being a detective. If a neutral wire was loose, it could cause crazy problems in the rest of the house. The trick was finding it—it could be in the switch box, an outlet, a light fixture, the attic, the panel, at the meter, or even out by the city. You had to think logically and test your assumptions. And working with electricity could be dangerous. Even deadly, if you didn't know what you were doing.

So why was this guy here? Why did he already know so much about Warren? He must be the mob or something. All right, Warren knew the mob was Italian, and this guy didn't look Italian. But still, he looked dangerous.

"And if I don't?"

"I don't think we want to go there, do we, Warren?"

"But what if everyone else votes guilty?"

"That doesn't matter. Just keep saying you don't think he's guilty. If you stick to your guns, they can't force you to say anything different." He slid over a paperback. It was a thriller about a hit man. "And here's a little food for thought."

After he left, Warren found ten one-hundred dollar bills tucked in the middle of a scene where the hit man took out a juror who refused to cooperate. He got the message.

It hadn't been easy. In the jury room, they had all yelled at him. Warren had just gone to that place he had started going to when he was a kid and his parents were fighting. Or when they were mad at him over something he had broken. Turned their voices into white noise, like an ocean. When the real Warren was tucked away inside, safe. It had only hurt a little when that pretty girl, Naomi, had gotten so mad at him.

He wasn't a dummy. Had Leacham killed that girl? No doubt. But she was dead. There was nothing Warren could do to bring her back. He had looked up online what would happen next. If Warren stuck to his guns, there would be a hung jury, and the prosecutor could refile the charges. Meanwhile, Leacham wouldn't dare do something like that again. Not when he would go to prison. A man like that—how long would he last in prison? He was soft.

Warren finished buttoning his shirt, then tried to fluff his hair just the right amount. He checked his phone for the time and swore. Song might already be there. She had wanted to meet him there, which he guessed was smart. Someone who looked like she did had to be careful. He slipped on his coat and hurried out of his apartment.

He saw her as soon as he walked in the door, as pretty as he remembered and even more petite, despite the high, high heels. She had already ordered a pitcher of beer, and as he slid in across from her, she handed him a glass. She kept pouring, and soon she was ordering another pitcher.

With every sip, Warren let himself relax. He bounced his feet, more or less in time to the music. Finally he coaxed her out onto the floor and started swiveling his hips. For as pretty as she was, she wasn't that good of a dancer. Jerking her limbs, her face a mask behind those plain black glasses that just made her look sexier. It made him feel protective. She was clearly as nervous as he was. Had been. Because with every glass of beer he felt a little more sure of himself.

Finally during a slow song, she leaned closer. And closer. Until he felt her lips grazing his ear.

"Tell me a secret," she whispered. "Tell me a secret nobody knows."

CHAPTER 32

SUNDAY

Bo drifted up from sleep. Where was she? She was lying in a warm bed, her breath slow and rhythmic. She sniffed. Why did the sheets stink of cigarettes?

She jerked fully awake. With difficulty, she pushed herself up on one elbow. Her left hand, which had been curled under her cheek, was asleep, as dead as a fish. She flexed her fingers, trying to get the blood flowing, then pushed herself up a few inches farther.

Warren was behind her, his body spooning hers, fast asleep with his face half mashed into his pillow. He didn't stir.

It came back to her now, how they had ended up back here, at Warren's apartment. Warren had been so drunk he was stumbling. Bo, on the other hand, had been clear-eyed and clear-minded. Willing to do whatever it took to get Warren to confide in her.

He had wanted more than kissing and fumbling, but he had also been so intoxicated he could barely walk, let alone get his thoughts straight enough to try to persuade her to have sex. In the end they had fallen asleep on his bed, cuddling.

In her sleep, Bo's body had forgotten who he was. What he had done. Betrayed her. She had a sense memory of curling into the sheer animal warmth of another body in bed. They had slept entangled, as innocent as two puppies, but she should have been watchful. Awake. While he was sleeping, she should have slipped out of bed and searched for evidence.

The sheets were pale blue. They seemed clean, and she was grateful for that. Only partially covered by the top sheet, Warren was wearing a wrinkled white shirt, blue plaid boxers, and socks that were both black but of different lengths.

Bo was still fully clothed except for her shoes and coat. But what had barely covered her when she was standing upright and tugging it all down or up into place was now doing a less than adequate job. Her special glasses were on the bedside table.

Last night Bo had thought Warren would confess. "Tell me a secret," she had whispered in his ear on the bar's dance floor. Waiting until he was so drunk he could barely keep to his feet. He was swaying from side to side, nodding his head, shuffling in place and letting his arms swing in what she guessed he thought passed for dancing. Bo hadn't gone out dancing since she was young. And she hadn't been young for years and years. "A secret no one else knows."

"You want to know?" he slurred. "You really want to know?" A musky perfume surrounded him like a cloud. Sickeningly sweet, but not quite enough to mask the smell of his cigarettes. And underneath, the sharp, earthy scent of his anxious sweat.

"Yes." She only had eyes for him, for this man with the ugly hair and the sad eyes. It was only later that she realized that if he had told her something, the recording device hidden in her glasses would probably not have worked. Not with the din of the band playing and the other patrons' shouted conversations.

"I like you." He grabbed her wrist and looked deeply into her eyes, his own eyes almost comically wide. "I really like you."

And then Warren planted a wet, slobbery kiss on her mouth. Beer and cigarettes and cologne, all right under her nose.

She had had to bite her tongue to keep from heaving.

The thing was, she had thought he might really have been on the verge of saying something. That he had considered it, but he hadn't been quite drunk enough to think it was a good idea.

Now she slipped her glasses back on.

"Hey, Song," he said softly from behind her. "So you're awake? Good morning, gorgeous." He patted the top of her hip and then let his hand rest there.

She forced what she hoped was an appropriate smile on her face and rolled over to face him.

"Hi," she said softly and reached out to push his ridiculous two-tone, two-length hair out of his eyes. She should be grateful he hadn't tried anything while she slept. Although watching him wake up, smacking gummy lips, softly groaning as he put a hand to his head, it was clear that he might not have been capable of anything.

"It's been a long time since I've had anyone up here," he said. "And never anyone so beautiful."

That wasn't much of a surprise. For an answer, she giggled. Bo had done that a lot last night. A giggle bought her t me to think, to craft the right answer. Sometimes it distracted War en enough that she didn't have to answer.

He rolled away from her and grabbed a pack of cigarettes and a lighter from the night table. The table was a giant wooden spool that must have once held wire.

"Do you mind not smoking?" She hated the smell.

Warren put them down. "Sure, babe." She could see his desire for a smoke warring with his desire for her. "If it bothers you."

"After I met you yesterday, I googled you, you know," she said.

"What? You did?" He looked pleased. And also nervous. "What did you find?"

"Your Facebook page, for one thing." Warren had sixty-seven friends. "But mostly I found articles about a trial that just ended. You were on the jury."

He looked away from her, running a thumb over one eyebrow. "Yeah, that was a tough case."

"What was it about? I don't really follow the news." What would she reply if he asked what she *did* follow? But Warren kept silent, so Bo added, "I didn't really understand it."

"The case was about a girl who died. She worked in a massage parlor. But she did a lot more than give massages, if you know what I mean."

He was looking at her with his head tilted, so Bo nodded to show that she did understand. Her heart was a stone.

"She got into a fight with a customer. He said she tried to rob him, that she held a knife to his throat. The prosecutor said the customer was the one who brought the knife and that he was the one who attacked her, not the other way around. Both of them pretty much agreed that there had been a struggle and the girl ended up getting stabbed. She died. The customer said it was self-defense and the prosecutor said it was murder."

"According to the article, you thought he was innocent." Bo

tried not to let any heat show in her voice. Inside, she was crackling with anger, but she kept her voice soft. "You were the only one."

"No. I voted that he was not guilty. There's a difference." He took a deep breath. "I don't want to talk about that now. Not when I've got such a pretty girl in my bed." He moved closer. "Here, let's take off those glasses. We don't need them getting in the way."

He reached out before she could stop him, his fingers pinching the hinges as he pulled them free. "Hey, these things are heavy!"

Her heart stilled, a bird trapped in the cage of her bones.

"Why in the world do they weigh so much?" His eyes narrowed.

The words came to her, saving her. "Because I have a strong prescription."

He turned the glasses around and put them on his own nose. He squinted as he scanned the room. Then he turned to Bo, his features bunching together. "How come if you have such a strong prescription, everything looks exactly the same when I put them on?"

Bo opened her mouth to explain.

She just didn't know what she would say.

CHAPTER 33

It was a Sunday morning like any Sunday morning. That's what Marvella Lott would later tell the homicide detectives. At least it was until the stranger walked in.

When he came in, Marvella was still standing outside the doors to the chapel, holding her stack of programs. Church was about to start, and no one had come in from the street for the last couple of minutes. Richard, the other greeter, had already gone in, complaining that his hip was killing him today. On the other side of the swinging doors, Abigail Endicott started playing the melody of the choir's first hymn.

Marvella was just about to slip into the chapel when the visitor walked in the church's main doors.

She didn't recognize him. His bald head reminded her of a peeled potato. It was topped with a wide-brimmed white knit cap. He was a big man, more muscular than anyone she had ever seen.

A chest as broad as a tree trunk. Not young, not old. Dressed in an open jacket that didn't look warm enough for the weather.

In the chapel, the choir started into "Our God Is a Great God."

"Would you like a program?" Smiling, she held one out to him.

The man didn't put out his hand. Didn't even really look at her. He just kept walking forward, looking almost mechanical. Had she not spoken loudly enough? Marvella's smile wobbled a bit.

"They're free," she said. Sometimes new immigrants or people who had never been to church were reluctant to take one, afraid there would be some kind of quid pro quo.

She glanced down at his hands as she waited for him to reach out for one of the programs. His gloved right hand began to reach inside his jacket as he walked past her. But what was that under the jacket? Tan, leather—it looked like a shoulder holster. A snake uncoiled in her belly.

Marvella's eyes flashed up to the stranger's face just as he swiped his left hand down from his forehead to his chin, flipping the brim of his hat inside out. The hat had now become a white balaclava mask, covering everything but his eyes. The nose was marked with two dark dots of yarn, and more black yarn had been used to make it look like the mouth had been stitched shut. The stranger now looked like a ghost or a skeleton. Something dead and reanimated.

And what was he now holding in his right hand? It was small and black. *No*, she thought. *No, please, God, I'm not seeing this.* It wasn't a Bible, like so many of the other congregants carried. It was a—

"Gun!" Marvella screamed from behind the stranger as he shouldered open one of the swinging doors. She felt her heart unzip. "He's got a gun! He's got a gun!"

Instead of running outside to the relative safety of the street, or at least barricading herself in the office, Marvella let her pamphlets fall to the floor and followed him inside. Later some of her grandchildren would lecture her for her foolhardiness, and others would praise her bravery. When it hadn't been either. It just had been the desire to *see*.

What happened next passed with a curious, dreamlike slowness, even though it was over in an instant.

At the sound of Marvella's shout, some congregants hunched their shoulders and froze in their pews. As if they thought if they stayed absolutely still, no one would notice them. Others began screaming and running toward the other exits, scrambling over people who were too slow or too stuck.

In a nearly empty row, Derron Phillips scuttled forward on hands and knees, the pew back providing him with a partial shield. Gayle Oliver tried to climb right over John Kim, but when the toe of her high heel got hooked on his thigh, she fell headlong, tumbling in between the pews. Meanwhile John never moved from his customary seat in the third row on the far left, never even blinked as Gayle fell over him. He only had eyes for the gun. Not the man holding it. Not Marvella, scurrying in his wake.

Marvella was praying now, mixing snatches of the 23rd Psalm with bits of the Lord's Prayer and other half-remembered verses. "Lord Jesus, protect us, save us from violence, even though we walk through the valley of the shadow of death, we fear no evil, O Lord, deliver us, you are our refuge, you are our present help in times of trouble." Her mouth was dry and chalky, her thoughts as disjointed as her prayer. A little girl, Hannah Lee, had appeared by her side. Marvella had no idea where Hannah had come from, but she put her arm around her, steadying herself as much as she steadied the girl.

Toward the front of the room, Abigail was taking shelter in the overhang of the keys. In the first pew, Hu Shen was on her feet but not moving, her hands pressed against her mouth, her head turning from side to side as she tried to figure out the best course of action. Brett Rockwell, who was always talking about new fad diets, had gotten stuck half under a pew, his feet madly paddling as he tried to scoot his bulk underneath. Chrissie Proulx was stabbing at her cell phone, but Marvella knew in her bones that whatever was going to happen would be long over by the time 911 was able to send cops here.

As he walked, the stranger began to raise the gun.

"What do you want?" Pastor Bob managed to say. Because of his microphone, he had an advantage, and his words rang out even over the screams and shouts and panic. His voice caught only a little. Afterward, they would all agree about how brave he had been.

The man didn't answer. He just kept moving forward, as inexorable as a tsunami.

Pastor Bob stepped out from behind the lectern. His arms were open, his hands empty. To Marvella, he looked like Jesus in one of the stained glass panels that was set in the wall, the one where he welcomed the little children to come to him.

Pastor Bob slowly stepped down the blue carpeted stairs. One, two.

"Whatever is wrong, we can talk about it. We can work this out. Let's just go someplace quiet." He spoke as if there weren't bedlam and chaos around them.

The man veered off. Away from Pastor Bob and toward the choir.

There was a mad scramble among the few people left in the choir stall. Sheet music flew in the air. Metal stands were knocked over with a clang. Jennie Wood whimpered and raised her hands as if in surrender. A man—Marvella thought it was Steward Steele—shouted.

The stranger stopped, then raised his left hand and wrapped it around his right to steady it. He braced himself.

His first shot took out the flower arrangement on top of the piano. It shattered into dozens of shards of vase, water spraying out, the flowers scattering in all directions. The sound roared and faded.

The second shot hit Abigail, who was still cowering underneath the keys. Her body jerked, then uncurled itself. Slowly, slowly, she sprawled back on the carpet. Her dark wig came off, exposing the vulnerable bones of her skull topped with thinning white hair. Blood, red and shiny as paint, spread from the point where the bullet had entered her skull.

The stranger froze as if he himself was shocked by what he had done. He turned on his heel, unleashing a fresh round of screams. Marvella pushed Hannah behind her. But he paid no attention to any of them. As he strode quickly toward the door, he let the hand with the gun drop to his side.

As he was leaving, Pastor Bob ran to Abigail and fell to his knees. He leaned over her, speaking quietly into her ear, holding her hand, gently stroking her bloody head.

But Marvella could see that it was too late for Abigail to hear him. Too late for Abigail to hear anything.

CHAPTER 34

Hey, Mia," her dad said as she slipped in beside him on the pew. "I didn't expect to see you here." From his other side, Luciana leaned forward and offered a shy smile.

Mia answered with nothing more than her own smile, not sure how much of the truth, if any, she wanted to offer. Last night she had been unable to sleep. What was going to become of Gabe? Would he really stop using? How much of a price would he end up paying for those muscles of his?

Clearly, the apple hadn't fallen far from the tree. In the years before he died, Scott had gotten in the habit of taking shortcuts. From the outside, their life had still looked picture perfect: a big house, a new Suburban, vacations to tropical beaches. After he was gone, Mia had realized their life had actually been an illusion, bought but not paid for.

Scott had always liked to look good, secretly delighted in

making people jealous. And now it seemed that Gabe was following in his father's footsteps.

Or maybe it was Mia's fault for sticking by Scott for far too long. For letting him expose their children to the wrong lessons. And for not having taught Gabe anything herself that had stayed with him.

The church service began, and along with the rest of the congregation, Mia got to her feet to sing a hymn—barely aware of her dad's slightly off-key bass and Luciana's soft soprano—then sat back down for announcements and scripture readings. Obediently, she closed her eyes for the prayers.

But her thoughts continued to spin in tighter and tighter circles.

What would happen to Gabe now? Was this the point where, when Mia looked back, she would realize things had already gone too far? That there would be no turn-around? Could he become a drug addict? A thief? Or just the kind of guy who could aim no higher than a minimum wage job?

Remembering how she had praised Gabe for how his hard work was finally paying off, Mia flushed. She had been a fool. A fool.

How could she have been so blind? Willfully blind, just as she had been with Scott. And like Scott, learning the truth too late. *Oh, dear God*, she thought, *please make it not be too late.*

As a prosecutor, Mia accepted no nonsense. But she tried to have a softer side at home. Tried not to cross-examine, not to suspect, not to trick Gabe or Brooke into admitting the truth. Tried to believe they already were being truthful. Because these people were her family, darn it. Not strangers. Not people who did bad things.

Only maybe Gabe was both. Family. Who did bad things.

As the pastor launched into his sermon, Mia barely heard him.

Instead, she kept second-guessing how she had handled things yesterday. Should she have hidden her discovery from Gabe until she had more time to research steroids? Had it been a mistake to let Charlie talk to him?

She didn't know what he had said, just that he had left as soon as he was done. Before he did, Charlie had taken Mia out on the porch and talked to her in a low voice.

"Just because he says he's quitting doesn't mean that he is, or that he's going to stay quit. He knows you're watching him now, though. So he'll either stop using or he'll try to get better at hiding it. You just better hope he keeps feeling guilty. But if I were you, I wouldn't assume anything."

"Okay." Mia wished she could just go into her room and close the door, pull the covers over her head and not get out of bed for a year or two. Maybe not until Gabe was twenty-five. "Thanks. Thanks for everything."

"I can remember what it was like to be a teenage boy." His mouth twisted, and he looked down at his shoes. "Sort of." He raised his head, and his eyes met hers. "I think he'll probably be okay. His brain just needs to catch up with his impulses."

Did Charlie think she was a terrible mom not to have noticed anything? Did he think she had been hiding her head in the sand? She didn't really want to know.

"I sure hope so." Mia sighed. "See you Monday." Then she took a deep breath and went back inside and up to Gabe's room, the place to which he had retreated after talking to Charlie. She opened the door without knocking. Gabe was sprawled on his bed, tiny white earbuds screwed into his ears.

"This probably comes as no surprise," she said in a voice designed to penetrate, "but you're grounded."

He yanked out one earpiece and pushed himself up on one elbow. "For how long?"

Mia pinched the bridge of her nose between finger and thumb. "I don't know for how long. In the interim, I want you to research and write a four-page, double-spaced report on the drawbacks of steroids. A minimum of a thousand words. I want you to cover not only the medical aspects but also people whose lives got messed up. Who lost their sports careers or even their lives."

Then she had spent the next half hour playing dolls with Brooke, wishing life were as simple for her as it was for a four-year-old.

Now Mia tuned into the sermon and realized it was about the prodigal son. Either God had a sense of humor or he was taunting her. Gabe had squandered his gifts, come close to throwing them away. Would he ever return to the fold? She couldn't pray for herself, could barely pray for Gabe. She realized it was because she lacked any certainty that it would turn out okay. But maybe that was what prayers were for, to make you realize you had no control, to make you let go of the notion that you controlled your destiny.

Maybe the future was best approached on your knees.

"Mia?" Her dad touched her arm. "Church is over."

With a start she realized everyone was getting to their feet and gathering their things.

"Sorry!"

"Would you like to go to lunch with Luciana and me?"

"I would love that." She was in no hurry to return home. Gabe had still been in bed when she left. Kali was looking after Brooke.

They met at a diner a half mile from the church, the kind that served breakfast all day. The food looked basic, and probably most of it started out frozen in some kind of industrial-size packaging, but how badly could you mess up breakfast? Remembering her vow to eat better, Mia ordered her toast dry.

Her dad leaned forward. "So how are things going with the kids?"

Mia opened her mouth, but no words came out. To buy time, she took a sip of her coffee. It was scalding, burning her tongue. She waved her hand in front of her mouth, hoping her dad would think that the coffee explained the tears that had flooded her eyes. "Let's just say it's been . . . interesting."

"I remember your brother when he was Gabe's age. You know what they say. When you're fourteen or fifteen, your parents don't know anything, but by the time you're twenty-five, it's amazing how much they've learned."

"I hope you're right." She stopped herself from sighing.

"And work? How's that going?"

"I've been helping a homicide detective with a case. We're pretty sure that the victim is the same guy who asked for my help outside the Chinese restaurant where he worked. He didn't speak very much English, so we couldn't really communicate. He came to America illegally." She paused while the waitress set down their plates. "I would guess that everyone who works at that restaurant is undocumented. And probably as a result, the people who work there have never even heard of the minimum wage. And they all live in a run-down house where four or five people share a room."

Her food forgotten, Luciana was listening with interest. "Maybe they are more than just illegal," she said carefully. "Maybe they are slaves."

"What?" Clearly, Luciana did not have a good grasp of English. "There aren't any slaves anymore. Not in America."

"There *are* slaves in America," Luciana insisted. "Even slaves in Seattle."

Mia remembered a story she had seen on the news, a couple from Indonesia who had brought over a servant and then never let her go outside, never paid her, made her sleep on the floor.

"I guess I've heard of maids being treated like slaves."

"It is not *like* slaves," Luciana insisted. "It *is*. And there are slaves in factories and on farms. In restaurants. Anyplace you need a lot of people and they don't need to speak much English."

"The people from the restaurant that we talked to live in a house in a regular neighborhood. They talk to the public every day. They're free to go wherever they want. They're not being sold at an auction. I mean, it's not like they're chained up or anything." But as Mia spoke, she wondered. How free were the people they had talked to, really?

"They don't need to be chained up." Luciana's words were an urgent hiss. "They chain themselves. The bosses take their papers. The bosses say, if you go to the police, you will be beaten, raped, maybe even killed. You will be jailed. You will be deported." She nodded, agreeing with herself. "That's what the police do to people in their home countries, so it makes sense. So there's no point in asking anyone for help. Plus, these people are told they owe money to the smugglers and they have to work to pay it back. Only when you are paid a dollar or two an hour, you will never pay it back. It is called"—she looked up, trying to recall the correct term—"debt bondage. But what it means is that you are a slave." Her lips pursed. "Even if they *aren't* sold at auction."

"How do you know all this?" Mia asked.

"Because that's what happened to me."

Mia looked at her dad. Food forgotten, he was listening to Luciana with one hand across his mouth. She could still make out his expression. Pain, sadness.

"When I was offered a job in America," she continued in her soft voice, "I felt like I had won the lottery. I was living in a little town in Mexico with my family, but there was no work. When a woman said she had a job for me, I thought, *I can earn money and send it back to my family. I can help my parents. Everyone knows you make good money in America.* I felt so lucky. This lady told me, 'You help me, and I will help you.' She said I was like a daughter to her. But then when I was brought here, she told me I owed her twelve thousand dollars for passage. And she charged me for every bit of food I put in my mouth, the bed I slept on. Everything."

Luciana sighed and was quiet for a long moment. Neither Mia nor her dad moved.

"To pay her back, I had to be with men. Man after man after man. The people who ran the whole thing were from Mexico, like me. So were the other girls. The only Americans I met were my clients. You are told you have to earn back the money you owe before you can leave. Not that you know where you are. Even if you've been there for months. Maybe you know the area code. Or the state. But not the city. And you get passed around, you get traded. Like a slave. You can still be bought and sold. Even in 2015. Even in America." Her eyes shone with unshed tears. "One time I tried to tell a man who seemed nice what was happening. But he told the madam. I was beaten until I almost died. Then they put me in a locked closet for eleven days. And then I was put back to work. If a neighbor hadn't eventually called the police, I think I would have died. One way or the other."

Luciana blinked and a single tear ran from her eye.

Mia's dad reached out his thumb and wiped it away.

CHAPTER 35

Gabe's fist throbbed, the pain flashing red with every beat of his heart. Crimson blood seeped from his knuckles. A fist-shaped dent cratered the wall right next to where he was lying on his back on the upper bunk.

Staring at the hole, Gabe put his knuckles to his mouth and licked them. His mom hardly ever came in here anymore, not since Eldon had moved in. With luck, it would be a long time before she even noticed it. Still, that had been pretty stupid, punching the wall. He hadn't even decided to do it. He had just done it.

It felt like there was a pit inside his chest, and it was getting wider and deeper. Or maybe he was already inside the pit, having fallen in.

Eldon had gone down a little earlier to fix himself breakfast, so for once Gabe was alone in the room. The room that was supposed to be his. Now the only thing in this room that was his and his alone was this upper bunk. A three-by-six-foot piece of real estate.

The rest of his room was now shared with Eldon. Eldon who had fifty pounds on him, easy. Even now, even after the steroids had given Gabe the body he always wanted. Pretty soon it would disappear, and it would be back to being more like an eighty-pound difference between them.

Once that happened, how would it look when they walked down the halls at school? Probably like Gabe was some little dwarf capering in a giant's shadow.

People had remarked on his weight gain, his new muscles. They would surely comment when he dwindled back to nothing. Back to being the boy who wasn't much bigger than a sixth grader. Girls would roll their eyes when he tried to talk to him, the way they had before.

But that's what his mom and Charlie were dooming him to. They wanted him to go back to looking like the little kid they treated him like. His thoughts circled and looped the way they had all morning.

Five minutes ago, when Gabe thought about what had happened yesterday, about how his mom had snooped through his things, hot anger had surged up in him. Before he realized what he was doing, he had hit the wall with his fist. Now he flexed his hand, hoping he hadn't broken anything. The way his mom had looked at him, her mouth twisted as if he had just betrayed her. He had wanted to curl up so tight that he would just disappear.

Last night she had told him that she loved him, that she would always love him, but the words had sounded rote. Stripped of all pride, of all joy. It was pretty clear she figured that she *had* to love him. Love as a burden. Love as shame.

He blinked away the sudden spark of tears and tried to find the anger again. His mom was always after him, saying that he was the man of the house. But now that he looked like a man, she wasn't happy. But wasn't that what she had wanted? Wasn't it?

And what did Charlie think about him now? Did he think he was a loser? An idiot? A jerk? A few weeks back, Charlie had been talking about the two of them taking in a Seahawks game. Clearly, that would no longer be part of the picture.

Was Charlie right about what steroids could do to you? His mom could be counted on to get freaked out, to go all worst-case-scenario, but Charlie not so much. So if Charlie had said those things, maybe they were true. Or true-ish. Rolling over, Gabe slid off the bunk and headed into the bathroom, hoping that for once he would be left in peace for a few minutes. His mom had a bathroom all to herself, but between him, Eldon, and Brooke, it felt like someone was always waiting.

In the bathroom, he locked the door, then took off his shirt. His pecs were so much bigger now. But could some of it be because he was actually developing breasts? He poked at them, and they seemed firm. But did that mean anything?

He picked up a hand mirror and tried to see the back of his head. It took a lot of contorting and working the angles to get it right. Did he have less hair? Maybe? Yes? No? Between spiky brown strands, he could see tiny spots of white skin, but it was hard to know if that was new, since he couldn't remember ever looking at the back of his head before.

Still, even if his body was changing in a few hardly noticeable ways, it was a small price to pay, wasn't it? Not when he could see the respect in people's eyes when he walked down the halls at school. Not when he could challenge himself to do nearly anything physically, and his body would respond like a machine, only one made of muscles and tendons.

He slid his T-shirt back on. When his head popped out of the hole, for a disorienting second Gabe thought he saw his dad staring back at him from the mirror. Like he was back from the dead.

Was it wrong that a big part of him still loved his dad, given that he had been such a jerk? Gabe wasn't supposed to know what his dad had done, but he did anyway. How many of the commandments had his dad broken? Nearly every one except for "Thou shalt not kill."

Instead, his father was the one who had been killed.

When he was little, Gabe had wanted to *be* his dad. His mom had an old scrapbook, and in it was a photo of Gabe wearing nothing but a diaper, his dad's big shoes, and a grin.

He had his own memories from when he was a little older. His dad showing him how to build a birdhouse. Teaching him how to play guitar. Playing catch with baseballs and footballs and Frisbees. Pride had flooded his chest when his dad nodded or smiled at some achievement or accomplishment. His mom was all about words, while his dad hadn't been big on talking. Still, you could tell when he approved.

The last year before his dad died, his parents had fought a lot. Even though Gabe hadn't really known what it was about, he had been angry at his mom. She was such a nag.

Now he realized she had been desperately trying to turn his dad around before he crashed. And it hadn't worked.

Was that what she was trying to do with Gabe? Turn him around before he crashed?

With a sigh, he unlocked the bathroom door. When he opened the door, he started back. Eldon was hanging out in the hall, clearly waiting for him to leave, although he hadn't made a sound to let Gabe know he was there.

Gabe just hoped he hadn't been muttering to himself. He went back to their room and sat at the desk. He wasn't planning on doing any homework until this evening, not until the last possible minute, but he still didn't want Eldon taking up one more spot that was actually supposed to be his.

When Eldon came into the room, Gabe blurted out, "My mom found my supplies yesterday."

Eldon's eyes went wide and he swore under his breath. "What happened? How did she find them?"

"She was going through my stuff and she found my kit. She threw away the needles and flushed the drugs down the drain."

"Are you serious, man?" Eldon winced. "Does she think I was taking them too?"

Gabe's face got hot. Guilt by association. The idea made him feel even lower. "No worries. She knows you're just naturally a big dude."

"You must be in a lot of trouble."

"She even had that cop she works with, Charlie Carlson, yell at me."

Eldon's eyes got even bigger. "Did he arrest you?"

"No. I wouldn't be sitting here if he had." Gabe's sarcastic tone covered up a sudden jab of fear. He hadn't even thought about that, about how Charlie was a cop. Taking steroids had never seemed illegal, exactly. More like a secret.

"So what are you going to do?"

Gabe started to say that he had promised his mom that he wouldn't take them, but then he realized that didn't mean much. After all, he had been using them before, knowing full well that his mother wouldn't approve.

"I'm thinking about stopping." As he said the words, he realized he might mean them. Maybe. "At least for now. Mom will be giving the evil eye, so I won't be able to get away with anything."

Eldon bit his lip, then said in a rush, "Maybe that's a good idea. Since you started taking them, you've changed."

"Of course I've changed. I can do stuff I never did before."

Eldon gave him a look. "I mean, you seem like you're angry all the time."

"No, I'm not. That's ridiculous."

And then Gabe followed Eldon's gaze to his hands, which had become fists again without his even noticing.

CHAPTER 36

D o you know why my business works?" Kenny was so angry the tops of his ears felt hot. He was in his office, along with the idiot he had made the mistake of counting on. "It is because I am careful not to make mistakes." He sliced one hand through the air. "It is definitely not, how do they say it, because I shoot first and ask questions later."

"I was taking care of *your* problem," Chris Atkinson said sullenly. "And she was just where you said she would be. Ten forty-five to noon every Sunday, playing piano at the front of the church." His lower lip jutted out like a spoiled child's. And with his shaved head, his face did look something like a baby's. Not the rest of him, though. He was nearly as wide as he was tall, muscled in places no one who didn't use steroids even had muscles. "It's not my fault it wasn't her."

Three years ago, Atkinson had been a security guard. A wannabe cop who wasn't even allowed to carry a gun on the job. Then he had started buying steroids from Kenny. That had allowed him to gain fifty pounds of muscle on his five-foot-nine frame, leaving him so brawny he looked like a cartoon caricature. He started selling to guys at his gym, got a concealed carry permit, and eventually left his job and started working for Kenny on a freelance basis.

Kenny had enforcers, yes, Chinese men who made sure that those he smuggled over paid their debts. But Atkinson also had his uses. He had tapped into markets Kenny had only guessed at, gym rats and ex-cops and even boys in high school. And it was amazing how much better certain meetings went when you had someone standing behind you, someone menacing and muscled and with a gun openly displayed in a shoulder holster. It was only a bonus that he did not understand a single word of Chinese. No plans or pleas ever entered his ears.

And there were times when it was necessary to have someone get his hands dirty. Kenny preferred it if those hands did not belong to him. Kenny made the threats, and his enforcers or Atkinson carried them out. It was Atkinson who had shot Lihong.

But there were more fish in the sea. Atkinson could be replaced by another American looking for an opportunity to flex his new muscles. To be asked to act on his new aggression.

"You shot an old *white* woman. Not Bo Yee."

"She was wearing a black wig and she had her head bent over the keys when I came in. Anyone could have made the same mistake."

"Maybe anyone could, but you are the one who did. You were supposed to kill Bo Yee. Half that congregation is Chinese. They would understand the lesson and they would know to be quiet. They would know not to cross me in the future." It was like the parable: "Once bitten by a snake, a person is scared all his life at the mere sight of a rope." "Only it's a lesson no one is ever going to understand." Kenny made a sound of disgust. "Because the wrong woman is dead."

"But you're the one who told me she was going to be there. Basically, I did what you wanted me to do." Atkinson stared right back at him with a sullen expression. Stupid and sullen. But something about his tiny eyes—even the man's *face* appeared too bulky—looked sly.

And stupid, sullen, and sly could become a bad combination. What if one day Atkinson had what he thought was a bright idea? A bright idea that might end with Kenny lying on the floor, a bullet through his heart.

"The police may not be able to figure out why that old white lady died. The congregation might not either. But you can be sure that Bo Yee will." Kenny gritted his teeth in frustration. "And now she will go into hiding. Now she will be a lot harder to kill."

"All right, all right. Give me another chance and I'll make sure I get her. And I'll even do another job at no charge."

Kenny heaved a sigh, massaging his temple. "Spilt water cannot be retrieved. Let Bo Yee go, for now. With luck, she will leave Seattle and never come back."

Should he take Atkinson up on his offer? He did not know Mia Quinn well, but well enough to know that she would not stop. She wanted David Leacham in prison. And now that she was wondering and worrying about Lihong, now that Chun had given her some more pieces of the puzzle, maybe she would start putting them together. Having Mia Quinn taken care of would put a stop to that.

It would have to look like an accident. A tragic accident.

But he wouldn't use this fool to do it. He had to find another way. First he had to get rid of Atkinson. Before he talked. Or before he decided that the best way to solve Kenny's having a problem was to kill Kenny.

He could hire another killer to take care of Atkinson, but where would that end? Anyone he hired might be reasonably afraid that they would be next.

He had decided it would be better if no one else was involved. Luckily, there was a way to have the man solve the problem himself.

"Give me a day or two," Kenny said. "Let me think about the best course of action."

"Whatever it is, I'll do it. Just tell me what you want." The big man nodded his head.

"Understood." Kenny reached into his desk drawer and snagged a small blue-topped vial with his fingernails. He tossed it to Atkinson, who caught it with one meaty paw.

"What's this?"

"I received something new this week from China. It's supposed to be especially effective, but with no acne or hair loss. It's not even available in the States yet."

Atkinson held up the vial to the light. It was filled with clear liquid. Aside from the blue top, it looked like all the other ones he had sold.

"No hair loss?" he asked, running his hand over his shaved head. By the stubble, Kenny could see how his hairline had receded, one of the typical side effects of steroids.

"It's even supposed to reverse any previous problems." He shrugged, as if it didn't matter to him. "That's what they told me, anyway. Why don't you see what your customers think?" With the back of his hand, he nudged forward a white paper takeout bag filled with a couple dozen vials.

The truth was that they didn't contain steroids, but an animal tranquilizer. Some animal tranquilizers were used as club drugs. People said they liked how far away and blurry the drug made things. How uninhibited and full of love they felt.

Only this tranquilizer wasn't made for just any animal. It was used to sedate elephants. Injected into a human vein, it would stop the heart.

Wearing gloves, Kenny had carefully wiped down the surface of the vials with antiseptic wipes before he put them in the paper bag. He wanted to leave no trace of himself. No partial fingerprint. No DNA.

Atkinson would want to be the first to sample this new wonder drug. He would be found with the needle still in his arm and with old track marks on his elbows and ankles. The authorities would wonder, but in the end, it would be chalked up to an accidental overdose.

And now all Kenny had to do was to take care of Bo and Mia himself.

CHAPTER 37

As he waited for the church's pastor, Bob Ho, to get off the phone, Charlie's thoughts went in circles. He believed that the key to solving a murder was to start with the victim. Why had the killer chosen that particular person? If you could pick out that first thread, you could start pulling it until it led back to the murderer.

Whoever had killed Abigail Endicott this morning had clearly sought her out. The killer had walked past dozens of other potential victims, ignored the people who fled screaming at the sight of his gun. Paid no attention to Marvella Lott, the greeter who had followed on his heels and shouted out a warning to the congregation. In other circumstances, Charlie might have said her actions had saved dozens of lives, but the more he heard, the more he was certain this man had come with only one purpose: to kill Abigail Endicott. He had been a man on a mission. And once he had succeeded, he had fled without trying to harm anyone else or even uttering a single word.

Confronted by chaos, the first responders had radioed for additional units to help question witnesses and search the area. A lot of the congregants had already fled in a mad panic, resulting in sprained ankles and even a few broken bones. They had run down the street until they could run no more, or piled into their cars and peeled out of the parking lot.

The first officers on the scene had herded those who remained into the social room, the place where coffee and cookies were normally served after the service. Officers had questioned each person briefly, getting names and addresses and a quick description of what they had observed. Unfortunately, no one seemed to have witnessed the killer leaving.

Their best lead was Marvella, the only one who had seen the killer before he pulled down his ski mask. The rest had focused on the eerily embroidered white balaclava with the black stitches across the lips. What else they remembered: about his height, weight, and even ethnicity varied dramatically from person to person. Marvella was working with a sketch artist, but Charlie was afraid that her fixation on the gun had pushed aside anything else.

They had no suspects, Charlie thought as he shifted on the hard bench. No leads. There was no video camera in the foyer, and none in any nearby business that focused on the street. The little information they had on the suspect was being broadcast. But you couldn't get very far putting out a BOLO for a white male in his thirties or forties, about five foot nine, wearing a black winter coat and dark pants, and who was believed to have fled in an unknown vehicle in an unknown direction of travel.

Marvella had said he was white and had a stocky build. She also thought his head was shaved, but Charlie didn't know whether that was true, because the balaclava he had worn like a hat had covered his head. The lady had paged through mug shots, but so far not a one had been familiar. And the spectacular MO certainly did not match any other recent crimes in Seattle or even in surrounding states. Charlie had checked.

The only clues the guy had left behind were the spent brass from his gun and the bullet in Abigail's head. The best Charlie could hope for was that the guy had ditched the balaclava—and his DNA along with it.

So Charlie's first job was to start with the victim and learn everything he could about her. It was like a spiral, the beginning of the yellow brick road. It was here at the church that she had died— and also where she had spent a big chunk of her life.

On the other side of his office window, the pastor raised one finger to indicate to Charlie that he was almost done. Charlie nodded in return, his thoughts still consumed with Abigail.

The problem was that the road seemed more of a dead-end. Why would someone want to kill a seventy-two-year-old widow? She had no history with the criminal justice system. Not even a parking ticket. She had lived in the same house for thirty years and seemed to have had no disputes with the neighbors. Abigail had a forty-three-year-old married daughter who lived in Missouri, a daughter who loved her and who was bewildered.

She was a retired piano teacher. It was hard to imagine that the killer was a former student, come back to wreak revenge for being forced to spend their formative years playing "Fur Elise."

Her social life revolved around her church. So it seemed the most likely suspects would be found here, at the very place where she had been killed. A rival Sunday school teacher? A jealous spouse? But then why hadn't Marvella recognized the killer?

Charlie's mind circled around the problem and tried a different angle. If you wanted to kill someone, the last place you would do it would be in front of hundreds of witnesses. Unless you wanted to be showy. What if this was a murder for hire, designed to send a message to someone else in the congregation?

The door to Bob Ho's office opened, and the pastor stuck his head out. Ho was in his midforties, stocky, with black hair parted on one side and the hint of a double chin. "Sorry that took so long. I don't think my insurance company is used to claims arising from a murder and its investigation. In fact, none of us is used to any part of this. Not like you must be."

"Every case is different," Charlie said as he went into the pastor's office and took a seat. "And even I've never had one like this." He leaned forward, resting his elbows on his knees. "Why don't you tell me more about your church."

The man had said to call him Pastor Bob, but Charlie was trying to avoid calling him anything.

"We've been around for over a hundred years. When we first started, we mostly served Chinese people who had been brought over to work on the railroads and in the coal mines. Men like my grandfather. The Chinese still come to this area of town for herbs, for advice, or for jobs. They like to go someplace where people will speak their language, where they can buy bok choi and roast duck."

Charlie nodded.

"But over time Chinatown became the International District, and something similar has been happening with the church. We've branched out. Now we have members who are Filipino, Japanese, Vietnamese, Korean, and Thai. And there are a lot of people who just live in the neighborhood who come to services here, people who like a dynamic church. We're growing, and not a lot of churches can say that. Two services on Sunday, Bible study classes, men's and ladies' groups, a youth group, even a food pantry and clothes closet."

"And how long has Abigail been a member?"

"As long as I can remember. She and her late husband lived a few miles away. Jack had a heart attack when he was sixty. Died before he even got a chance to retire." Bob let out a shuddering sigh. "I guess it's good he wasn't alive to see this. If he weren't already dead, it would have killed him." The sound the pastor made wasn't quite a laugh. "And she's got a daughter who lives in Missouri or Mississippi."

"Missouri," Charlie supplied. "St. Louis."

"That sounds right. They get along well. And that girl has a daughter of her own, a three-year-old. Abigail's always showing off new photos of her." He shook his head. "The whole thing just seems senseless. And so wrong. The Bible says that where two or three are gathered in Jesus' name, he is there. It's a terrible sin, taking a life, and it was committed here in front of God."

Charlie went off script. "Do you believe God should have protected her?"

After a moment's hesitation, the pastor said, "Maybe he did, by taking her in the place where she would feel closest to him. And it was fast. By the time I got to her, she was already gone."

After he was done with his questions, Charlie thanked Bob for his time and then kicked the man out of his own office, which he had temporarily commandeered. As he left, Charlie asked him to send in Gwen Lin.

While he was waiting for the woman everyone agreed was Abigail's best friend, Mia called.

"Hey," Charlie said, "I'm afraid I don't have time to talk. I'm in the middle of another murder investigation."

"Another one?" Mia sounded surprised. It was unusual for Seattle to get two murders in a single week.

"And this one really doesn't make any sense. Retired piano teacher gunned down playing piano at church. It's so public I'm starting to wonder if it was murder for hire." There was a soft knock on the door. "Sorry, gotta go."

Gwen Lin wore her too-black hair pulled back in a tight bun. "We talked every morning at seven," she told Charlie. "Two widow ladies, living on their own. It was nice to check in with someone, to have someone to talk about the news with, or who knew if you had a cold, or if your son was coming to visit. I guess I won't have that anymore." Her eyes, caught in a net of wrinkles, shone with tears.

"Can you think of anything she was worried about? Anyone she was angry with or who was angry with her?"

"You obviously never met Abby. She was all about giving. Helping people. Even though she was retired, she gave free lessons to anyone who loved music. She said it gave her joy."

"Did she ever have trouble making ends meet?"

"Abby had her savings, she had her Social Security, but that was about it. So not a lot." Gwen managed a half smile. "If you wanted to get together for lunch, it had to be a place that had coupons in the Sunday paper."

"Do you think she was in any debt?" Charlie asked.

"Abby? No way. Besides, even if she did owe someone some money, what good would it do to kill her? She's certainly not going to be paying anyone back now."

After Gwen left, Charlie scrubbed his face with hands. He was not getting anywhere.

How big of a risk had the killer actually taken? Even though he had done it in front of dozens of witnesses, he had been the only one who was armed. And the only one who had seen his face was Marvella. Charlie was more and more convinced that this hadn't been a murder. It had been an execution.

Charlie read back over the witness statements that had been gathered the day before. And then he realized the one thing that was missing.

He thought back to Abigail's body, vulnerable and small in death. He had seen only one entrance wound in the victim, the one just above her ear. But many of the witnesses had described hearing two shots. Some had talked about seeing a flower vase on top of the piano explode.

He went back out into the main part of the church. The wall behind the piano was papered with a small blue-and-white geometric print, the kind of thing that was designed not to show dirt if people rubbed against it in passing.

Moving his head back and forth, he scanned the wall. And finally he spotted it. A hole in the drywall. Charlie took out his phone to call the crime scene tech back.

He would make sure the guy didn't get his saw anywhere near the bullet.

And then he would tell Bob Ho that the insurance adjustor had one more thing to adjust.

CHAPTER 38

What the heck kind of glasses are these, anyway?" Warren had stopped looking around the bedroom and was now staring directly at Bo with a puzzled expression. Looking at her through her spy glasses that pretty obviously only held clear glass. How long until he noticed that the part over the bridge of the nose was oddly springy? That was the spot where the recording unit could be toggled on and off.

"It's just that . . ." Bo let her voice trail off. She had run out of lies, and a giggle would not serve her.

The lines between Warren's brows smoothed out. "It's because guys don't take you serious, right? I mean, you've got that rocking body, but nobody pays attention to your mind!"

Understanding dawned. He thought the glasses were a kind of cover, that the carefree girl in heels and a too-tight sweater was the real her.

"Exactly right." She plucked the glasses from his face and slid them on. "How about if I go to the store and pick up a few things while you sleep in a little? Then I can come back and make you breakfast in bed."

The corners of his mouth turned down. "Are you just saying that because you want to get out of here? That's okay. You can go. You don't have to lie."

"I swear to you, I'm not lying, Warren."

He smiled, but his eyes were wary. "Then sure. And if you really want to make me breakfast, I would love it."

"See you in a bit," she said as she pushed her feet into her high heels, ignoring the way they protested. She leaned down and picked up her coat.

"I sure hope so, Song. And maybe while you're out, you can get them to turn the sun down. It's hurting my eyes." Warren pulled the pillow over his head.

Before she left, she checked out his kitchen. It was surprisingly neat, but maybe that was because he owned so few dishes, cooking utensils, or pantry items. He had the sad, half-empty kitchen shelves of a man who had no idea how to cook.

After making sure it wouldn't lock behind her, she pulled the apartment door closed. She had to get Warren talking again. And the best way to do that, it seemed, was to get him drunk. At the store, she got coffee, tomato juice, celery, Bisquick, maple-flavored syrup, a bottle of cheap vodka, and a bottle of Everclear. Warren shouldn't be able to taste the Everclear, but the vodka would hide any lingering taste—and explain why he was going to start feeling drunk. As she walked back to his apartment, she rehearsed explanations if he saw the Everclear and asked why she had bought it. But he was still snoring gently when Bo let herself in.

She filled one glass with tomato juice and the second with half Everclear, a splash of vodka, then the rest tomato juice, and stuck a stalk of celery in each. She mixed up the pancakes and cooked them in a frying pan she unearthed. In lieu of a breakfast tray, she set everything on a cookie sheet. Before she carried it in, she pressed the glasses at the bridge of her nose to start the recording.

Warren woke up as she was setting the cookie sheet down next to his cigarettes. He smiled sleepily at her. He looked as happy as an American child might look on Christmas morning.

"You came back," he said simply.

She handed him his glass. "O ye of little faith."

He smiled uncertainly, and she guessed he didn't know the Bible verse. "What's this?" He took a sip before she even answered.

"Bloody Mary."

Groaning, he started to put it back on the cookie sheet. "Not for me."

"Oh, please, Warren." She fake-pouted, leaning over to give him another glimpse of her cleavage. "A little hair of the dog, isn't that what they say?"

He grunted, but he did hold on to his glass and take a sip. And then another. While she waited for the alcohol to take effect, Bo asked him easy questions in between bites of pancake. About his job. About the giant spool that served as a table, which Warren told her had come from an industrial job site. He grew more animated, more red-faced, and Bo returned twice to the kitchen to pour them new drinks, upping the proportion of Everclear each time. And slowly she brought the topic back around to the trial.

"The articles said that no one understood why you voted no." She tilted her head. "So why did you?"

He licked his lips, looked from side to side, then set down his plate so he could learn closer to her. "Here's the *thing*." He slurred the word *thing* so it stretched out forever. "If I tell you, you can't tell anyone, okay?"

"I won't," she lied. "I promise."

"As the trial was beginning, a man came to me. Big guy. Built like . . . like a mountain. He threatened me. He said I had to vote that that guy who was on trial, that David Leacham, was not guilty. He said no matter what the other jurors said, I could never change my mind. I would have to keep voting that he was not guilty." Warren took a shaky breath. He looked around as if someone might be listening and then lowered his voice. "And he said that if I didn't do what he said, he would have me killed."

Bo got to her feet. She was exhilarated, as if she were the one who was drunk. "You need to go to the police." Now she had the proof. Now Mia would be able to persuade her boss to reopen the case.

"No, Song." He caught her wrist. "I need to be honest with you. There's something else that he said."

"What's that?" Her eyes didn't leave his face.

"He said that if I voted the way he wanted, he would also give me money. More money than I'd ever seen in my life. But if I tell anyone what happened, they'll take that back. And then they'll kill me."

"But you can't really believe that guy was innocent!"

"I didn't say innocent. I said I voted not guilty." Warren emphasized this as if it were an important distinction. "I mean, it *is* possible Leacham didn't mean to do it, that it really was an accident. And besides, I was the only one who voted not guilty. There were eleven other people on the jury. Before I decided whether to do what that guy wanted me to, I looked up what would happen. If the jurors can't all agree, it's called a hung jury, and it goes back to trial. Basically, they just start over again. Which means that in the end, Leachman will be convicted. So no blood, no foul. Only now I've got more money than I know what to do with." He managed a sick sort of grin. "I'm hoping you can help me spend it."

"But he's free." Bo crossed her arms, making sure she covered her chest in the process. "He could even be killing other girls right now!"

"He won't be out for long. Besides, they've got him on an ankle monitor. And I'm sure that wife of his is not going to let him out of her sight."

"But what if they don't try that man again? They don't have to. In fact, I've heard they're not going to."

Warren looked stricken. "What do you mean?"

"It is optional. It is not like the rules say they have to put him on trial. They could choose not to re-try him. And I heard that was what the prosecutor was going to do. I heard she was going to let him go free."

Warren was so drunk it took a long time for the information to sink in. When it did, he buried his face in his hands. "Oh no. What have I done?"

"You can go to the authorities." One way or the other, she would make sure the police learned what Warren had done. If he was the one who told, he would probably get in less trouble than if she did. "Tell them what you told me."

"I can't do that! If I do, I'll be the one on trial. I'll be the one going to prison."

"Not if you explain that he threatened you," she said, not knowing if it were true or not. "Not if you give the money back."

"Maybe," Warren said, but she could tell he didn't believe her. "But this guy also promised to have me killed if I told. And I'm pretty sure he meant that."

"Together, we can figure out what to do." She squeezed his hands, then released them. "But first I'm going to stop by my place, change clothes, and then come back here." She leaned in and kissed his cheek. "I'll see you in a bit. And then we'll sit down together and figure out what to do."

"What?" He stared at her blearily. "No! Let me take you."

"I'll be back soon," she lied.

"It's just that I still can't quite believe that you're real." For some reason, his words stung.

"I promise I am real, silly. But I think you should take a nap and I should take a cab. My apartment is kind of a mess." She couldn't let him see her photos of Dandan.

"Let me pay for it, then." She tried to argue, but he wouldn't listen. Instead, he got to his feet with a groan, went into the bathroom, and emerged a second later with a hundred-dollar bill. Bo took it and kissed his cheek, feeling a bit like Judas. Once she was home, she would download the recording, then call Mia and tell her what had really happened at the trial.

CHAPTER 39

Gabe wanted to put it off forever, but he knew that once his mom came home from church with his grandfather she would ask him if he had started researching that stupid report she wanted him to write. Telling her no was not going to help his chances of getting un-grounded.

Only once he started to research the report, it turned out not to be so stupid.

Since his mom told him he had to cite his sources, Gabe went to different websites from the ones he had used to research exactly what steroids to take, how much, and when. Those had painted steroids as miracle drugs that piled on muscles, with few if any side effects.

The new websites might as well have been discussing a different drug. They talked about liver damage, heart disease, impotence, sterility, breast enlargement, premature baldness, acne, benign tumors, and violent behavior. They sounded like Charlie, only scarier. The new websites made it sound as if steroids ruined your body and destroyed your mind.

Gabe read for a long while, then went back to the original sites and message boards he had first looked at. Only now he imagined what his mom would say if he showed them to her.

On one board dedicated to taking steroids, a guy complained about how everyone around him was acting. "My gf and my parents keep saying I get more angry now, and claiming I didn't used to be like that." His response was to rant and swear about them online while other people on the boards urged him to ignore them and called them names.

Gabe saw posts from other guys saying any side effects were worth it. Talking nonchalantly about taking testosterone or having to rely on Viagra. Even about having cosmetic surgery to get breast tissue removed.

Next he checked out news websites. The pro-steroid boards all said the mainstream media exaggerated things, especially the link between extreme emotional disturbance and steroids. But it was hard to be nonchalant when he read about a guy his own age who had come home from school and told his mom he was going upstairs. Only he never came down again because he had hung himself from his closet rod with a belt. Then Gabe read about a pro wrestler who killed his four-year-old, his wife, and then, after sitting with their bodies for a while, himself. He read about men who beat people unconscious for doing things like cutting them off in traffic.

Could Charlie be right? Could the steroids have changed more than Gabe's muscles? Could they have changed not only his body but his mind? His mom and Eldon had said he was more angry now. Was it true?

From where Gabe sat, he could just see the shallow, fist-shaped crater he had left in the wall. He looked from the dent to his still-swollen knuckles to the big muscles in his arms. Were they really worth it? Worth risking his own life—and maybe the lives of more people? What if he snapped again like he had when he hit the wall, only when he had something more dangerous than his own fists available to him?

Gabe had a sickening image of himself arguing with his mom in the kitchen, the knives in the butcher block within easy reach. But he would never do that. Would he? He remembered how before he hit the wall it had been like a red mist descending. How he had gone blind and deaf and dumb to anything but the urge to do some damage. And it didn't sound like those people who killed themselves or killed other people had been depressed or angry before steroids.

When he made the decision to start taking steroids, he had acted just like a kid. Like a stupid kid. Wanting something for nothing. If left to her own devices, Brooke would have Doritos for breakfast and follow that up with a candy bar. Was he any more mature?

But he wasn't a stupid kid. He was nearly an adult. Maybe he should act like the adult he now nearly was. The adult he already looked like, at least for a while.

It wasn't enough to say he was sorry. It wasn't even enough to stop using. But maybe, Gabe thought, feeling something unfurl in his chest, maybe there was a way to redeem himself. Maybe even to become a hero.

CHAPTER 40

In the cab, Bo leaned back against the black faux leather seat and closed her eyes against the weak late-afternoon sun. She wanted to hate Warren, but found she couldn't. Why hate the puppet? It made much more sense to hate the man who had pulled the strings. Who had made the puppet dance. And clearly, that was David Leacham.

After the cab let her out, she pushed open the door to the apartment lobby with a sigh. She went up the shallow stairs to the second floor, her feet screaming at every step. At the top of the stairs, her elderly neighbor, Georgina Frye, shot her a suspicious glance and then darted back into her apartment. Bo was sure she was still staring at her through the peephole, probably judging the scantiness of her outfit.

Mrs. Frye lived to complain, to find fault. If she didn't have anything mean to say, then she just avoided Bo altogether. She didn't like the smell of the garlic and ginger that Bo cooked with—or, as she put it, "all those foreign spices." Mrs. Frye had complained to the manager about Bo keeping her bicycle outside her apartment, even though the hallway was eight feet wide. So now Bo kept her bike in her living room, where it always seemed to be in front of something she needed to get to, like the bookcase or the closet.

The first thing Bo did after she walked in the door was to take off her shoes. As her feet tried to settle down into place, her arches began to cramp. Moaning a little at every step, she hobbled forward, her shoes dangling from her fingers. Before she called Mia, she needed to download the recording from her glasses into her computer, make sure it was clearly audible. And while she was doing that, she would try to massage some life back into her feet.

She paused at the door of her bedroom. Where was her laptop computer? She thought she had left it on the little desk, but she didn't see any sign of it. In fact, she thought she had left the bags from Macy's in the bathroom, but there they were on the bed. Now why would—

Without any warning, something pink and white dropped in front of her eyes. Bo blinked in surprise. Before her eyes even opened again, unseen fingers viciously yanked whatever it was straight back so that it bit into her neck.

She stumbled backward. One of her shoes fell from her hooked fingers. Her heavy glasses tumbled from her face and landed on the carpet. Then her bare foot came down on them and she felt them snap in half.

Her attention had narrowed to the thing wrapped around her neck. The thing that was killing her. It was, Bo realized, a scarf.

In fact, she recognized it as her own long silk scarf, patterned with pink peonies. When she wore it, she liked to loop it loosely around her neck. Now someone had taken it from her bedroom drawer and was using it to strangle her.

With her right hand, she tried to claw the fabric away from her neck, but it had already sunk deep into her flesh, cutting a groove. The world began to spin around her like water swirling down a drain.

"Let go," a voice hissed in her ear. A man's voice. She didn't recognize the voice, but she did the language. His words were in the Guandong dialect. "Go and join your daughter. Everyone will understand. Go join Dandan."

In an instant, Bo saw what would happen next. First she would die. Then this man would drag her body to someplace where he could tie the scarf. From the ceiling fan in the living room, perhaps, or from the highest rail in her closet. He might take one of the chairs from the dining room and knock it over, as if Bo had stepped off into death.

In China, by far the most common method of suicide was hanging. And there, suicide was considered not just an act of grief but of revenge. The spirits of the dead were thought to torment the living. It would be easy for people to think that Bo had believed killing herself would make David Leacham suffer, or that she was striking back against the authorities for not avenging Dandan.

Everyone would shake their heads, not in confusion, but in sorrow. With Dandan dead and her daughter's killer set free, why shouldn't Bo Yee take her own life?

Years ago, Bo had taken a self-defense course offered by the church. The whole time she had pictured the enemy, not as some stranger in a dark alley, but instead as the people who had killed her baby. Now if this man killed her, then Dandan's death would never be avenged.

Shifting her hips to the left, she made a fist with her right hand and thrust her elbow back as hard as she could into the man's solar plexus. She was rewarded with an explosion of air. But the scarf did not loosen in the slightest. In fact, it tightened. Her vision was going fuzzy.

Then she remembered the single shoe she was still clutching in her left hand. Pressing it against her thigh, she shifted her grasp until the tall pointed heel was turned back. Then, summoning the last dregs of her strength, she hammered it back over her head. She heard it knock against her attacker's skull, but his grip didn't loosen.

"No. Let go," he whispered. "Stop fighting."

Bo's knees began to sag and she let them. At the same time, she arched her back. Mouthing her daughter's name to give her strength, she swung one more time, only this time she aimed farther back—

And was rewarded with the man's high-pitched scream, right in her ear, as the heel met something soft and yet substantial. It stuck. And then it slid.

Finally, finally, the scarf loosened. She dropped the shoe, yanked off the scarf, and stumbled around to face her attacker. Her breath was coming in ragged gasps that hurt her throat. The man was slender and about her height, with his hands cupped over his eyes. Blood as red as paint was running between his fingers. But how soon until he straightened up? How soon until his pain turned to anger?

She had to get out of here. Were there more men out there? Waiting to make sure the deed was done?

Her bike was leaning against the wall. Bo yanked open the door, threw one leg over the seat, and began to pedal out the door and down the hall.

Heedless of the fact that in about ten feet she was going to come to a flight of stairs.

CHAPTER 41

MONDAY

W hat *is* that?" Gary Newman asked Charlie with a curled upper lip. Gary had recently been promoted to homicide detective, and he hadn't quite acclimated to the squad room yet.

"It's a sandwich." Charlie didn't look up. On a sheet of scratch paper he had written *Abigail Endicott* and circled it. Around it were other circled words and phrases with lines leading back to the dead woman's name. One said *Revenge?* Another *Money?* A third read *Jealousy?* and a fourth *To hide a secret?*

"But there's no bread," Gary said.

Charlie shifted a mouthful to one side. "It doesn't need bread. It's got two chicken breasts instead."

Gary leaned closer. Charlie had seen the guy regard spattered blood and brain with more enthusiasm. "With what in between? Cheese and bacon?"

Charlie took another bite. "And special sauce." Which, like most special sauces, seemed to be some variation on Thousand Island dressing. The result was still delicious. His eyes went back to his paper. Picking up his pen, he added *Shooter mentally ill?*

Gary finally looked at the paper, which was the only really interesting thing on the desk, in Charlie's opinion. "That's the case of the lady killed in the church?"

"Yeah. My problem is that there doesn't seem to be a good motive. No one generally goes around killing little old ladies."

"Unless it's a by-product of the real crime, like stealing their purses or their cars."

"This guy gunned her down in front of dozens of witnesses and walked away empty-handed."

"At least it's interesting," Gary said. "I keep getting the people who get drunk and do stupid things cases."

"There's something to be said for the simple things," Charlie said, taking the last bite of his sandwich just as his phone rang. The caller ID showed that it came from the medical examiner's office. This morning he had attended Abigail's autopsy, but it had not revealed much. For someone in her early seventies, the victim had been in fairly good shape. Doug thought she might have lasted another fifteen or twenty years if the bullet had not gone ricocheting around in her skull.

"This is Carlson." He swallowed the last chewy bite.

"You're not going to believe it," Doug said.

There was not a lot Charlie didn't believe. "Try me."

"It's about our dead organist."

"I think she actually played the piano," Charlie said.

Doug was undeterred by this minor detail. "You saw that bullet I took out of her brain. Too mangled to be any good. Luckily drywall is a lot softer than bone. The bullet you got forensics to pull out of the wall was in excellent shape. She was definitely shot with a .22."

So why did Doug sound so cheerful? Saying the gun was a .22 was about as useful as saying the shooter had been a white man. Hundreds of handguns and rifles were chambered for that round. Both .22 ammunition and the guns themselves were cheaper than guns that fired bigger rounds. Lots of shooters also liked them because both the noise and the recoil were less. The crime lab had already looked for fingerprints on the cartridges and found nothing.

"And?" Charlie prompted. The other man was clearly enjoying drawing out the suspense.

"The crime lab scanned the bullet into NIBIN, and it came up with a possible match to another crime. One of the techs just confirmed it."

"To what crime?"

"That's the crazy thing. It matches to the last murder you and I worked." When Charlie didn't rush to fill in the blank, Doug clarified, "The dead Chinese guy."

Charlie's mind was working overtime. What did a quiet retiree who basically only went to church and the grocery store have to do with a young Chinese illegal immigrant who worked twelve hours a day, seven days a week? He thought of how many immigrants attended the church. That had to be the connection. Lihong must have been one of the people who attended services there. Maybe he had managed to go to an early Sunday service and met Abigail there? Although even if they had known each other, why would someone have killed them both? For different reasons? For the same reason?

The moment Charlie had looked at the young man's body, he

had had the feeling that it was not a one-off. But he hadn't expected this. It still felt to him like the two victims had little to nothing in common. The next step would be to show the pastor the photo of Lihong's face. See if he could help him connect the dots.

He called Mia. "Want to take a field trip?"

CHAPTER 42

As soon as Mia got in the car, they both started talking. Mia let Charlie go first. It only took him a couple of minutes to drive to the church, which wasn't enough time for them to update each other. They sat in his car parked at the curb so that he could tell her about the matching bullets and about how he could find no reason for Abigail's murder. In turn, Mia told him what Luciana had said.

"I'm starting to think that Lihong and Chun and the others were trafficked," she said. "What Luciana said got me thinking: Kenny Zhong's only been here for seven years and yet he already has four restaurants. That would be a lot easier to do if you didn't have to pay for labor. If your workers were paying you for the privilege of being here in the first place."

After talking to Luciana, Mia had seen everything in a new light. The crowded, unsafe house Lihong had shared with Chun and the others was not the result of new immigrants seeking out a cheap place to live, but instead something closer to slaves' quarters. The men who had taken Lihong from the coffee shop had been the modern version of slavers hunting down escaped property.

"Maybe Lihong has been coming to church here," she said. "Maybe Abigail was trying to help him." With a flush of shame, she imagined the older woman being more patient with his queries than she had been. She sighed and started to open her door. They were parked next to the reader board, and now she focused on the church's name, which was printed on the top.

She turned back and clutched his arm. "Charlie?"

"What?"

She shivered. "I'm 99 percent certain this is the church Bo Yee attends."

His brow furrowed. "Really?"

"And more than that—she told me once that she played the piano for services."

The pieces in the kaleidoscope were falling into a different pattern, but Mia couldn't quite see it yet.

"Abigail was wearing a black wig," Charlie said slowly. "She's got to have thirty years on Bo, but from a distance . . ."

Mia completed the thought for him. "The shooter might have seen what he had been told he would see. Bo Yee at the piano."

"The witnesses said that after Abigail was shot, he stopped in his tracks and stared at her, then fled. I saw the body, and her wig came off when she collapsed. He must have realized he made a mistake."

They hurried into the church, where they found Pastor Bob Ho in his office. He got to his feet to shake Mia's hand while Charlie introduced her. He was wearing a turtleneck and jeans, the casualness undercut by the fact that the jeans had been ironed into sharp creases.

Before the pastor had even settled back behind his desk, Charlie asked, "Does Abigail normally play the piano for services?"

The pastor's eyes widened as he grasped the meaning of Charlie's sentence. "She always plays for the early service, but it's another woman who plays for the second. Her name is Bo Yee."

Before he even had time to ask why, Mia had turned away and was dialing Bo on her cell phone. It went straight to voice mail. "Bo," she said. "It's Mia. Mia Quinn with the King County Prosecutor's Office. Please call me right away. You may be in danger." Fear squeezed her heart.

"No," she heard the pastor say. He looked bewildered and afraid. "Dear God, no."

Next she tried the tea factory where Bo worked, but a woman in human resources told her Bo was still out on leave. As she listened, Mia pinched the bridge of her nose and hoped against hope that Bo was still okay.

"Do you think Bo was the real target?" the pastor asked after Mia left another message for her. Another message she feared Bo would never hear.

"It's hard to say," Charlie said, "but it's definitely a possibility we need to explore. And there's someone else we need to ask about." He took out his phone and scrolled through his photos before selecting the one of Lihong's face and handing the phone over. "Do you recognize this man?"

He looked at it for a long time. "No. I've never seen him before."

"He worked at a restaurant called the Jade Kitchen," Mia said.

The pastor's expression changed.

"So you know that restaurant?" she asked.

"I've never eaten there."

"That's not exactly what I was asking."

His mouth crimped. "One hears things."

"And those things would be . . . ," she prompted.

"A lot of his workers might be undocumented. It's not the kind of thing I concern myself with. But I hear rumors."

"Could they be more than undocumented? Could they be trafficked? Enslaved?"

He pressed his lips together. "I don't know about that."

But Mia thought he did.

They excused themselves and left. "I know everything is connected," Mia said. "I just don't know how. All I know is that I'm really worried about Bo. We need to warn her." If it wasn't already too late.

Charlie was already on the phone with the phone company's security division, asking what they could tell him about the location of Bo's phone. Since this was an exigent circumstance, they didn't need a warrant to get the information. Charlie listened to the answer and said thanks. He turned to Mia. "Her phone has been turned off. It's been off since Saturday afternoon. The last recorded location was at her apartment."

Bo lived in an apartment building that had seen its best days more than a century ago. An overhang sheltered the first-floor apartments and the stairs leading up. As they went up narrow, shallow steps, Charlie unbuttoned his jacket. He reached back and rested his hand on the butt of his gun. Once they got to Bo's door, he motioned for Mia to stand on one side while he took the other. He rapped hard with his free hand. Mia held her breath but didn't hear anyone. He knocked again. "Bo? It's Charlie Carlton. Bo?"

"I don't like this," Mia whispered. "Not one little bit."

As they were standing in front of the door, an old woman with a small, white dog on a leash walked past them, looking at them with narrowed eyes. She was putting her key into the lock of the apartment two doors down when Charlie flashed his badge.

"Excuse me, ma'am, can we talk to you?"

The woman walked back to them. Mia tried to ignore the dog's small wet nose snuffling her ankles.

"What is this about, Officer?"

"Do you know your neighbor, Bo Yee?"

"Just by sight, I guess." Judging by her expression, she didn't even like looking at Bo. "I didn't know her name until just now. Just that she's one of them Chinese people."

"When was the last time you saw her?"

She looked up, remembering. Her dog suddenly licked Mia's ankle, causing her to let out an involuntary squeak as she jumped backward.

"Oh, Rascal, stop that!" The older woman jerked on his leash, but not enough to actually move him away from Mia. "Friday? The thing is, I saw someone going into her apartment a few hours ago, but it wasn't her. Some young Chinese girl with lots of makeup and clothes that looked like they were spray-painted on, if you know what I mean. She wouldn't even look me in the eye. In fact, she seemed to be in a real hurry."

Mia and Charlie exchanged a look.

"What apartment number does the landlord live in?" Mia asked.

"Downstairs. 1F."

"Thanks," Charlie said. "We might need to talk to you again. Maybe have you work with a sketch artist to get a drawing of that girl you saw."

"I'll try to help if you need it." The woman shrugged. "But I have trouble telling those Orientals apart."

Mia waited until they were out of the woman's earshot. "Bo's already dead," she hissed. "She's already dead and someone came by to search her things."

"Don't borrow trouble," Charlie said. "Maybe . . . maybe Bo has taken some girl under her wing, a girl forced into prostitution like her daughter was?"

For once it was Mia who was dubious and Charlie who was clutching at straws.

When he knocked on the door to 1F, a man with a long white ponytail and a white beard answered the door.

"I'm Charlie Carlson with the Seattle Police." Charlie pulled his badge off his belt and passed it in front of the guy's eyes. "This is Mia Quinn with the King County District Attorney. We need you to let us in so we can do a welfare check on one of your tenants, Bo Yee." He pushed the badge back into place. "And your name is?"

"Nelson. And let me see that badge again."

With a sigh, Charlie pulled it off and handed it over.

"This says 'detective.' What kind of detective are you?"

"Homicide."

Nelson's eyes widened, but he still said, "You're not with immigration? Because she's legal."

"That would be ICE, Nelson, and it's federal. I don't care about anyone's immigration status. I just want to make sure this lady is okay."

Once they were upstairs, Nelson knocked and called several times before he finally put a key from his huge ring in the lock. He started to step in, but Charlie put up his arm, barring the door. "Step back and don't touch anything else. This is a crime scene."

Mia saw what he had seen. In the middle of the living room floor were two high-heeled shoes, a matched set, except they were twenty feet apart. And in between them were fat, round drops of blood. Someone had been bleeding—and bleeding hard.

"I'll go in and see if Bo's here," Charlie said. Left unspoken was whether she might be dead or alive. "We need to minimize who goes in until after the techs have been here."

He was back a few minutes later, shaking his head.

"Did you check the closets and cupboards?" Mia knew it was a dumb question, but she still asked it anyway. What if she had been injured and tried to hide?

"She's not there, Mia. It's kind of a mess, though. Makeup scattered all over the bathroom counter. And shopping bags with no clothes in them. And a silk scarf with blood on it. Soaked with it."

Mia's heart sank. In all the months she had known Bo, she had never seen her wear makeup.

CHAPTER 43

The crime scene techs had just arrived to process Bo's apartment when Mia's phone rang. It was Eli Hall. Before she could tell him it was a bad time to talk, he said something that changed her mind.

"I've got a client I think you might want to talk to," he said. "Her name's Jiao. She's Chinese, and in the country illegally. She was picked up for prostitution. But the thing is, she says she used to work with your victim. The case where the jury hung?"

"Dandan Yee," Mia supplied. For a moment she forgot her worry that she would never see Dandan's mother again.

"Yeah. Dandan. Anyway, I think you need to talk to her. She says she was there the night Dandan died."

The words jolted Mia. She tried to be cautious. "Is she looking to cut a deal?"

"Well, it's starting to look like she might have been trafficked, so you putting in a word with ICE wouldn't hurt. But she's very anxious. Very afraid."

Charlie decided to come with her. Uniformed officers had started going door to door in Bo's neighborhood, asking if anyone had seen her. The crime scene techs were swarming over the scene. But until there were new leads, there wasn't much that he could do.

Eli met them after they went through the metal director. He and Charlie exchanged a wordless look. It wasn't particularly friendly.

"Dandan's mother, Bo Yee, is missing," Mia told Eli. "We just came from her apartment. There was blood on the floor and signs of a struggle, but no body. It's possible that whatever happened to her is related to the trial. Bo's been pretty adamant about wanting to see justice."

"What about my client?" Eli looked from one to the other. "Will this mean she's at risk?"

"It's hard to say." Mia was worried the girl might not talk. "I'd rather you didn't mention it to her. And we won't take any notes. That will give her some protection. If she ends up implicating someone and they are charged, then at some point any notes we made would have to be turned over to that person's defense. If there's no records, that won't have to happen. If she ends up not making a deal, I don't want to put her life at risk for nothing."

"Hmm." Eli gave her a half smile. "First of all, I appreciate you looking out for her. And second of all, I have to say that's a pretty tricky way of doing it."

"Don't tell me that you don't use the rules to your advantage," Mia said. "Because we all do."

The Chinese interpreter, a woman named Kwong, came hurrying

down the hall toward them. She looked to be in her fifties, with a flat face and square bangs. They went into the interview room. A few minutes later, a deputy brought in the girl. Jiao couldn't have been older than eighteen or nineteen. She was petite, with a high forehead, hunched shoulders, and nervous, heavily lidded eyes.

Kwong took a notebook and a ballpoint pen from her purse.

"Why do you have those?" Mia asked. "I don't really want you taking notes about what we say here today." As she spoke, Jiao's eyes went back and forth between them.

"It's just for me. If her sentence is complicated it helps me remember parts of it so I can translate it the right way in English."

"Okay," Mia said. "You just have to destroy whatever you write before you leave this room." Then she turned to Jiao and focused solely on her. Over the years, she had learned the best way to work with interpreters. You looked at the person you were questioning, not the interpreter who provided the English words. That way you did not turn them into someone being talked *about* rather than someone being talked *to*. Just because they weren't able to speak much English did not mean they didn't understand some. Facing Jiao also meant that she and the girl were less likely to miss any nonverbal communication—expressions, tone of voice, or body language.

"How did you come to be here in the United States?" she asked and kept looking at Jiao even when it was Kwong who answered.

"On a plane. The snakehead gave me a fake Thai passport and told me to pretend to be a Thai citizen. Only I don't even speak Thai. No information in it matched with me, except the photo only. When the plane landed, I called a phone number I had written on the inside band of my bra." Jiao's eyes welled with tears as Kwong spoke for her. "If I had known what would happen next, I would never have called that number."

"And what happened?" Mia prompted.

Jiao's tone was halting, while the interpreter kept speaking at a steady pace.

"A man picked me up. I was very excited. I was looking at all the cars and the houses and thinking that soon I would have those things for myself. He took me to a business. A massage parlor, only it was not really for massages. Do you understand?" A fine tremble washed over the girl.

Mia nodded.

Jiao's words began to stumble and hesitate, but Kwong continued to speak evenly in a near monotone. "He took me in the back and he raped me. And then he threw a towel at me and told me to clean myself up. He said that this was to be my life now. That I owed them money, and I had to earn it back by letting men have sex with me."

The trembling increased as Jiao slowly shook her head. "At first I said no. I said I would not do it. I was stupid"—Kwong corrected her own interpretation—"no, naive, naive to think that I had a choice. Because there was no choice. I had to do what the man said. Sooner or later. Now I wish I had done what he said sooner."

Jiao held out her empty hands, and it took a second for Mia to see past the shaking fingers, to focus on the scars circling her wrists. "They handcuffed me and put me in a closet for six days. Finally I agreed."

The girl's next words were so low that Kwong had to lean forward to hear them. "Besides, where was I going to run to? I had no money, no papers. No English." Mia heard the girl say the word *English* a half beat before Kwong. She thought of Lihong, desperately seeking her with only his handful of words.

Jiao hugged herself, but it didn't stop her shivering. "I am in

America, but all I've seen are a bunch of ugly white rooms. When we didn't have customers, we slept on the massage tables. And sometimes the customers did not come there for us but to buy other things."

"What things?" Charlie asked.

"Drugs."

Charlie leaned forward. "What kind of drugs?"

The interpreter conferred with Jiao, making a few Chinese characters on the paper and pointing at them, then turned to Charlie. "Pills to make men able to have sex. It sounds like Viagra. And some kind of drug to make men strong. Not sexually. To give them muscles."

"Steroids?" Charlie asked.

"I think so." Kwong nodded.

Mia froze. Charlie had said that Gabe had gotten his steroids from someone he met at a restaurant. He couldn't have really gone to a massage parlor to get them—could he? The palms of her hands were suddenly slick, and she rubbed them over her skirt.

"The men who come to those kind of places probably are looking for ways to feel more manly," Eli said. "Viagra, steroids, prostitutes—it all makes a kind of sense."

"How many times can you sell a pill?" Charlie answered his own question. "Once. But a human being? You can sell them over and over again."

Mia imagined the head of this operation as a spider sitting in a web. Profiting from every base instinct. He had most of the seven deadly sins covered: lust, sloth, greed, anger, gluttony, envy, and even pride. He had found a way to make an enormous amount of money.

"What about Dandan Yee? How long did you know her?" Mia

asked as Kwong translated. The girl's story of how she had come here and what she had been forced to do would probably differ from Dandan's in only a few details.

Jiao's mouth drew down and she blinked away tears. "You are moved around. Every couple of months you are someplace new with new girls. I think it's so you don't make any friends. I've been in eleven or twelve different places. But I was working with Dandan the night she died. She was new. She was still in shock. She cried a lot. She said her mother lived in Seattle, had come to America years ago. But she was too ashamed to try to get word to her. Besides, she owed so much money she figured there was no way her mother would be able to buy her freedom." Jiao paused, her hands twisting in her lap. Her eyes darted around the room.

"I know this is hard," Mia said, "but by telling us what happened that night you can help us make sure this never happens again. And of course we will explain to ICE how helpful you have been to us."

"It was early in the evening when the man came in. I recognized him, but I didn't know his name until later." Jiao then said the name, giving each syllable equal weight. "Da-vid Leach-am." She put her own hands to her neck as the interpreter said, "Once he tied me up and put his hands around my throat until the world got dark. I thought I would die. When I woke up, he was smiling at me."

To demonstrate, the girl pasted a dead grin on her face, and Mia shivered inwardly.

"So when I saw him come in that night I was just hoping he would not pick me. I think he liked girls who were sad. Who were afraid. Maybe that was why he picked Dandan. I do not know. I was just glad he did not choose me." Jiao's trembling was becoming more pronounced.

"The other girl and I, we were still waiting for customers. About fifteen minutes later, we heard Dandan shouting, 'Help me! Help me!' and then we heard a fight.

"The woman who was our boss ran in. The man was yelling that it was not his fault, that she shouldn't have moved. That he hadn't really planned to hurt her. The other girl there that night was too scared to look, but I looked. Dandan was still alive, or sort of alive. She was moving a little and making these bubbling sounds." Jiao pressed her hands to her mouth, as if she were seeing it again and had to stop her own screams.

Out of the corner of her eye, Mia saw Eli wince. "What happened then?" she asked gently.

"The madam pulled the knife from her chest and wiped the handle clean on a towel, then wrapped Dandan's hand around it before letting it fall on the floor."

Mia didn't let her expression reflect the elation she was feeling. David Leacham would certainly be going back on trial now, and this time she was sure he would be going to prison.

"What was David Leacham doing while she did this?"

"He ran outside. We could hear his car racing out of the parking lot."

"What happened after that?"

"We had to gather up our things and leave in a hurry. All of us. We just left her there." Jiao's face was a mask of sadness and fear. "Then they put the other girl and me in different places. Told us if we ever talked about what had happened they would kill us. Because . . ."

Kwong stopped even though Jiao was still speaking. And in the welter of words, Mia thought she heard two she knew.

Kwong seemed to be asking the girl a question. Or maybe she

was telling her something. All Mia knew was that there was now a torrent of words from both sides, so fast that Mia couldn't pick out a syllable.

Moaning and whimpering, Jiao pressed her fists to the sides of her head.

"What's the matter?" Mia asked, while Eli said, "What's wrong?"

Suddenly one of Jiao's hands shot out and grabbed the pen from Kwong's hand. She threw her head back and without hesitation drove the pen into her own throat. Everyone was on their feet, yelling. Except for Jiao, who lay sprawled back in her chair, the pen buried deep in her neck as her body began to convulse.

"Don't pull it out," Charlie yelled.

Just as Kwong did.

CHAPTER 44

Yesterday, as she had careened down the sidewalk, peddling with bare feet, one knee throbbing from banging into the lobby wall after she bounced down the apartment stairs, Bo had frantically thought about where she could go. Who she could trust. After all their promises, the police and the prosecutor had let her daughter's killer walk free. She was not confident that the police would do any better job of protecting her now.

If she went to friends from work or church, she would just be putting them in danger. And her purse with her money and her ID was still back at her apartment, so she couldn't hide out in a hotel, even one that took cash and didn't ask questions.

So she went to the last place they would look for her.

Outside the building, Bo's hands were shaking so badly she barely managed to wedge her bike into a corral, and she completely forgot about the lock. All she could think about was whether people were driving down this street right now, looking for her, hoping to finish her off.

Inside, she took the stairs with legs almost too weak to hold her. One of her feet felt oddly wet. When she looked back down the stairs, she saw a red smear of blood on every other step. She must have cut her foot when she stepped on her spy glasses.

On the second floor, she pounded on the third door.

No answer.

Her heart was beating nearly as loudly as her fist. She tried again. What if there was no one there? Where would she go? Where could she be safe?

And this time Warren answered, mouth half open in a yawn. His eyes widened when he realized it was her and he started to smile. Then he took in her tearstained face, wild hair, and bare feet.

"What's the matter, Song?" Warren put his hands on her shoulders.

His touch tore a sob from her chest. And then another. He tried to pull her toward him, but instead she doubled over. Reliving those terrible moments when she had been unable to think. Unable to breathe. Unable to do anything except realize that she was dying.

Warren put his arm under her elbow and steered her inside. The bolt thunked when he shot it home.

"What happened?" He began to stroke her hair. She was still bent over, her elbows braced on her knees, one hand on her hot, wet cheek, the other stroking her poor neck. "What's wrong? Song, talk to me." He tried to pull her upright, but she wouldn't straighten up, wouldn't take her hands away.

Finally she managed to choke out a few words. "When I walked into my apartment, a man was waiting for me. He tried to strangle me."

"What?" Warren's voice cracked. "Are you all right?" When she didn't answer, couldn't answer, he put his hand under her chin. This time she let him raise her head. "Let me see." He sucked in his breath. A fingertip lightly brushed her throat's skin right above the line that still throbbed. "That almost looks like a cut. That can't have come from his hands."

"He used a scarf. A silk scarf." She made a sound like a laugh. "My silk scarf."

He sucked in air with a hiss. "It looks deep. We need to get you to the hospital and get an X-ray or something. See if your throat is damaged."

"No." Bo shook her head. Now that she was in Warren's apartment, she didn't want to leave. The man who had tried to kill her could be anywhere. Anywhere but here.

"Then we have to call the police." He started to pull his cell phone from his pocket.

She grabbed his wrist. "No. Don't call. I don't trust them. I don't trust anyone. The only one I trust is you."

"But Song, he needs to be arrested. He could have killed you."

On legs that suddenly wouldn't hold her, she stumbled over to his couch and nearly fell on it. "That was what he wanted. He wanted me to die. And he won't stop until I do."

Warren followed her to the couch, but he sat a half cushion away, as if giving her the space to collect herself. "Who? Who did this to you, Song?"

"I don't know who he was. But he knew me. And I know he'll hunt me down. He won't rest until I'm really dead."

"Song, you're not making any sense." Warren scrubbed his face with open hands. "If you don't know this guy, then why will he hunt you down? If he's like some serial killer or whatever, can't he go out and find some other girl to kill? Some girl who will be easier? I mean, why would he come back for you?"

"Because he's not a serial killer. And I'm not really Song."

His brows drew together. "What do you mean?"

"Song's not my real name."

"Not your name?" His face cleared. "Do you mean that's not your Chinese name?"

"No. My real name is Bo Yee. Do you understand? My name is Bo Yee."

"Yee," he repeated, leaning away from her and crossing his arms. "That's the same name as the girl who was killed."

"I am her mother."

"That's not possible." He exhaled sharply. "You're a student."

"I lied. I'm not a student. I am her mother. I am Dandan's mother." She thumped a hand over her heart. Saying the words made her back straighten. Gave her strength.

"I heard that Dandan's mother was the one who was always sitting right behind the prosecutor. She had long hair and she wore long dresses. She was a lot older than you."

"Hair can be cut. Clothes can be changed." Bo took a deep breath. "But I will always be my daughter's mother. And I will do whatever I can to help her. It doesn't matter that she's dead."

Warren's expression changed, and she could tell he was starting to believe her. "How old are you, anyway?"

"Thirty-seven."

"And is this about the money? Is that why you went out with me?"

"It has to do with David Leacham. I want him to pay for killing my daughter. I needed to get proof of what happened with the jury. How you voted not to convict him."

He bit his lip. "And did you get that proof?"

She nodded. "You told me. And I recorded it."

"Then why are you here now? Why did you come back now, knowing I was bribed to hang the jury?"

"Because this is the only place they won't look. And what you did was bad, but you're not evil. And David Leacham is. He is pure evil." She took a shaky breath. "And I knew that you liked me. Really liked me."

"I liked Song," Warren said plaintively. "I don't even know you."

And that night, Warren insisted on sleeping on the couch, while Bo took the bed.

The next day they moved around each other like polite strangers. He told her when he needed to go out, what he needed to do, and how long he would be gone. He went to the grocery store, and when he came home, he found her in tears. She showed him the news story she had found online, about her friend Abigail.

"I asked her to play the piano in my place. And instead she was killed. They must have realized they made a mistake. And then they tried to fix it." Wincing, she rubbed the line on her neck.

"You can't hide here forever," Warren said.

Bo knew he was only speaking the truth. But she didn't know what else to do.

CHAPTER 45

If you wanted to learn how to do pretty much anything, Gabe knew what the first step was. Go to YouTube. There you could count on finding a video showing you exactly what to do, step by step.

How to do a kickflip on a skateboard.

How to fix a leaky faucet when it turned out your mom didn't know how and your stupid dad had gotten himself killed before he could ever teach you.

How to videotape someone without their knowing.

How to secretly gather evidence for the police so they could bust a steroids ring.

Okay, so maybe there *wasn't* a video about that, but Gabe figured the YouTube videos on making secret recordings he had watched last night fit the bill.

One of the ways involved putting your phone in a shirt pocket with the top edge, the part that held the tiny camera aperture, just peeking out.

Gabe didn't actually own a shirt with a breast pocket, but his dad had had a bunch of them. Once he got home from school, he tiptoed down the upstairs hall as if someone might hear him, even though the house was empty. His mom was still at work and would be for hours. Normally Gabe would have already picked up Brooke from preschool, but today he had called and said he wouldn't be there until late, maybe not until just before they closed at six.

Kali had a doctor's appointment and Eldon had gone with her. Gabe hoped whatever the doctor had to tell them was good. Or at least not terrible.

He opened the door to his mom's room, which he still thought of as his parents' room. The covers were pulled up but still a little messy on his mom's side. On the side where his dad had slept, the blue-and-white quilt was taut and smooth. His mom tried to pretend like she was over his dad's death, but Gabe still saw a million clues that she wasn't. Like always keeping to her side of the bed.

And, Gabe thought, as he pulled open their closet door, she still hadn't gotten rid of his dad's clothes. As he flipped through the shirts, a faint smell teased his nose. A shiver traced his spine. It almost felt like he would turn around and his dad would be standing there, maybe holding a towel around his waist, his hair still damp from the shower. Maybe this was why his mom held on to the clothes, so she could pretend.

"I'm trying to be a better man than you were, Dad," Gabe said aloud to whatever ghost or memory was in the room with him. "I'm trying to be the man you should have been."

He pulled out a dark-blue shirt. Some of his dad's shirts were too nice for a kid to wear, made of silk or with contrasting cuffs, but this one was just plain sturdy cotton. He pulled off his T-shirt and slipped on his dad's shirt. Just a few months ago, it would have hung on him. Now it was a little snug through the chest and biceps.

He was going to miss that feeling. But he was starting to think that Charlie was right, that what made him a man was what he thought, what he did. Not how he looked.

After buttoning the shirt and tucking it in, Gabe set the phone in his pocket, with the pinpoint of the camera pointing out at the world. In the mirror, he checked it out. Against the dark-blue shirt, the black phone was nearly invisible. And he himself looked almost unrecognizable. Like an adult.

And now he was going to act like one.

He took the bus to the Jade Kitchen, the same place he had met Tyler before, a meeting he had arranged after texting him this morning between classes. Every time the bus driver hit the brakes, his stomach lurched. His hands were starting to sweat. Even the bottoms of his feet. Gabe unzipped his down jacket and tried to blame it on the overheated bus. He hoped he wasn't pitting out the shirt before he even got to the restaurant. At least it was a dark color. After he got off the bus, he turned on the video camera, then carefully slipped the phone back in his pocket and took off his jacket.

"Takeout order?" the hostess asked after he came in the front doors. It was too late for lunch and not yet time for dinner, so the restaurant was nearly empty.

"Um, no. Can I have a table for two? My friend will be coming soon."

While Gabe waited, he tore tiny strips off his napkin. Despite his churning stomach, he ordered some pot stickers, but didn't touch them when the waitress set them down.

Even though he had been waiting for him, Gabe still jumped when Tyler pushed open a swinging door in the back of the restaurant. In one hand was a white paper bag. He wore jeans and an open, blue down vest over a skin-tight, pale-gray knit shirt that showed off every muscle on his torso and arms. He pulled out a chair and sat down across from Gabe. The bag was out of sight now, in his lap under the table.

"You're not done with your cycle yet, are you?" Tyler shifted his bulk. "Because it's not a good idea to up your dosage when you're just starting out."

"Actually, what happened is that my mom found what you sold me before and flushed it down the toilet."

Tyler swore as his eyes went wide. "What? Where did you tell her you got it?"

"Don't worry, I didn't tell her I got it from you. I didn't tell her anything. I just need to replace what she flushed."

Tyler was already pushing back his chair. "I'm sorry, man." He got to his feet. "I can't help you out. You're on your own. Because I do not sell steroids. And I never have."

He sounded like he was speaking for an audience. Which, Gabe realized, Tyler thought he was. He thought Gabe was wearing a wire. Which was more or less true.

"What are you talking about? I need you to help me. I'm going to get small, man." At the thought, real emotion colored his voice. "I mean, what am I supposed to do?"

"You lift weights and eat protein. Like I said you should."

Gabe lunged across the table and tried to grab for the bag, but Tyler clutched it to his chest and pivoted away from him. He made for the front door at something close to a run. The hostess stared after him as the door banged shut.

Now what was Gabe supposed to do? Had his plan just crashed and burned?

But Tyler, for all his muscles and swagger, was probably the end link in the chain. And every time Gabe had gotten steroids, Tyler had come out from the kitchen area holding a white takeout bag. Gabe was pretty sure this was where the drugs were coming from. Maybe he could still salvage things.

He got up and went toward the restaurant's kitchen, pushed open the same swinging door Tyler had walked out of. If someone caught him, he could say he was trying to find the bathrooms, even though they were actually near the entrance.

The kitchen was straight ahead. Two Asian guys were tending huge blackened woks set over leaping flames that hissed and sputtered. Along the back wall, a third guy was using a hose to spray off dishes on a black rubber conveyor belt. All three men were engrossed in their work and didn't appear to notice him. Gabe darted down the short hallway to his left. None of the doors were marked.

He opened the first door. An office. An empty office, with a desk, a computer, and even an abacus. But looks could be deceiving. He stepped inside and closed the door behind him. With shaking hands he started yanking open drawers in the desk and then the filing cabinet. All he found were papers. Papers, papers, papers. His heart felt like it would beat out of his chest. He slammed the last drawer closed.

Gabe went back to the door and peeped out. The hallway was still empty. He slipped out and tried the next door. It opened, revealing a very startled Chinese guy. He started yelling at Gabe, putting his hands on his shoulders to push him out. But not before Gabe had made sure that his torso—and his phone—had been pointed in the direction of the two plastic bins, one filled with blue pills, the other with tiny red-topped clear glass vials.

Suddenly an arm went tight around his neck, the elbow right underneath his chin. He felt another hand cup the back of his head, pressing him forward, ratcheting down on the space that was already too small for his neck.

And then everything went black.

CHAPTER 46

With every beat of his heart, Kenny's eye throbbed, the pain sharp and red. All the fault of a stubborn woman who didn't know when to let go, when to give up. When to admit that her stupid whore of a daughter was dead and nothing she could do would bring her back.

Instead of accepting her fate and dying quietly, Bo Yee had hammered back with her high heel, leaving a rapidly swelling dent on the top of Kenny's head. The last strike caught his eyebrow, like a hook piercing a worm. A millisecond later, continuing its downward trajectory, the heel impacted his eye. The pain had been like a live electric current zapping his eyeball.

And then the heel had torn through.

"Follow my finger," Guangli Lo said now, holding up his index finger and moving it back and forth.

After the attack, Kenny had balled up the scarf he'd planned to strangle Bo with and instead pressed it to his bloody eye. Unsure, at that moment, if he even had an eye. He had driven home with his one good eye and one free hand, then called Guangli.

Guangli had been a doctor back home in China, at least until he had been removed by the Health Ministry for accepting "red envelopes"—money and gifts given in exchange for treatment. By that point he had made enough that he could afford to pay up front to be smuggled to the US. Now he provided homesick Chinese immigrants, legal and not, with traditional Chinese medicine, especially herbs and acupuncture. He could also be counted on to deal with traumatic wounds and injuries without asking pesky questions. In addition to stitching the tear in his eyebrow closed, he had insisted on measuring Kenny's pulse and looking at his tongue.

Now he was back to evaluating how badly damaged his eye was.

Kenny must have adapted to American ways. For this injury, he did not want traditional Chinese medicine, with its emphasis on balancing yin and yang. He wanted to go straight to the emergency room, he wanted to see an ophthalmologist, he wanted high tech scans. But he couldn't take the chance of seeking out that type of care. He didn't know where Bo Yee was, just that she had taken off. Even though she didn't know his name and they had never met, what if the local hospitals had been alerted to be on the lookout for a Chinese man with unusual facial injuries? Injuries inflicted by a woman's high heel?

With difficulty, Kenny tried to follow Guangli's fat finger. Or was it fat? It was like trying to see through a red curtain.

Guangli stopped moving his finger from side to side and began to move it up and down. "Does it hurt to move your eye?"

"No more than it hurts to keep it still." Kenny supposed he should be glad that he could still see something. At first he had been afraid that his eye was completely destroyed. With his good eye, he had stared in horror at the blood trickling through his fingers and willed himself not to scream again. Kenny had heard Bo get on her bicycle and bump down the stairs, followed by some sort of crash when she reached the bottom, but he hadn't paid much attention.

"Cover your good eye and watch my finger again."

Kenny did as he was told, and immediately the edges of everything went soft and dull.

"Is it blurry?" Guangli asked.

Kenny sought the right word. "Watery."

Pressing his hand on Kenny's forehead, Guangli tilted his head back underneath the light, peering so closely that Kenny could smell the fishy odor of the man's dinner creeping into his nostrils.

"I believe you have a scratch on your cornea. It should heal, but you need to let it rest. If it begins to hurt more or if things get more watery or blurry, you may still need to go to a hospital emergency room."

"Will I lose my sight?"

"Probably not. But it is hard to say. Again, this is not my area. You should go to the hospital—"

"No." Kenny cut him off, even though it was what he wanted more than anything. "No hospitals."

"Then let me see if I have a patch."

Guangli dug into his bag of wonders—treatments and supplies that were half American and half Chinese—and came up with a black eye patch. He also left behind some herbs to swallow and others to make a poultice of, to be applied three times a day.

After he left, Kenny took stock of his situation. *Bad things never walk alone.* His eyesight compromised, maybe gone from his left eye for good. Bo Yee run off, who knew where? David Leacham out on bail, but how long would that last? Atkinson dead, or soon to be dead, leaving Kenny without anyone he could trust to solve his problems.

His musings were interrupted by a phone call. It was a woman named Kwong who worked as an interpreter. Whenever a policeman or a doctor or a lawyer hired an interpreter, they needed someone who spoke the right dialect. But that shared dialect meant they had grown up in the same region as the person whose words they were translating. Maybe in the same city. Maybe even on the same street.

Which meant that interpreters often knew a lot more than they might let on. Interpreters were supposed to be more machine than human, doing their jobs without favor or rancor. They weren't supposed to gossip. They weren't even supposed to acknowledge someone they had met through the job if they saw them again on the street.

Every month Kenny paid Kwong to report back on anything interesting she had learned. A lot of it wasn't interesting, of course. But now and again there was a hidden gem.

As had happened a few hours ago, with an arrested prostitute named Jiao. Kwong had not realized whom Jiao was implicating until the girl had said Kenny's name, at which point Kwong stopped translating. She had realized she had to put a stop to things before they got worse. So she had told the girl that if she kept talking to the police she was going to die, and die slowly, and so would all her relatives back home in China.

The girl had decided to end things then and there, and nearly succeeded, with a little help from Kwong. Without Jiao to testify, how far would they get, really?

"Do you think she will die?" Kenny asked.

"With luck."

"Maybe there needs to be more than luck," Kenny said carefully. "Maybe you should be very concerned about her. Concerned enough to visit her in the hospital. I would be most grateful."

He pressed the button to turn off the phone, but it rang again in his hand. It was the manager at one of his restaurants.

"We've got a problem."

"What kind of problem?"

"A guy burst into the back room. He saw the steroids. He was filming them on his phone. I thought he was a cop or something, and I panicked. I put him in a choke hold. Only it turns out he's fifteen years old. A kid."

"Did you kill him?"

"No. I've tied him up and gagged him. But now I don't know what to do."

The answer was clear. The manager just didn't want to face it. It was too late to go back now.

It reminded Kenny of the first time he had killed someone. It had been before he had hired Atkinson to be his bodyguard. A man named Longwei had owned the original Jade Kitchen, but he hadn't wanted to sell it, even though it had been in his best interests, the price more than fair. Kenny had simply meant to threaten Longwei, but somehow the gun had gone off, wounding him in the shoulder. They had looked at each other, both shocked by what had happened. The wound had not appeared to be life threatening. Except that it was. Looking at the blood pulsing out between the fingers Longwei was pressing against it, Kenny had seen what would happen. The hospital would call the police, and the police would not rest until they had answers. Once Longwei had been wounded, there was no way to go back to the moment before. And no path led to a good outcome for Kenny. In a split second, he had realized it was better to cut his losses, that there would be far fewer questions if the man simply disappeared.

So Kenny had taken one step closer, put the gun to Longwei's temple, and pulled the trigger.

Now Kenny sighed. "I'll come down and take care of it. What's the kid's name?"

"Gabe Quinn."

A long pause, during which Kenny's eye throbbed with every beat of his heart. "Did you say Quinn?"

"Yes."

"Is he conscious?"

"More or less."

"Ask him what his parents' names are. I'll wait."

A minute later, the manager was back. "He said Mia and Scott Quinn."

Well, well. This might have been useful information to have. Once. When he could have blackmailed her. Now it was too late. He could only hope that the disappearance of her son would throw her off her stride.

Only maybe it wasn't too late.

Kenny began to see how he could solve his problems. Didn't the Americans have a saying? "To kill two birds with one stone?"

CHAPTER 47

It was dark when Gabe woke up. His head ached and his neck felt weird.

Only he realized he hadn't woken up. Not exactly.

He had come to.

With a rush of panic, he remembered bursting into that room at the Jade Kitchen. The feeling of the arm coming across his throat and squeezing. After that, everything had gone dark.

Now he tried to get to his feet, to run, but found he could barely move. His knees were jammed up against his chin. His arms were pinned behind his back, and his hands were locked together. He was in some sort of small, confined space that pressed in all around him. That reflected every panicked, snorted exhale right back into his face.

Gabe couldn't scream. He couldn't even breathe through his mouth. It was sealed shut with some type of tape.

He managed to turn one hand enough that he could run his fingers across the bond that linked one hand to the other. A metal chain. His hands were cuffed behind his back.

Another jolt of adrenaline surged through him. Had he been buried alive?

But wherever he was, it didn't feel like dirt around him. It was hard and rubbery. And it didn't smell like dirt. The air was sour and hot, reeking of rot and mold.

He was, he realized, in a garbage can. A big one. Like industrial-size. One they hadn't bothered to clean before they handcuffed him and dumped him in here. It must belong to the Jade Kitchen.

But what if they had put him in here thinking he *was* dead? What if they never came back to get him out? How long would it take him to die? Overwhelmed by a fresh wave of panic, Gabe screamed twice, screams that left him shaky and sweating. Even though he had screamed as loudly as possible, he could tell it hadn't left the inside of his head, let alone penetrated the garbage can and gone out into the world.

He felt a sudden surge of nausea. Closing his eyes in the darkness, he fought it back down. If he threw up now, with the duct tape across his mouth, he would choke and die. He couldn't afford to cry either. Not if his nose might run and block his only way of breathing.

He had to calm down. He told himself that they wouldn't have bothered with the duct tape or the handcuffs if they had thought he was dead. And if they had wanted to kill him, they would have done it right away, without bothering to restrain him.

So maybe he was okay. Maybe they were just going to hold him for ransom or something.

But Gabe didn't really want to hang around to find out what

that something was. So where was the garbage can? Was it outside? Was anyone watching him? But any observer would have known he was conscious by now, and no one had kicked the sides or yelled at him to shut up. No one had reacted at all. So maybe wherever he was, he was alone, at least for now. If he could manage to knock the can over, he might be able to crawl out, stand up, and escape. Run clumsily because of his bound hands and numb legs, but still run.

Gabe shifted on his deadened legs, rocking back and forth. He thumped one side with one shoulder, then the other. Each time the garbage can moved a fraction but settled right back into place. Then he tried to stand up, but his legs had gone to sleep and he was too crammed in to get any purchase.

Did he hear something? He held his breath and tried not to panic. Was someone coming? Someone good—or someone bad? Should he try to make noise or should he try to keep quiet?

Make noise, he decided. Because the bad guys were the ones who had put him here. They already knew about him.

He tried again to scream, tried to put power behind it.

And in answer the lid swung back.

Gabe stared up. But he had no idea who the man was looking down at him. Just that he didn't look surprised.

Gabe realized he should have been ready. Tried to do something. Maybe he could have head-butted this guy. But instead he was just looking up at a short, slender Chinese man. Gabe could tell that he was taller than the man, and with his new physique, he had many pounds on him. Still, this guy was clearly a man, not a boy.

The man's face was hard. Expressionless. He wore a black eye patch, but it didn't look funny at all, not with the red divot running down his forehead and then disappearing under the patch. Gabe didn't want to know what was—or wasn't—under that eye patch. For a second he remembered the pirate party his mom had put on for his sixth birthday. The guests had all gotten foam swords and eye patches. Gabe had worn a pirate's hat, and they had followed clues to find a pirate's hoard of gold-foil-wrapped chocolate coins. Found them right here in the garage he was in now. The garage at his house. Because now he recognized where he was.

Behind the man was a white van with *Jade Kitchen* written on it. Why had they taken Gabe here?

He was still wondering when the man grabbed the handle of the garbage can and tilted it. Suddenly it went over. Hard. Gabe reflexively jerked his hands, trying to protect his head, but the back of his skull bounced off the side of the can as it hit the floor. While he was still lying there, stunned, the man put his hands under Gabe's arms and hauled him out. Gabe tried to get his feet underneath him, but his legs were boneless and numb. He lay like a fish on the deck of a boat, his back arched awkwardly over his cuffed hands. He could only watch as the man slipped off Gabe's Vans, toed off his own shoes, and slipped his feet in Gabe's.

The man reached out one latex-gloved hand and ripped the tape from Gabe's mouth. It should have been a relief, and it was, at least physically. He sucked in greedy gulps of air, knowing the man would only have done it if he had no worries about anyone hearing Gabe.

"Who are you?" Gabe said. "What do you want?" He wanted to sound strong, like a man, but his voice came out weak and hoarse. Were there other men here? Or was it just this one man?

"That does not matter. All that matters is that you caused a big mess and now I have to clean it up."

"Just let me go and I won't tell anyone what happened." The man didn't even bother to answer Gabe's plea. He tried another tack. "Whatever you do, you shouldn't try to kill me."

One side of the other man's mouth lifted at that. "And why not?"

"Because my mom is a King County prosecutor and her friend is a homicide detective. If you kill me, they won't rest until you're on death row."

"Oh, I know your mother, Gabe. Her name is Mia Quinn."

To hear his name in the other man's mouth made him flinch. And why wasn't this guy wearing a mask as well as those translucent latex gloves? Gabe could easily identify him. Especially with that eye patch.

At least he could if he were alive.

"Your mother has become a thorn in my side. That is what they say in America, right? She will not stop asking questions. Each time she takes away a little piece of information. Maybe the tiniest crumb. But she keeps coming back. Well, we have another saying in China. 'An ant may well destroy a whole dam.'" His mouth twisted. "So who else lives here? And do not lie to me, or it will go very badly for them."

Unable to work out if a lie was better, Gabe went with the truth. "Besides my mother, there's my little sister, Brooke. She's four. And my friend Eldon and his mom." What was going to happen to them? He prayed that none of them came home now. Because he realized they couldn't save him. And he couldn't save them.

"And where are they all now?"

"My mom's at work. My sister is at daycare. And Eldon and his mom are at the doctor's."

"How long until they are back?"

He still couldn't see any point in lying. "An hour or too. Maybe less." But not Brooke, he realized with relief. Because Gabe wouldn't come to pick her up.

The man put his foot on Gabe's hip and pushed him to one side. He leaned down and plucked Gabe's phone from the back pocket of his jeans.

"What do you have on here?" He swiped sideways, looking at all of Gabe's apps. "Facebook, Twitter, Instagram. And what kind of texts do you send?" He scrolled up and down. "Very good. Fully spelled-out words. I dislike the way Americans always have to have shortcuts."

Gabe didn't say anything. How could he get his hands on his phone? If he had it, he could try to dial it behind his back or press buttons with his nose. He was sure if he tried hard enough he would succeed.

"I think first we shall have you send a message to your mother." The man spoke aloud as he continued to type. "'Mom come home right away. Something bad happened.'" He hesitated. "No, if it ends there she might call the police when you do not answer your phone. So we shall make it"—he started typing again—"'Something bad happened that I need to tell you about.' Perfect. Just enough to make her curious. To make her hurry. To make her think it is something she will want to keep private." He tapped the bottom of the screen, pressing the Send button.

"What are you going to do to her when she comes home?" Because the man was right, Gabe knew. His mom would hurry home. She would be distracted. Worried. What would she be imagining? That he had been suspended at school? That he had taken some kind of bad drug?

"It is a sad story, really. A story about a boy who becomes addicted to steroids. You know what steroids make people do? They can make them get angry. Very angry. And so one day this boy snaps. He lies in wait and kills his family members one by one as they come home. And finally he turns the gun on himself.

"Then I will go to all your applications. What shall I say? 'I can't take it anymore'? 'It's all over'? 'They are better off now'? 'I'm so sorry for what I have done'? Or maybe something that sounds more angry or crazy. Perhaps—'I am the angel of death'? With a photo of your mother's body?" He gave Gabe a cold smile, as if pleased with his cleverness.

"They will never figure out where you got the gun, but kids have a way of finding the things they really want, do they not? Just like you figured out how to get steroids even though they are illegal." He stuck out one Vans-shod foot and regarded it. "And in case I go tracking blood, I am wearing your shoes. The story without words has to match the story I will use your phone to write. That is why you must die last. In case they can tell the order things happened in."

He picked up a roll of duct tape. Before Gabe could react, the man duct-taped his legs together at the calf. Then he tore off two new strips, which he slapped against Gabe's mouth.

With dawning horror, Gabe realized that it would work. Even if anyone tried to run, even if they fought back, even if they tried to hide—they would do all those things whether they were running from Gabe or Kenny. The evidence wouldn't change.

His mom was going to die today. Maybe Eldon and Kali. And of course Gabe himself. And it would all be his fault.

But at least Brooke would be safe. His mom would think Gabe

had already picked her up and she wouldn't go by the daycare. So his little sister wouldn't die today. He tried to hold on to that thought as the man turned off the light, closed the door, and left Gabe alone on the garage floor.

CHAPTER 48

Mia sat in the hospital waiting room with Charlie and Eli. As soon as the operation to repair the damage to Jiao's throat was finished, the surgeon was supposed to come out and give them an update on her condition.

At the sound of a tinny chime, she started. It was her phone dinging, signaling a text. She pulled it from her purse.

MOM COME HOME RIGHT AWAY. SOMETHING BAD HAPPENED THAT I NEED TO TELL YOU ABOUT.

What little adrenaline Mia had left flared up. What kind of trouble had her son gotten himself in now? She took a deep breath and tried to tell herself it couldn't be that bad. At least he wasn't calling her from the police station. Or a hospital. The front of her suit jacket was still stiff with blood from when she had placed her hands on Jiao's neck, tried to stop the girl from dying.

She must have made a sound because Charlie lifted his head from an old issue of *Entertainment Weekly*. "What's wrong?"

She handed over her phone. Charlie read the message and grunted, then handed it back. "Something bad? He's a teenager. It could mean that he asked a girl out and she said no."

Eli was looking back and forth between the two of them. She knew he wouldn't judge her, not after the troubles he had had with Rachel smoking pot. She handed the phone to him.

"Gabe just sent me this."

Eli read it and then handed back the phone with a quizzical look.

"Things with Gabe have been kind of fraught in the last couple of days," she explained. "Right now he's grounded, big-time. Because on Saturday"—part of her still could not believe what she was about to say was true—"I found steroids in his backpack."

Eli's eyes widened. "Gabe is using steroids? Those can have some pretty serious side effects."

Mia bit back on her impulse to snap at him. "Which is why I'm treating it seriously. As you know"—she underlined the word *you* with her tone of voice—"it's impossible to police a kid twenty-four/seven."

Deciding not to say anything more, Mia called Gabe's phone. But there was no answer.

When it went to voice mail, she said, "Gabe—can you call me back? I need to know more about what's going on."

A million possibilities ran through her mind. Had he been expelled? What could be so bad he had to ask her to come home right away? And could it be that something he defined as bad was not nearly so bad after all? Had he gotten in another fight with Eldon? Her breath caught. Was it possible he had hurt Eldon? Mia called Kali, but again got nothing but voice mail. Then she remembered that Kali had had a doctor's appointment late in the afternoon and that Eldon was going with her. She decided not to leave a message. Kali already had enough on her plate.

A new, even more terrifying thought seized her. Had something happened to Brooke? Was Gabe so young, so panicked, that he would text Mia rather than call 911? She pictured Brooke cartwheeling down the stairs. Lying unmoving at the bottom. She knew she was assuming the worst, that she was conjuring nightmares from fifteen simple words. Then again, earlier today she had watched a girl try to kill herself with a pen.

Before she hit the speed dial for Rocking Horse Preschool, she relived what had happened. It still confused her. Jiao and Kwong had been talking fast, their words running over each other. The thing was, Mia had thought she heard Jiao say two words she knew. *Kenny Zhong.*

But she had checked with both Eli and Charlie afterward. They hadn't heard it. And surely Charlie would have picked up on it.

Kwong/Kenny Zhong—said fast, one could sound like the other. Or Jiao could have said something else entirely.

"What did she say to you?" she had demanded of Kwong after the ambulance had taken Jiao away. "Right before she did it?"

Kwong was trembling. Blood freckled her broad face. She had screamed, "Sorry!" over and over as they scrambled to save Jiao's life. She was still clutching the bloody pen she had plucked from the girl's throat.

"She was saying that she was afraid and she did not want to testify. She was saying she should join Dandan."

"And she did not say anything about Kenny Zhong?"

"Who?" Kwong's expression didn't change.

"Kenny Zhong."

Kwong's flat eyes met her gaze without wavering. "No. Who is that?"

Mia answered her question with a question. "Then what were you telling her?"

"That there was hope. That life was worth living." The other woman sighed heavily. "That's when she pulled the pen from my hand."

Mia still wasn't certain she believed her. But the conversation between Kwong and Jiao hadn't been recorded by the jail because any conversation that involved Jiao's lawyer was privileged. And she and Charlie hadn't recorded it because they were trying to keep Jiao safe. They only had Kwong's word for what had been said in the interview room. And maybe Jiao's, once she regained consciousness.

Now she pressed the Call button beside the name of the preschool.

"Rocking Horse. This is Sarah."

"Hey, this is Mia Quinn. I was just wondering if you were there earlier when Gabe picked up Brooke?" She would ask about his demeanor. If he had said anything.

"Actually, he hasn't yet. He said he was going to be running late today and that he wouldn't pick her up until close to close." Sarah added pointedly, "Which is, like, only seventeen minutes from now."

Rocking Horse charged a dollar a minute for any parent who was later than six. It didn't matter if traffic was terrible or the car had broken down. The staff had heard all the excuses before. You could still say them, but sooner or later you would also be opening your wallet.

Why had Gabe said he would pick Brooke up late? And why hadn't he? Stomach churning, Mia called his phone again. And left another message. "I guess I'm going to have to pick up your sister.

I'll be home as soon as I can. Please call me back and let me know what's going on." She hesitated and then said in a rush, "I'm really worried, Gabe."

"Let me go with you," Charlie said after she pressed the button to disconnect and started to put on her coat. Eli held the back of the collar so she could slip her arms into the sleeves.

"No, that's okay, Charlie. This is probably something he wants to stay in the family. He already felt like you were taking on too big of a role on Saturday when you talked to him about the steroids. He kept telling me afterward that you're not his dad."

Charlie shrugged, seeming unruffled. "Gabe's right about that, of course. But with Scott dead, your son probably needs a bunch of dads, not none. And if something *is* really wrong, Mia, you'll want someone else there."

She did not want to think about how bad it could be. "How about this?" She looked from Charlie to Eli. "I'll call one or both of you if I get home and think it's something I can't handle. And meanwhile, can you two stay here and let me know what you hear about Jiao?"

"Deal," Charlie said, and Eli nodded.

She got to Rocking Horse a minute before close. Brooke was the last child there. Saying hello and good-bye to Sarah, buttoning Brooke's coat, and putting her in her car seat kept a tiny bit of Mia's anxiety at bay.

But it all came roaring back once she was in the car again, her damp hands sliding on the wheel.

CHAPTER 49

After Mia left, Eli looked over at Charlie, trying not to let his distaste show. The guy had never been a parent. He had only been a husband, and he clearly hadn't been any good even at that, since he had also been divorced three times.

"So Mia had you talk to Gabe after she found the steroids?" Eli felt a pinch of jealousy. Was she already trying Charlie out for the role of father to her kids?

Charlie shot him a look, and Eli guessed that the other man knew exactly how he felt. "I happened to be there when she found them. So I asked if I could talk to Gabe, man to man, about how they can affect you. I figured she wouldn't know those kinds of details, and even if she looked that stuff up on the Internet, it would be pretty awkward talking to her kid about it." He snorted. "Hey, it was awkward for me."

And how exactly did Charlie know these details? Was it from personal experience? Eli only said, "How did he take it?"

Charlie's mouth twisted. "Gabe was angry. Really angry. I just hope that underneath he was listening. You know what it's like at that age. Everything's a big deal. Everything's life or death. It's all the best of times, or the lowest, and there's nothing in between."

That was certainly true for Rachel, and she wasn't taking steroids. "Steroids mess with your emotions, don't they?" Eli asked.

"For sure. Mostly they can make you irrationally angry. They can also make you pretty depressed. Even suicidal."

That gave Eli pause. It sounded like Mia was right to be worried. What if Gabe had overreacted to something small that still seemed overwhelming in the moment that it happened? Teens were so impulsive. Would Gabe kill himself rather than face it—or face his mom?

The shiny silver doors to the surgical area opened automatically, and an African American woman dressed in green scrubs walked between them. She came over to them. "Are you two the cop and the lawyer?" she asked. A surgical mask dangled around her neck.

This was the surgeon, Eli realized as Charlie nodded, not the scrub nurse. How often did he only see what he expected to see?

"How's Jiao doing?" he asked.

"We had to give her five pints of blood, but she'll make it." The doctor touched her own throat. "She's going to have some pretty significant scarring on her neck. And the pen nicked her vocal cords, so her voice will probably be affected, but hopefully not too much. She might end up sounding a little husky. We're just lucky that she's so young and that her underlying level of health is pretty good."

"When will we be able to talk to her?" Charlie asked.

The surgeon pursed her lips. "Not for a while. We want her not only medically stable but psychologically stable. Which means it definitely won't be tonight. She's still sedated and won't be waking up from the anesthesia for several hours. We'll need to get an interpreter in tomorrow and assess her medical state."

"Do me a favor," Charlie said, "and make sure you don't use the one we did. Her name was Kwong something. She freaked out when this happened. She was pretty useless. And I don't want her around Jiao, reminding her that she almost died."

"I can imagine it was pretty intense," the surgeon said. "A girl shoving a pen in her own neck—hopefully that's something you never see in your life, or you only see once and never again. But I'll make a note of it. No interpreter or visitor named Kwong."

Even before she disappeared back behind the doors, Eli was pulling his keys from his pocket and getting to his feet. He knew Charlie wasn't going to like what he was about to do, but Eli didn't care what he thought.

"Where are you going now?" Charlie asked.

"The same place you are. I'm going to see if everything's okay with Mia. And if it's not, I'm going to help in any way I can."

CHAPTER 50

Ever since the man had left him lying on the floor of the garage, handcuffed, trussed, and gagged with duct tape, Gabe had been working on freeing his hands. He had been trying so long that now his hands were wet with either sweat or blood. Because they were behind his back, he didn't know which and he didn't much care. All he knew was that whatever it was, it was a lubricant. It might be just what he needed to slide one hand out of a cuff. Just one. And then he would be free.

Only neither hand would go. The metal rings refused to slide down any farther than the meaty part of his thumbs, despite how much he pulled and pushed. Finally he admitted defeat. He was going to have to find another way. If he could just get his cuffs in front, he could at least use his hands to get off the duct tape that bound his legs and sealed his mouth. He could at least open doors. He could walk out of here. Maybe even handle a weapon, like the rake that stood in one corner.

Moving like an inchworm, Gabe rolled and dragged and creeped until he reached the built-in cabinets at the back of the garage. He pressed his back against one and managed to scoot himself up until he could grab a cupboard door handle. He used that to lever himself to his feet. But the duct tape around his calves compromised his balance. For a long, terrifying moment he felt himself beginning to fall right onto his face. He staggered frantically forward in tiny steps until he managed to catch himself. Then he crouched, sliding his hands down behind him until they cleared his butt and were behind his thighs. His shoulders were already screaming before he half sat, half fell onto his back. Then it felt like they were being pulled from their sockets. A shriek was forced out of his lungs. He hoped the duct tape across his mouth had stifled it.

He had imagined that he could roll back and then kick his legs over his cuffs, but it turned out that wasn't possible. Maybe he could do it if he could step over the cuffs one leg at a time, but his legs were still bound together. He grabbed the back of his pants at the thighs and yanked and pulled, snorting with exertion, his desperation giving him strength. Finally the button at his waist popped off and the pants began to slide down his butt. Inch by inch, Gabe wrangled his pants down, tugging with first one hand and then the other, until he finally managed to get them down his legs and over his stocking feet.

Now he just had to get his feet back over the cuffs one at the time. Gabe rolled himself up as tight as he could. He strained and stretched, trying not to grunt even as his shoulders felt like they were being twisted off as if he were one of Brooke's Barbies.

If that man came back in the door and saw what Gabe was doing, he would surely shoot him. The one positive thing—if you could even look at it that way—was that Gabe had to be giving himself wounds that could not be explained away as injuries consistent with suicide.

Finally he got his right leg over. Now he was straddling the cuffs. But when he tried to do the same with his left leg, it did not seem able to bend as much. *No, no, no.* Any second the man was going to walk in and find him, awkward as a pill bug, squirming, the handcuffs still stuck behind his left knee. With a final burst of energy, Gabe pressed his right foot on the cabinet and rolled so far back his weight rested on the bones in the nape of his neck. He managed to get his left leg up and over, painfully scraping the back of his bare calf on the metal chain linking the cuffs.

Gabe was still lying on the floor, breathing hard through his nose and trying not to make any noise doing it, when he heard his mom's car pull up in the driveway. *No,* he thought. *No, please, God, no, I'm not hearing this.* He heard the sound of his mom's footsteps climbing the stairs to the porch. Fear pierced his chest like a needle.

And then, to his horror, he heard the high, piping sound of Brooke's voice on the front porch.

"Where's Gabe, Mommy?"

And Gabe's heart broke.

CHAPTER 51

When Mia turned onto their block, the house was completely dark. Not even the porch light on. Her heart contracted. She turned off the car and pinched the house key between her fingers before she unbuckled Brooke from her booster seat. Should she have raced out of the hospital, let the charges pile up at Rocking Horse, and hurried home? What if her son was lying dead somewhere inside the house and these last few minutes could have made all the difference?

Brooke must have picked up on her anxiety. "Where's Gabe, Mommy?" she asked as Mia carried her up the front porch.

"I'm not quite sure," she said, hoping the answer wasn't going to prove to be too awful to bear.

Unlocking the door, she went inside. "Gabe?" she called out, then held her breath. Did she hear a faint thumping noise? Or was it just the beating of her own heart? Before she turned on the light, she bent over to set Brooke down. Just as a shot split the darkness and sang just overhead.

———————

Charlie followed Eli out. There was no point in trying to argue him out of going. The man was stubborn. Stubborn as a mule.

He had to admit that maybe they had that in common. That and their affection for Mia. Once in the hospital's parking structure, he lost sight of Eli when the other man kept climbing the stairs to a different level. Charlie hurried to his car, dialing Mia's cell phone as he went. No answer.

It was against department policy, but that didn't stop him from putting on lights and sirens as soon as he pulled out of the lot. Charlie flew down the highway, past all the other cars, which were forced to pull over to the shoulder. But then he picked up another vehicle, drafting in his wake.

He squinted at his rearview mirror. Eli Hall. Doing what he wasn't supposed to be doing either.

Maybe they had more in common than Charlie thought.

Once he hit Mia's neighborhood, he cut the sirens. Sometimes if a person was on the verge, the sound of sirens could make a bad situation infinitely worse.

Mia's house was dark, without even the porch light on. But the front door gaped open, as wrong as a missing tooth in a mouth.

Charlie got out of his car and hurried to Eli's. "I need you to stay back," he whispered. His hand was on the butt of his gun. "You can't just go running in there. You don't know what you'll find. And you're not armed."

From the house came the sound of a gunshot.

And then they both went running.

———————

Moving faster than thought, Mia put her mouth close to her daughter's tiny ear. "Stay right here, baby. Don't move. And don't make a sound." Then she half opened the hall closet door and shoved Brooke inside.

Her ears still roaring from the sound of the gun, Mia was reacting on pure instinct. On hands and knees, she scuttled toward the kitchen. She needed a weapon. Something to fight back with. She mentally rehearsed how she would lunge for the knife block while praying that the knives were actually in the block and not, say, scattered all over the counter.

She had just put one knee on the tiled floor when Eli, shouting her name, ran in the still-open front door. Mia turned to call out a warning.

A thousand things happened at once. The lights flared on overhead. Charlie was standing in the doorway in a half crouch, his gun drawn and held out before him in both hands. Kenny Zhong had one hand fisted in Eli's dress shirt, yanking the taller man down to his level. And he was holding a gun to Eli's head, pressing hard enough that Eli's forehead had turned white where the barrel pressed against his skin.

Eli himself was standing very, very still.

Into the sudden silence, Brooke's small voice came from the closet. "Can I come out now, Mama?"

And at that moment Gabe, pantless and silent in his stocking feet, slipped up behind Kenny Zhong, looped his handcuffed arms around the man's neck, and jerked backward.

CHAPTER 52

TWO WEEKS LATER

Mia lit the cinnamon-scented candle in the holly centerpiece on the dining room's sideboard. Shaking out the match, she stepped back, feeling satisfied. Everything looked perfect.

Well, maybe not perfect in the traditional sense of the word. There was a stain on the carpet in front of the TV where Brooke had once tipped over a glass of milk, and the furniture showed signs of being well used. She had gathered up all the unopened mail and shoved it into the junk drawer. But the house was still hers, and it was going to be filled with her friends and family, and that was all that mattered.

The Saturday before Christmas she always had an open house. But this was her first one without Scott.

So many things had changed in the past year. She had lost her husband. Gone back to work. Learned truths she would have said would be too hard to bear, would bring her to her knees and then smear her face in the dirt. But here she was, still standing.

Arranged on the sideboard, the kitchen counters, and the living room coffee table were trays of crackers and cheese, just as she always had. But this year there were also trays of cut vegetables. And some of the crackers were made of nutty whole grain. Some. But not all. Mia had realized it was impossible to eat perfectly, or for that matter to do anything perfectly. But it was possible to do better.

Better didn't mean that Mia wouldn't sample Kali's contribution to the party: traditional Samoan *panipopo*—sweet coconut buns. The doctor had said Kali's tumor was shrinking dramatically. Soon she would be done with chemo and have her mastectomy behind her. She would be able to start working again. Once Kali had more money, maybe she would want to move out. But for now she and Eldon were here, and part of Mia's improvised family.

A hand reached past Mia and snatched a piece of Swiss cheese before she could swat it away. "Gabe!"

"It's only one piece, Mom." He stuffed it into his mouth. "And Coach says I need to eat a lot of protein."

After stopping steroids, Gabe had gone to his old football coach and asked him for help designing a strength regimen. Coach Harper's plan included a diet of real foods only, no supplements, no weight-gainer shakes. Gabe hadn't told the coach what had happened, but Mia was sure he must have guessed. After all, how many kids would get smaller even as they lifted weights every day?

Smaller, but somehow happier. And Gabe had managed to hold on to some of his muscles. Yesterday he had told her, "Now if I get results, I'll know it's natural, that I did it myself. I don't have to be one of those guys who need drugs to get big. Now it will really be me."

Kenny Zhong's empire—the smuggled steroids and Viagra, the restaurants and massage parlors staffed by illegal immigrants who were really slaves—had started to crumble the night he tried to kill everyone Mia loved and had been foiled by a fifteen-year-old boy. Now Kenny was facing dozens of felony charges, including the murder of his former hired gun, the man who had shot Abigail Endicott.

On the day Kenny was arraigned, a dozen television cameras had been waiting for him outside the courthouse. As soon as he spotted them, he lifted his head and straightened his shoulders. Even so, he barely reached the chins of the federal agents escorting him. His expression was proud and unapologetic, despite the fact that his hands were cuffed behind his back, despite the two agents who had their hands hooked in his elbows and were dragging him forward. In fact, if it were possible for a man to strut in such circumstances, Kenny had strutted.

Kenny was also facing charges for the assault and torture of Chun, the waitress who had talked to Charlie and Mia. Cops had discovered her, handcuffed to a pipe, in the basement of the house the workers from the Jade Kitchen shared. Beaten badly, but alive. Just.

The one thing Kenny hadn't been guilty of was killing Sindy. He had tried to lure her through Atkinson, but she had gotten leery and then spent a few weeks hiding from everyone until news of Kenny's arrest made it clear she was safe.

Facing retrial for Dandan's murder, David Leacham had accepted a plea bargain. But for twenty years, not two, thanks to the information Jiao and Warren had provided. Kwong was also facing charges for threatening Jiao.

When Jiao was discharged from the hospital, Bo Yee had offered to take her in. When Mia last saw them, Bo had seemed to have found some measure of peace.

For his cooperation, Warren had gotten probation. With his bribe money confiscated, he had gone back to his job as an electrician. Mia had heard that he had also started attending Bo's church, but she didn't know if that stemmed from a real conversion or was simply the most twisted crush ever.

The one question Mia had not been able to answer, not even for herself, was whether Frank had been pressured not to re-try Leacham. Either way, there was a distinct chill between them, and she wasn't sure it would ever lift.

But she wouldn't think about that tonight. Tonight was for celebrating. She had invited everyone she knew, and most were coming. People from work. Her dad and Luciana. Bo and Jiao. Eli and Charlie. Eli was bringing his daughter, and even though Rachel was two years older than Gabe and emotionally light years ahead, Mia had caught him hanging a sprig of mistletoe over a doorway.

"What?" he had said when she raised an eyebrow at him. "A guy can dream, can't he?"

Yes, she concurred silently, as she looked at the food and thought about her friends, *we all can dream.*

READING GROUP GUIDE

1. Before you read *Lethal Beauty*, were you aware that there were modern day slaves in America and that they work in all different types of industries?

2. One of the key witnesses, Sindy, goes missing after being in foster care. Have you ever considered being a foster parent? Do you know anyone who has been one or someone who spent time in foster care as a child?

3. Today, even teenagers can turn to legal drugs and supplements to help them concentrate, loose weight, gain weight, be less anxious, etc. Do you think too many normal issues are being turned into medical problems, or that it's good that today's teens have more options for help than kids did twenty or more years ago?

4. When Gabe first goes online to read message boards about steroids, he gets a one-sided picture of the truth. Have the Internet and other targeted media become an echo chamber, presenting information that isn't balanced? Should we as individuals try to do something about it? How can we get the full picture when we seek out information about controversial subjects?

5. Mia decided to go cold-turkey on junk food, purging her house of any foods she thought her family shouldn't be eating. How do you balance the need to eat healthy with the desire for something fun and/or fast? Do you have tricks for keeping a kitchen that helps you support a balanced diet?

6. At first when Eli sees the African American woman come out to talk to them about Jiao's surgery, he think she's a nurse. *"This was the surgeon, Eli realized as Charlie nodded, not the scrub nurse. How often did he only see what he expected to see?"* Have you found yourself making assumptions about people based on how they dress, the color of their skin, or other externals? How can we train ourselves to not jump to conclusions?

7. Even though David Leacham is guilty, Warren is able to bring the trial to a halt by refusing to vote to convict him. Do you think the jury system is the best way to go about deciding cases? If not, what would you propose in its place?

8. Who do you think Mia should end up with? Charlie? Eli? Neither?

9. Have you ever wondered about the working conditions of a foreign-born worker whom you encountered? What would you do if you suspected that the man at the convenience store or the woman at the dry cleaners had been trafficked? If you have information about a potential trafficking situation, please contact the National Human Trafficking Resource Center at 1-888-373-7888 or text BeFree (233733). The hotline is open all hours, all days. They take reports from anywhere in the country related to potential trafficking victims, suspicious behaviors, and/or locations where trafficking is suspected to occur. All reports are confidential. Interpreters are available.

ACKNOLWEDGMENTS

My warmest gratitude and thanks go to the readers of the Mia Quinn mysteries. Your enthusiasm for Mia is inspiring and humbling.

Thank you O'Reilly, from Wiehl. And thank you to my "sister from another mother", Deirdre Imus. Thank you to Roger Ailes, for hiring a certain legal analyst, and to Dianne Brandi. And thank you to Robin Burcell, former police officer, for answering procedural questions.

Thank you to this amazingly wonderful publishing team! Daisy Hutton, vice president and publisher, wise beyond her years; Ami McConnell, senior acquisitions editor and friend; Amanda Bostic, editorial director, brilliant; LB Norton, line editor, with the keenest of pens and the sharpest of wits; Becky Monds, editor, keeps the whole team on track with a smile on her face; Jodi Hughes, the ever on-target associate editor; Karli Jackson, associate editor; Kristen Vasgaard, a brilliant manager of packaging; Laura Dickerson, marketing manager, is inspired; Kerri Potts, senior marketing associate, and the inspiration behind my Facebook page; and, of course, special thanks to my friend Katie Bond, director of marketing and publicity. What a great team!

Special thanks to our book agents, Todd Shuster and Lane Zachary of Zachary, Shuster, Harmsworth Literary and Entertainment Agency and Wendy Schmalz of the Wendy Schmalz Agency, who have worked tirelessly.

Thank you to my friend and collaborator, April Henry.

And always, Mom and Dad, thank you does not even begin to express how I feel.

All the mistakes are ours. All the credit is theirs. Thank you!

ABOUT THE AUTHOR

Photo by Kyle Widder Photography

L is Wiehl is a *New York Times* bestselling author, Harvard Law School graduate, and former federal prosecutor. A popular legal analyst and commentator for the Fox News Channel, Wiehl appears weekly on *The O'Reilly Factor, Lou Dobbs Tonight, Imus in the Morning, Kelly's Court,* and more.

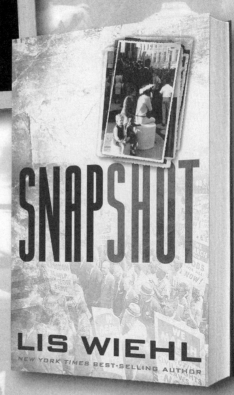

LIS LOVES TO HEAR FROM HER READERS!

Be sure to sign up for Lis Wiehl's newsletter for insider information on deals and appearances.

Visit her website at LisWiehlBooks.com
Twitter: @LisWiehl
facebook.com/pages/LisWiehl